FUTUREDAZE

An Anthology of YA Science Fiction

A delightful surprise—young stories of a new sort: stories with a sense of wonder and a wary, expectant look at the universe.

—**C. J. Cherryh**, award winning science fiction and fantasy author

Some of the stories are thought-provoking, some of the stories are charming, and some of the stories are poems. A fine anthology for young adults of every taste.

— **Mike Resnick**, award winning science fiction and fantasy author

A fine assembly of science fiction stories that are provocative, entertaining, and sometimes nervously mind-stretching.

—**Piers Anthony**, author of the Xanth series

For dreamers and armchair adventurers of all ages.

—**Kevin J. Anderson**, *New York Times* bestselling author of Star Wars Jedi Academy trilogy

Brilliantly powerful and/or amusing tales. I came away dazzled, and you will too.

—**Michael Bishop**, author of *Count Geiger's Blues* and *Brittle Innings*

Opening this amazing collection is like visiting one of those All-You-Can-Eat restaurants, except everything in Futuredaze is freshly-made and yummy. [T]his is exactly the kind of book I would have loved when I was a teen.

—**James Patrick Kelly**, winner of the Hugo, Nebula and Locus awards

FUTUREDAZE

An Anthology of YA Science Fiction

Edited by
Hannah Strom-Martin and Erin Underwood

UNDERWORDS PRESS
Marblehead, Massachusetts

Exterior cover design by Deena Warner Design, LLC.

Copyeditor Robert Stauffer.

Proofreader Heather Magaw.

Futuredaze's mission is to inspire a love of science fiction in today's teens and young adults—providing them with a launching pad that will encourage them to further explore the many branches of the genre.

UNDERWORDS
48 Hawkes Street
Marblehead, MA 01945
www.underwordsblog.com

ISBN 13: 978-0-9858934-0-8

Printed in the United States of America
by Lightning Source, LLC.

First Edition: 2013
10 9 8 7 6 5 4 3 2 1

Acknowledgments

Hannah Strom-Martin would like to thank her coeditor, Erin Underwood, whose literary hijinks have enriched her life and without whom absolutely none of this would be possible. Thanks also to the community of talented writers around the world who contributed their prose and enthusiasm to this project. Hannah would like to dedicate her half of the editing credits to her very patient husband and to the children they hope to have in future days.

Erin Underwood would like to thank Nancy Holder and Jack McDevitt for contributing more than just their fiction to this anthology. She would also like to thank the people who have helped to make *Futuredaze* a reality by supporting our Kickstarter campaign and who helped to spread the word to their friends and family. Erin also thanks her coeditor and friend, Hannah Strom-Martin, whose talent and eye for story has always been an inspiration and who has been there every step of the way. She also gives special thanks to her husband Tom whose patience and love mean the world to her.

Contents

Introduction

Hannah Strom-Martin & Erin Underwood

The Hunger Games isn't the only reason that the young adult section is the coolest place in the bookstore. (And we're talking any bookstore, mind you, from brick and mortar to digital cache.) From future dystopias to good old-fashioned teen romance that's light years beyond Sweet Valley High or Hogwarts, young adult fiction (also known as YA) is experiencing a publishing boom. Teen fantasy and paranormal romance in particular have emerged as the dominant YA genres *du jour*—but, like a certain Katniss Everdeen, Suzanne Collins has a bead on Stephenie Meyer, and the science fiction works of Scott Westerfeld (the Uglies series), Beth Revis (Across the Universe series), and Dan Wells (The Partials Sequence) have further opened the possibilities for the adventurous reader in the ever-expanding realm of YA. (Interestingly, estimates by publishing experts suggest that as much as a third of all YA fiction is bought by adults, further contributing to the YA upswell.[1])

It's an exciting time for young adult fiction—though the careful observer may have noticed one downside. While fantasy or paranormal romance anthologies (edited by such authors as P.C. Cast and Melissa Marr) have proliferated, when it comes to the search for short science fiction for young adults, you could be in for a bit of a trek. However, we are pleased to see the recent anthologies by editors

---

1   Thomas, Liz. "Boom in young adult fiction as sales jump 150 percent in six years thanks to hits like Twilight and The Hunger Games." The Daily Mail. July 2, 2012

Ellen Datlow and Terri Windling (*After*) and Tobias Bucknell and Joe Monti (*Diverse Energies*) hit the market in late 2012, but these anthologies primarily tackle the science fiction subgenres of post-apocalyptic and dystopian fiction. And with a noticeable lack of a wider selection of short science fiction for young adults in the market, the genre has had few opportunities to formalize itself.

We created *Futuredaze: An Anthology of YA Science Fiction* to help fill the void. (If the anthology helps to better define the burgeoning genre, we're okay with that, too.) At a time when the YA market is dominated by novel-length fantasy, we hope to inject the short-fiction market with a measure of rocket fuel, a dash of dystopia, and an extra serving of undisguised wonder at the possibilities that the future may hold.

Since the inception of the science fiction genre, young readers have been given adult science fiction that was considered "safe" for them to read. However, books like *The Outsiders* by S. E. Hinton and *Charlie and the Chocolate Factory* by Roald Dahl helped to pave the way for the emergence of a new genre: young adult fiction. As YA literature came into its own through works such as Madeleine L'Engle's *A Wrinkle in Time*, Ursula K. Le Guin's *A Wizard of Earthsea*, and Judy Blume's *Are You There God? It's Me, Margaret*, YA became synonymous with teen-centered stories that are usually told from the unique viewpoint of a teen protagonist (*a la* close first person narratives of *The Hunger Games* and *Twilight*). Of course, adult science fiction novels like *The Hitchhiker's Guide to the Galaxy*, *Dune*, *I, Robot*, and other classics by the likes of Jules Verne, H. G. Wells, and Ray Bradbury remain staples of young adult reading lists—which may explain why the subgenre of YA science fiction has been slower to emerge in its own right.

Whatever the subgenre (fantasy, science fiction, paranormal romance), YA at its best is far from "safe," and is frequently constructed with the same level of emotional honesty and intensity that is found in the best adult fiction. The work of the late Maurice Sendak, author of such children's classics as *Where the Wild Things Are* and *In the Night Kitchen*, provides us with a good example of this. Presenting Sendak with the National Medal of Arts in 1996, President Bill Clinton noted that: "His books have helped children to explore and resolve their feelings of anger, boredom, fear, frustration and jealousy." Sendak himself admitted an "obsession" with the "heroism of children" and with their urge toward "survival" in an often hostile world.[2] In this respect, Sendak's work offers us a window into our own obsession with the exploits of such enduring YA protagonists as Harry Potter, Bella Swan, Artemis Fowl, Ender Wiggin, and the aforementioned Miss Everdeen.

The level of violence and adult themes found in much of YA literature continues to be a topic of discussion—but the ability to tackle thematic material is the badge of any story worth reading. Indeed, it is YA's refusal to talk down to its audience that makes it so appealing to people of all ages—and the lens of youthful experience that makes it so relatable: whether you're sixteen or sixty, who among us can fail to relate to the (often fraught) experience of growing up?

If the sales figures for *The Hunger Games* are any indication, the answer to the above question is "not many." It is therefore puzzling that Suzanne Collins's novel, with its basis in such classic future dystopias as *Brave New World* and *The Handmaid's Tale*, has yet to revive the science fiction genre for younger audiences the way the Twilight and Harry Potter series revived paranormal romance and fantasy. Despite science fiction's endless possibilities (near and far futures, alternate timelines and planets, for a start) there is nothing in current YA science fiction on par with the cultural phenomenon of *The Hunger Games*. And while today's speculative fiction writers have drawn inspiration from such classic short stories as Ray Bradbury's "The Veldt," Kurt Vonnegut's "Harrison Bergeron," (and, dare we say, "little known" author Richard Bachman's novel *The Long Walk*), there seems nothing comparable for today's younger readers wishing to explore short science fiction from their own perspective.

With *Futuredaze* we hope to give the next generation of speculative readers and writers a taste (as it were) of the infinite possibilities inherent in both the science fiction genre and the short story form. Short fiction, with its suppleness and experimentation, is a great way for new readers to experience any genre—and, as we've seen a wave of epic fantasy and paranormal fiction on the market, we thought it was time to ask: where's the short stuff?

Also, where's the diversity? "There Need to be More Nonwhite

2   Krystal, Becky. "Maurice Sendak dies; author and illustrator wrote about children's survival." The Washington Post. May 8, 2012

Protagonists" was the title of a recent *New York Times* "Room for Debate" piece by YA author Sharon G. Flake (*Pinned*). Like many of today's writers she was expressing the need for more diverse YA characters. More nonstraight and other underrepresented minority protagonists could also help today's readers to—as Ms. Flake has suggested—"find their voices, [and] share their insights and questions."[3]

When developing *Futuredaze*, we too wished to represent a wider range of viewpoints than is typically seen in American popular culture, and to attract culturally diverse stories that reflect an equally diverse readership. This was, in all honesty, easier said than done as the majority of submissions we received did not venture beyond a white/Western perspective. Still: we remain hopeful that we've made a positive start and that the stories collected herein will prove wide ranging enough to begin awakening readers to the possibilities of viewpoints and experiences beyond their own. Ideally, literature should be for everyone, and science fiction in particular, with its themes of progress, should strive to provide new perspectives even as it allows us to encounter new frontiers.

Diversity for *Futuredaze* also includes the diversity of form. Outside the speculative fiction niche not many people have experienced science-fiction poetry. Gleefully, we correct this phenomenon—and then some. Having originally planned for a mere twenty pieces, we were quickly inundated with more quality submissions than we had dared hope to receive.

Futuredaze contains twelve poems and twenty-one amazing tales that run the gamut from heartbreaking to hilarious, interstellar to terrestrial, and "hard" to subtle. In "A Voice in the Night" by Jack McDevitt, a young Alex Benedict takes his first step toward becoming the inquisitive antiquarian of the award winning Alex Benedict novels. In "String Theory," Danika Dinsmore takes the idea of time travel and mines it for its comic and tragic potential. Dale Lucas's "Out of the Silent Sea" is both a pulse-pounding tale of military combat and a meditation on love. And (with a nod to Anthony Burgess's *A Clockwork Orange*) Chuck Rothman takes a day at the mall and uses it to reinvent teenage speech in the ultra-funny "Spirk Station."

---

3   Flake, Sharon B. "There Need to Be More Nonwhite Protagonists." The New York Times. March 28 2012.

Speech itself, whether inventing new languages or struggling with current modes of expression or self-identity, has become a kind of theme for this anthology both on and off the page:

Our co-editor, Erin Underwood, recently met a delightful twelve-year-old *Hunger Games* fan at a dinner party.

"So you like science fiction?" Erin asked.

The girl wrinkled her nose and gave an emphatic, "No!"

"But ... you know the *Hunger Games* is considered science fiction?"

"No, it's not," the girl said. "It's Future Fantasy."

Future Fantasy? We like that: a term once applied to early works such as Edgar Rice Burrough's Barsoom novels is given new life by a young reader who re-envisions science fiction as a more elastic and welcoming genre. It is this sort of elasticity that we have tried to represent in *Futuredaze*. While we haven't been able to include examples of every possible subgenre, we feel the stories within these pages provide a solid overview of what science fiction has to offer. Future fantasy, dystopian fiction, alternate history, speculative fiction, slipstream, steampunk, space opera—whatever we call the branches, they all derive from the same literary tree. In *Futuredaze: An Anthology of YA Science Fiction* we embrace those gnarled, yet sturdy roots and allow the new buds to keep growing, reaching upward toward the skies.

Hannah Strom-Martin and Erin Underwood
—August 2012

Things to Consider
When Choosing a Name for the Ship You Won
in a Poker Game Last Night

Irving

Have you got yourself some big freighter
that will never stray far from home base,
or a faster, sleeker smuggler's dream,
that will win through each thrilling chase?

How long has it been since you flew one of these?
Can your eyes and your hands work out how?
Can you run life support, the controls—the guns!
Or should you be greeting the passengers with a bow?

Are you worried the law might catch up with you soon
(though it was a crime you didn't commit)?
Are you anxious to see the next frontier beyond,
before civilization takes the fun out of it?

How far away is the planet you came from?
Do you long to return now and then?
Is the atmosphere gone? Are you the last of your kind?
Will you ever go home again?

IRVING

Have you seen all the worlds you ever wanted to see
and grown tired of the infinite black,
or are you still curious about some legend you heard,
in some bar a few parsecs back?

Will you be marrying your job as the captain,
or will your children be born here on board?
Is it a hideaway or a city you'll build,
or just a shell where cargo is stored?

If you plot a course straight on till morning,
do you dream of the wonders you'll find?
Or are you trying to forget you're in mourning
for the true love you left far behind?

Have you finally had an inspiration,
thought the one sound that sounds just right?
What name for the passion that will carry you on,
from this star to each star in the night?

Clockwork Airlock

Nancy Holder

I wish to tell you a story because I value your opinion. It concerns love, betrayal, and mutiny, and it has already affected your lives. It begins this way:

The *Plongeur* had reached the outer belts and the starfield sparkled in the ether. Thousands of superstitious crewfolk counted the sky diamonds as the clockgears ticked; for it was said that when they triangulated Primoris Astrum, the star at the center of the universe, their sailing days would be over. Landfall was a centuries-old legend, but it was a religion for many, and with the Judgment coming on, the pressure aboard the vast ship rose to near breaking point.

It was either the best of times or the worst for plotting a mutiny. On the one hand, the many-thousands-fold crewmen were distracted by the glittery vastness; on the other, they were hyperalert because the Captain's catchers were culling the population for Judgment fodder. Who would be plucked?

It was not the Judgment ritual that caught you. Nor was it the airlock that killed you. It was you, committing the blunder that got you caught. You could hate the Captain for her barbarism, her cruel sense of whimsy, her repression. But you could not hate her for your own acts of stupidity.

Was mutiny an act of stupidity?

When one's life is at stake, one must know how to assess the situation. Such powers of observation had kept Jinquine alive for sixteen years, even though she had been an orphan and a ship's urchin for most of them. Now she thought of the airlock and shuddered. It was agony to die in airless space. Your blood turned to vapor. Your lungs exploded. But before all that, you were pushed through the beautifully adorned brass airlock by a burst of steam that scalded you past any previous knowledge of pain.

The Captain—the mother of Jinquine's boyfriend, Jean-Marais— already had cabins filled with victims for Judgment Day. Some of them would die via the airlock. For those who escaped, there would be various "rewards"—many of them unwelcome, but some quite delightful.

The Judgment would be held concurrent with the meteor shower—approximately six days hence—and everyone aboard the *Plongeur* was going a little crazy in anticipation. Legitimate businesses were shuttering early in favor of more dubious activities: dressing in outrageous finery, drinking, gambling, consorting in dark alleys and darker stairwells—in these times, the enormous space vessel of bronze and gold rollicked and rolled like a floating Terran Gypsy camp as it clicked and whirred its way through the stars.

Or so Jinquine was told. She had never been to Terra. No one had in over a thousand years. It was a radioactive desert. Like all her fellow crew folk, she had been born on the *Plongeur*. Her mother, a whore, had died young, as whores often do. It was difficult to mourn what one could not remember, and the Ladies' Pleasure Guild had looked after Jinquine until she had informed them on her thirteenth birthday that *merci,* but she herself would not be seeking membership into the trade. Good thing, too, as the Captain had dissolved the Guild during last year's Judgment. This year, were any whores found plying their trade, they would be sent to the plank, there to choose their own fate—the airlock, or a reprieve.

Banning the Guild was just another of the terrible things the Captain had done. Taxes and mandatory hard labor—scraping the hull in the big brass-helmeted suits, repairing the steam engines— were doing everyone in. But the crew was too worn down and hungry and frightened to disobey.

Enter Jinquine and the other mutineers. And the secret weapon Jinquine had kept from everyone, even Jean-Marais. But tonight, the Captain had instituted a horrible new law. The infirm and the vagrants without work must walk the plank, even if they had not been arrested for a crime. Never had Jinquine been more grateful for the rough calluses, earned from hard labor, on the palms of her strong dark hands. But others she knew were not so lucky, and they were being rounded up.

Something had to be done. Now, she decided. The time was now.

So she crept deep down into the lowest of the holds, inching her way to the secret meeting place of the mutineers. There she tiptoed to the shadowy corner, pushed away the pile of junk she'd made there, pulled the canvas tarp off her secret weapon, and spoke his name.

"Watson," she whispered to him. "Wake up."

Activating, he clicked and whirred.

Watson. She had traced his lineage in his construction. His face and the shell of his body had once been completely covered in lovely bronze and brass, though several sections had broken off. Those she had been forced to replace with aluminum, since she, poor as she was, did not have access to such fine metals. The result was a patchwork automaton. His gearworks were iron and steel, mostly intact, though she had taken out the rusty bits and successfully replaced them with more aluminum.

She had found him while foraging in the dustbins for more flintlock gears to fill a repair order for Findhorn, the foppish cabin boy. Amid gouts of steam, shooting up from dangerous fissures and punctures, she had uncovered Watson's inert, filthy chest cavity and in the rapture that occasionally came on engineers when presented with novel problems, she cracked him open. She had seen the wheels and the cogs, the pins and the threads, and figured his works out on her own. She'd wondered if he'd had any dreams while he'd been shut down. If his memories swirled around in his sleeping mind like hers did, so that sometimes she awakened smiling and sometimes with tears running down her cheeks.

She wondered now if, when he said that he wanted to help her and would always be loyal, he understood what he was talking about.

Now, with time pushing in on her like barometric pressure, she shined his face one more time with the sleeve of her buckled jacket. He sat there impassively, in the rough clothes she had brought for him, and submitted. Beyond Watson's profile, the brass porthole revealed a night most ethereal. The Ambergris Nebula swirled like the seven veils of Salome, bathing his metal face and her dark brown skin with colors. He was a marvel, a wonder, a force for the cause.

She stood back, appraising him. It *was* time, wasn't it? She cleaned him some more, as if the sight of him so shiny would dazzle her fellow conspirators into action.

Then footfalls rang on the brass grate farther aft, ringing like the jackboots of the Captain's catchforce, and Jinquine thrilled with terror. She ran to gather her camouflage, a huge canvas sheet on which she had tacked hundreds of pieces of detritus.

"Friend or foe?" she asked Watson as the footfalls grew louder. Sometimes he could tell these things. She didn't know how.

"Difficult to tell," Watson replied. His French was not the best but then again, neither was hers.

She was about to throw the canvas over the two of them when a voice whispered her name and then the code word:

"Paradise," he said.

She caught her breath. It was Philippe Dardon, whom she called *le Tigre*—the Tiger—because of the soundless way he snuck up on people. He was an excellent spy. He had discovered the blueprints for the *Plongeur* and he had verified that try though they might, the shipwrights would not be able to maintain the steam engines much longer. They were falling apart. It was one of the Captain's dark secrets. There were others.

And because le Tigre was an excellent spy, she paid better heed to his jealous character assassination of Jean-Marais than other girls in other love triangles might do. Jean-Marais's loyalty had limits, le Tigre insisted. The spoiled aristo was only playing at mutiny. If forced to choose between his mother the Captain and his girlfriend the itinerant engineer (and patriot), well, Jean-Marais often snuck away from his palatial cabin for their revolutionary meetings with sugar and brandy still on his lips while Jinquine and le Tigre had dined on rat in the leanest of times. When forced to choose—and Jean-Marais would be forced, once the mutiny began—he would choose his mother.

In fact, le Tigre often argued, he would *warn* his mother. He would go to her and tell her everything.

And then ... the plank.

"I knew you would be here. Somehow I knew," le Tigre said, and he almost kissed her when she put down the tarp. He was always almost kissing her. Then he looked past her to Watson, gleaming in the nebulous glow, and caught his breath. He put his hand to the inside of his vest, where he kept a small air pistol.

"It's all right, le Tigre," Jinquine said, drawing Watson forward. "Look at him. A mechanical man! He can speak. And he has such a secret!"

"*Bonjour,*" Watson said in his terrible French.

Jinquine rapidly told le Tigre how she'd found the automaton, and activated him, and how Watson had told her that he'd once been part of a difference engine far superior to anything in the seven known steamful galaxies. He and all his brethren had fit together into a recursive pattern of sums and conclusions and useful commands until one day they had fallen into an infinite feedback loop and had all blown up.

But before that, ah, yes, before that … grand days for the landfallen ancestors of the aeronauts. There had been centuries of plenty. No wars, and no spacefaring, because Terra was still habitable. If Watson and his siblings could be reassembled and rejoined, they could begin the work of universal improvement—and he knew where to find them. So Watson said.

"And he says that the Captain knows this," Jinquine interrupted Watson. "All the superior officers do, and they've kept it a secret for *centuries.*"

"*C'est vrai,*" Watson said. It is true.

"Oh, Jinquine, perhaps you have discovered our patron saint," le Tigre declared fervently. "Watson will teach us how to create a new world—"

"But with the safeguards that were lacking," Jinquine said, dizzily imagining a ship where no one would have to eat rats to survive. Where, as Watson had told her, no one contracted tuberculosis or scurvy and died.

Where people dropped anchor and lived on planets.

It was miraculous that they had chosen the word "paradise" as their code, *non*?

"Jinquine, you are a marvel. As marvelous as Watson," le Tigre declared, and took her in his arms. His eyes filled with tears and he kissed her, hard, and for one instant—two, three—she returned his kiss because she was bubbling over with joy and yes, fear too. It was one thing to plot a mutiny, another to begin it.

His arms were taut, his kiss, impassioned. They were brother and sister in the cause, and yet, as multitudes of stars glittered in the belts, she was not thinking of him as a brother …

Zut, what was she doing? She was the girlfriend of Jean-Marais, and so she pulled away. Their triangle would be a distraction, and so she had to make her stand. Le Tigre gave a soft groan and reached for her. She caught her breath.

"Someone comes," Watson said, and le Tigre and Jinquine took three steps away from each other. She grabbed one end of the canvas and he took the other.

But the new arrival was Jean-Marais himself, attired in the finest of aristo wardrobe—large feather in his hat; an embroidered waistcoat of sea-green and a ceremonial rapier at his waist. Velvet trousers, and the finest wide-brim slop boots that money could buy. He had the natural elegance to carry such ostentatious gear. Tall, very dark, with eyelashes longer than a whore's and lustrous black hair that tumbled down his shoulders, he glowered at the two of them.

He saw us kissing, Jinquine thought anxiously, but he must know that she had chosen him. She knew le Tigre loved her, and le Tigre knew she loved Jean-Marais. *Zut*, all this must be put away! They had a mutiny to conduct.

Still, she twisted her hands and le Tigre stared at her with wide, frightened eyes. One word, *one*, to his mother, and their mutiny would be over before it had begun.

"Look, sweetie," Jinquine said a little too cheerily, lacing her fingers through Jean-Marais's and drawing him toward the porthole, where he would be able to see Watson in all his gleam and glory.

"*Bonjour*," Watson greeted the son of the Captain.

"*Merde!*" Jean-Marais cried, in perfect French. "What is this?"

"Sit," Jinquine urged him, arranging the tufted velvet pillow Jean-Marais had given her as a birthday gift in the shelf of the porthole. She gave it a suggestive pat. "And listen, please."

With a grand gesture, Jean-Marais consented to sit. It was clear he was shocked, but his aristo upbringing took over—circumstances rarely affected men like him because he was rich and powerful enough to buy his way out of any difficulty—and he sat composed, while Jinquine and le Tigre explained what Watson was, and what he meant to their people. Then they revealed their plans to take over the ship as soon as they could summon the other mutineers and set sail to find and repair the others like him. Joining the mechanical brothers together, the brave patriots would raise their world past the limits of steam to whatever it was that had come before.

Jean-Marais went entirely crazy. He began to yell, "Are you both sunstruck? Do you lack oxygen? That is not the plan! Not the plan at all! And this *thing* was thrown away for a reason—a good reason, if what it says is true. It has confessed that it and its brothers are destroyers!"

The original plan was to depose his mother and create a tribunal that would govern the ship, in due time. Le Tigre had always maintained (privately, of course) that Jean-Marais was using them. That once his mother was out of the way, he would take her throne by force and dispose of the mutineers. Jinquine had always defended him. He was loyal to the cause and would inherit the Captain's chair anyway, leaving him no need to betray them in such an unspeakable way.

As Jean-Marais bellowed and shouted when he should have been whispering, Jinquine began to wonder if le Tigre was right. The things he was saying—"When my mother is gone and I have a say"—not *we*, or *the tribunal*, but *I*.

They argued for so long, and things became so heated that Jinquine did something stupid. In her disappointment and fury she accused him of abandoning the cause. She said to Watson and le Tigre, "Let's go," and took le Tigre's hand.

Even le Tigre knew it was a bad idea.

And that was how she wound up imprisoned in a cabin, waiting her turn as fodder for the crew's amusement on Judgment Day.

For this was the Captain's cruelest tradition, one she had implemented when she had inherited the ship from her father: the one to be Judged stood in the crow's nest on the forecastle where all could see, and from there two planks extended to two doors in the hull.

Behind one door, the airlock would slide open and a geyser of steam would thrust the hapless victim into the vacuum of space. Behind the other door would lie a gift from the Captain—sometimes it was treasure, the cure to a disease, or freedom from taxation for a lifetime, or a year. Whatever she wished to bestow, the survivor was required to accept with gratitude and grace. Once and once only had someone rejected her offer, and the Captain had pulled out her flintlock and shot the idiot dead.

On Judgment Day, Jinquine would take her place in the crow's nest, and stare at the two doors, and try to learn which one would mean life, and which, death. She didn't dare think past that, didn't wonder what reward the Captain might plan for her. She spent each hour in terror, wondering if the Captain knew about Jean-Marais and her, or about the mutiny, or about Watson.

She had five days and nights to wonder.

And on each night, Jean-Marais came to her after bribing the guard and swore that he had not been the cause of her arrest. He had not sent the catchers to her hovel of a cabin to arrest her for sedition. He didn't know how she had been selected. In the absence of any proof of wrongdoing, the Captain could not execute her, only trust to the stars to proclaim her guilt or innocence.

He promised her that Watson was still hidden in the deepest, lowest hold. He hadn't told the Captain about the mechanical man with the explosive history. And he swore to Jinquine that le Tigre, as far as he knew, was still free. Of all the mutineers, only she had been taken.

"I will find out the secret of the doors. I swear this to you. I will save you. I will tell you which door hides the airlock and which, your new life." For of course there were two airlocks, and one would be sealed closed. The other would be open, to accept her.

Tears like falling stars glided down his black cheeks, and she closed her eyes in the desperate hope that Jean-Marais's heart hadn't hardened against her. She should never, ever have grabbed le Tigre's hand. It had been so foolish to stomp off the way she had. So unnecessary and rash.

"Only … tell me this," he said on the last night before the Judgment. He hadn't slept. Neither had she. Exhausted, disintegrating before her eyes, he looked at her with raw need, and a hunger laced with fury. "Tell me the truth. Did you kiss Philippe? Be honest. If you lie, I'll know."

He opened his teary eyes wide and stared at her as she nodded yes. And she remembered her misgivings the first time that the son of the Captain, in his palanquin with his officers, had seen her on the street. She had been repairing the engine in a conveyance for a stooped old lady who had no means to pay her, except with a scraggly brown skirt stowed in the machine's storage compartment. Amused, the Captain's son, who once told her he had never worn the same garment twice in his entire life, had watched the *ancienne* practically yank down Jinquine's rough trousers to force her to put on the skirt.

Jinquine had taken the garment to allow the widow her dignity, and the next time the Captain's son had seen the itinerant engineer—goggles pushed back, scuffed brown boot pumping on the bladder as she heated up some lead to mold a fitting—Jinquine had been wearing that scraggly skirt. Jean-Marais was charmed, and moved. Aristo she was not, but she had true steam in her heart, and he fell in love with her.

He informed her of his feelings, expecting her to be overcome at her amazing luck. The heir to the captaincy loved her! Instead, she informed him that he was a spoiled aristo who had no idea what it was to love. He protested. She sent him on a quest: he must prove his love by finding the old lady who had given Jinquine her skirt, and present her with enough coins to live out the rest of her days in comfort.

Eager to win Jinquine, he had unleashed catchers after the old woman, and the poor thing had nearly died of a heart attack. Her comfort cost him his pocket money, that was all, but the act of charity changed him, he swore.

"I joined the mutiny for you, did I not?" he whispered to her now in her cell.

She was alarmed, first that he would dare to discuss it there and then; and secondly, that he hadn't joined the mutiny out of belief in the cause. Le Tigre had always insisted that Jean-Marais's heart wasn't in it. That he didn't care two figs for the crew's welfare.

"I will save you," he told her as the guard approached to tell him time was up. A bribe only bought them a few minutes. "When I'm sitting with my mother, look at me. I'll move my hand just so, left or right. That will be where the safe door is. Left or right." He raised his hand and very discreetly canted his wrist to the right, then to the left. "When you've deciphered my meaning, blink. If you don't blink, I'll do it again." He took a breath. "If I can."

*

If I can, he had said, and now it was the Day of Judgment. She was certain that if Philippe had been in Jean-Marais's shoes, he would have said, *"I'll do it again until you are safe. I'll hide a knife in my boot and slit her throat."*

She knew then that she loved le Tigre and always had. She had lied to Jean-Marais and herself as well because he was the Captain's son. But she'd been bargaining with him, offering herself to him for the good of the cause.

Maybe she could do it so convincingly because she was the child of a whore.

Facing this terrible truth, she climbed the rope ladder to the crow's nest—old people were pulled up on a board and a pulley. The crowd cheered and jeered at her. They were ready for a good death. A hundred people had walked the plank ahead of her, but most of them had chosen the safe door, and the crew felt cheated. The judged had been accused of fudging their taxes, theft, violence—a hundred different infractions. Those who chose the airlock were then known to be guilty; those who chose the other door were clearly innocent. The insanity of the trial process was immaterial. It was the way things were done. It was what Jinquine must do.

She finished climbing and faced the Captain, who though older was very beautiful. The Captain wore a blood red silk dress with a bronze ruff, bronze gearwork ornaments braided into her hair and at her neck. Jean-Marais sat beside her wearing a sash of gold and copper medals. As they had practiced, Jinquine took a breath and stared blankly at a place between the Captain and her son. She appeared to be giving the Captain her full attention, but of course that was not the case.

Now.

As the drums rolled and the crowd roared, she stood stiffly. For her gaze only, Jean-Marais barely lifted his hand from his lap. So he did know. He had found out which door would spare her life. She felt time stop. Left or right? What would it be?

And then his mother cleared her throat and raised her ceremonial cutlass. Jean-Marais froze. The trumpeters sounded the call for silence. After a few moments, the throng hushed. Waited.

She has proof that I am a mutineer, Jinquine thought, terror-stricken. *I'll be instantly condemned. I won't be offered the choice of the doors.*

When utter silence had fallen, the Captain raised her chin and smiled her pretty smile. Such evil hid behind that lovely face. Though she shouldn't allow her mind to wander, Jinquine thought of Watson's face, metallic and unmoving. Was Jean-Marais right? Was Watson really a "destroyer"? What kind of heart cogged round and round in his chest? Would he have brought them paradise?

I will never know, she thought. She began to shake. She would be scalded and thrust into airless space.

"As in times past, once fate decides the innocence of the one who stands before me, then and only then does that lucky person learn what marvelous gift I have prepared for them. That is the custom. But tonight, we shall do it differently. For Jinquine." She favored the itinerant urchin engineer with her most condescending smile.

"I will tell you what awaits you behind the door of life," she said.

Everyone sat forward, including Jean-Marais. This part was news to him as well. He had no idea what Jinquine's "reward" might be.

"What awaits you," the Captain said, pausing dramatically to glance at her son, "is a husband. You will be married on the spot to Philippe Dardon."

Do not look at Jean-Marais. Do not look, Jinquine ordered herself. But his tormented features swam before her. He set his jaw just the same as when they had fought over the shape of the mutiny, and Watson. He was enraged. His mother would marry Jinquine to le Tigre! Jealousy was consuming him. She wanted to shake her head, to remind him that they were in public. That he was sitting beside his mother—whose cruel smile suggested a certain knowledge of their *amour.*

She heard murmuring, speculation, and some laughter. Taunts of *left* and *right* echoed through the chamber. A marriage was a pretty good reward. Especially for the daughter of a whore who had died young.

"Quiet, *silence,*" the Captain said indulgently, giving the crowd a moment to compose themselves. When that was accomplished, she raised a brow at Jinquine.

"So now you know what you might have, if you walk to the safe door. Step onto the plank of your choosing, and reveal your fate."

Jinquine's heart thundered. She was bathed in sweat. *Monster*, she flung at the Captain. Then she looked blankly between the Captain and Jean-Marais, and waited for his wrist to cant.

It did.

To the right.

But his head was down, and she couldn't see his face and he couldn't see her blink her acknowledgment. She looked down at the two planks, the left one and the right. She considered her savior—jealous to the core of the man she would marry, if she did not die today. Her fellow mutineer, who could implicate Jean-Marais as one of them. But Jean-Marais seemed as surprised as she that le Tigre was to be her prize.

Jinquine considered the character of Jean-Marais—a young, handsome man who claimed he had never loved anyone until he had met her. Who surely was considering that he could get rid of le Tigre after Jinquine was safe and marry his widow. Or would she be used goods to him? Was he remembering how she had taken le Tigre's hand in the hold?

Trust him, or not?

Left, or right?

All of this had clearly been orchestrated by the Captain to rid her son of Jinquine through one door or the other.

Around Jinquine, the crowd grew restive. "Get on with it!" someone shouted. Crewfolk began to stomp their shoes on the deck, to clap their hands. To jeer.

She looked up at the bubble over the masts of the *Plongeur*, and thought she saw the brightest star ever, dead center in the heavens. Primoris Astrum.

Legend or landfall? Paradise or Judgment?

Jean-Marais or le Tigre?

Yes? No?

Does he love me enough? She begged space itself to tell her as the last of the meteor shower etched the starry sky. She wished Watson were here to calculate an answer, but the automaton and his mysteries were hidden away. *Le Tigre, where are you? Behind which door?*

"Hurry up!" another crewmember shouted. Boos and catcalls accompanied her unbearable indecision.

The Captain reached down to a table and picked up her flintlock.

Jinquine began to walk the plank. So which was it then? Jean-Marais's hatred, or his mercy? Left, or right? Life, or death?

And so this is the place where I require your opinion, oh you who sail the ether these days. Tell me what you think: Which awaited Jinquine at the end of the plank—the airlock, or the Tiger?

Why

Evelyn Lumish

Why do we ask the questions?
The young ones ask
Sitting with their schoolbooks
At their metal desks
Listing to one side
With broken pencils
Too short to sharpen

Why do we question life?
The old ones ask
Sitting at their mahogany desks
Tallying up figures
Pens in hand
Red circles on paper
Too many to count

Why do we ask the questions?
Why do we question life?
For the young ones
Not sure of their place
Studying mathematics
Geometry
Physics and chemistry
Learning genomes and heart valves
Punctuation and French

For the old ones
So sure of their place
Too sure to ask questions
Running the world
On beliefs long-decided
From generations past
That never questioned at all

For the ones
Who make it to the moon
And turn on the first TV
And sequence the genome
Who write about great love
And imprint their legacy upon the heavens
With the Hubble or space station

For the ones who wonder
And the ones who break free
We ask questions for you
And seek answers for us

Spirk Station

Chuck Rothman

So here I was looking in the mallstores and wondering if there's anywhere I can manage to spend the creds the Maahm had dropped on me when this giant duck comes up to me.

And then things got weird.

Yeah, I guess I should have expected something like that. This was Adhara Station (Spirk Station, they should call it), crossroads of the Universe, where hundreds of races meet in harmony to work out their differences for the good of all.

You really believe that horse paska? Let me tell you—it's as spirky up here as a month with your grandparents. You know, like when they feed you bits of animals that no one in their right brain would eat, and the vid has only a hundred channels and they think that if you nuss a beer with a boy it's shameful and if they find you taking spree it's go to your room and no connection.

Yeah. Like that. Only worse.

I got to get a lawyer and declare myself emanced. I'm almost fifteen, and this is abuse.

But it's Reeni this and Reeni that and it's educational (spirk!) and a wonderful experience with a chance to learn from others (double spirk!) and you're being unreasonable and you'll meet interesting people and foods (triple spirk!) and young lady you'll do what we say and because we're your parents that's why and the next thing I know, I'm out here in a tin box in the middle of nogoddamnwhere, living with creatures that make you want to luff up lunch.

It's just not fair. But don't tell them that. They'll just make like parentese: "Life isn't fair."

Paska.

I spend the first week in my room. They let me bring my favorite cubics, but even Tommi Tenaka mysteries get boring three times a day. And I can't text anyone I know because, if you think about long distance on Earth, try texting from a mazillion miles away.

So I had to come out. The Dodd was gone, out negotiating with bugs or fish or starfish over some dumb trade agreement for Earth, but the Maahm was waiting for me and she makes like, "It's about time," and "You're missing a great opportunity" and "Here's a fifty cred chip. Go to the mall."

The Maahm ain't so bad at times, but I wasn't going to say anything about that or she'd get all mother-daughter on me. So I make like, "Thanks. Maybe a little shopping will be a little modern."

The Maahm frowns and makes like, "I wish you wouldn't use that slang. Language is important."

I heard that song before—she's a translator and gets all nutzy about words. I didn't want to sing it with her for hours, so I made like, "Like you didn't do it as a kid?" and was out the door, checking that my cell was charged. There was no one to call, but I never could imagine going cell-less. I even asked the Maahm about a 'plant, but she got all parentese and said I was too young. Hah! Once I'm emanced, that'll be the first thing I buy.

To be God's honest, I wanted to eye out the premises, but one look and I knew I shouldn't have bothered. The mall is at the center of the station, and was hardly mega. And it was filled with *aliens*. I'd seen them on the vids, of course, but up close is a whole new planet. You don't get any idea as to their size until a green-eyed bug stands next to you, and the sounds of their voices are ultracreepy in person.

But what you really miss is their *smell*. Some weren't all that bad, like the ones who smelled like green tea. But others smelled like a bag full of farts. Sometimes, I had to breathe through my mouth to keep from gagging.

And I'd be here for four years. My life was ruined.

So here I was surrounded by creatures who looked like they escaped from a children's horror vid, and I'm looking in a store window wondering how the frazzle you hang those clothes on your body and suddenly there's a voice next to me, coming out of nowhere like trekoporting or something. And the voice makes like, "Don't bother. The real good stuff is up the street," all scratchy and with "up" sounding like "ub."

So I look and this giant duck is grinning a toothless beak at me like I was a piece of pitza. Pervo.

(It wasn't exactly a duck; it had hands and other stuff. But it was ducky enough. Ask a biotech if you want the details, not me.)

He makes like, "You're from Earth, aren't you?"

Well, that was obvi—I'm the only one around here that looks normal, but I make like nothing because I wasn't brainless. Let the pervo stick with other ducks.

The duck pointed at one of the bits of clothing in front of us and makes like, "Besides, my mother would never let me wear anything like that. She thinks I should dress like she did back in the Boring Ages."

I pick up. "You're a girl?"

The duck gives a quacking sound. "You're still new, I guess. Here's the clue"—and she points to the feathers atop her head—"yellow. Boys are green."

"Are there many of them here?"

"Are you kidding? Just my ugly little brother. My name is—" and she gives off a sound like geese farting then makes like, "but everyone from Earth calls me Daisy and laughs. They won't explain it. Do you know why?"

I make like, "No idea."

She doesn't flinch. "Must be a parent thing."

I laugh. "Don't I know. I'm Reeni, by the way. Now, you made like there were some better stores."

"You bet. I'm quite a good shopper, if I do say so myself."

Well, I knew I had to put that to a test.

She was not up to superb, but wasn't bad for a duck. The clothes she found were weird but modern enough that my friends back home would be jealous (if they ever got to see them. Or remember me. I want to die.).

Still I found a few things I had to have. Hats were a good thing; if there's one thing all aliens have (well, most of them), it's heads. So I wandered through the shop trying to pick something and wondering if the one with the two holes for antennae or something were modern enough to buy.

That's when the giant bug came up to me.

Well, it looked like a bug to me. Whatever it really was, it was tall, with long arms and a triangular head and a smell like bleach. I was completely weirded when it held out something to me. Daisy was trying on some sort of something (I wasn't exactly sure what it was, but she said she had to have one), so I was on my own. So I played it modern and waited.

It was some sort of multicolored piece of glass, maybe a jewel or something, about as big as an eyeball. Pretty, definitely.

The bug gestured toward me again. It made like "Breasent."

Well the Maahm had taught me to never turn down a gift (except from Germans, she would add and laugh like it's some sort of joke. Parents are weird.). I took it.

I went to make like thanks, but it was gone. So I stuck it in my sidepak and went back to what I do best. I picked out a frilly fedora that would go nice on my head and Daisy oohed and ahhed over it enough that I figured it was worth picking up.

Then Daisy tapped me on the shoulder. "Do you know what will make this perfect? I've got some ethanol."

Well, I don't figure that, but I guess she understands my look so she makes like, "Fermented fruit flavor."

"Fermented?" That sounds good. "You mean, like wine?"

She makes like, "Alas, I do not know the names of your beverages. I think so."

"I don't care, as long as it's good for getting giddy."

She made like, "The same for me. But brain chemistry in warm-blooded creatures is surprisingly similar."

The Maahm doesn't like my drinking; neither does the Dodd. It's all "when I was your age," which is paska, since I know full well that they nussed down beer and worse back then. All our parents did; it's a known social fact. But tough. I liked the giddy it gave me. So I make like, "Sure."

So we're off to her quarters (which didn't smell bad, for a duck house) and two bottles of pale yellow were soon in our hands as we searched for a place for privacy—not easy in a giant can filled with aliens. And Daisy lifestories me on the way, how she grew up in

Duckland or whatever her world is called, and her trip here and how she had hung out with an Earthguy—even learning how to text with him, only then he left without even saying good-bye, even though he had known weeks before.

Boys are scum, we agreed as we reached a small service corridor that might give up a few minutes' privacy (not that most of the aliens would understand why we would be in trouble, but you never know) and turned into a side corridor and …

We came face to face with an alien. Only the alien's face was attached to its head, which was on the floor, detached from its body, which lay there, twitching a bit.

Quintuple spirk with paska on top.

I'll tell you I wanted to luff up lunch, dinner, and snacks. I don't even like bugs back home. Daisy managed to nine-one-one the police and I tried not to scream. The squids arrived in a blink; I couldn't figure anything they were making like—you'd think they'd learn to speak normal—but Daisy could.

And they made like it was some sort of routine, that they found headless bugs all over the station. Some sort of alien sex—biting the heads off the males like mantises at home. They went all parentese on us for wasting their time making like, "The Zegazans" (the names of the bug, I guess) "do this all the time" and "This isn't your home world" and a snotty, "Next time, call maintenance."

But I was creeped, so Daisy and I went our ways and I went home and showed the Maahm the new hat and she made like, "How nice," as though she almost meant it and I didn't mention the dead bug at dinner and then I watched vids until I grew sick enough to go to sleep.

And I woke up in the dark, knowing something was wrong. You know that feeling you get when you're standing in the street and you *know* someone is staring at you? Like that, only more intense. I clapped on the light.

A tiny black dot hovered in the air. Like it was looking at me or something. Taking pictures.

I made like, "Pervo!" and threw a pillow at it. It didn't have the brains to dodge and I caught it right on.

It only stunned it, but I was up before it could peep and stomped on it hard. It crushed beneath my foot like a little bug.

Now that was just spirky. I stood there looking at it, idly scratching a spot on my side. What kind of perv would camera me right in my own bedroom? OK, maybe about a dozen different kinds. Back on Earth, the Dodd got a screener when I was six; pervs are everywhere.

But that's back home. There are only a few dozen humans here, and I didn't think a perv would go for this sort of job (though you never know). If this was an alien perv, though …

I went searching for the probe, finally finding it smashed against the wall.

Too spirked up for words.

I did what any modern girl would do: celled up. But I paused. No one to call, and the Maahm and Dodd wouldn't be appropriately scandaled. All I could think was Daisy.

I don't know if ducks sleep, but they do love to hear the dirt. I made like everything to her, and she kept asking more.

She made like, "Probes are illegal," as though that was news to me.

I make like, "This place is just plain Spirk Station. The dead bug, and now the probe." And I remembered the incident in the store. "And the jewel."

"What jewel?"

I realized she didn't know, so I text her the whole story.

She makes like, "Strange." She didn't make like anything for a few blinks. "Maybe there's a connection."

"Connection?"

"We have a saying on …" and out came more geese. "Everything is connected."

Well, I cogited on that for a min or seven and I didn't like the result. It was like something out of a Tommi Tenaka chip. "Maybe someone wants the jewel."

"Wants it?"

I make like, "The alien wanted me to have it. Then he vanished as soon as I took it, like someone was going after him or something." The pieces started to fit. "I'll bet someone killed him. They wanted it. They killed him to get the jewel, then made it look like it was normal." Like headless bugs were normal. "They were willing to kill him for it, so why not me?"

I may have gone a little screechy, but Daisy made like, "Do you have the jewel?"

I made like, "Sure," and searched for my sidepak. It was on the floor where I had left it and I reached inside to find the jewel.

It was gone.

I turned the 'pak inside out. Not there, only there was a hole in the side.

I made like "It's gone."

"Gone?"

"It fell out. Could be anywhere."

She greeted the news with cheer. "Then you're safe. Even if you're right, and they want to get it back, you don't have it."

I was growing to like Daisy more. The Maahm says I jump to conclusions and overdrama things. Sometimes I think she may be right (but don't make like that to her, right?). It was modern to have a friend—even a duck—who could be a bit levelheaded. I made like, "You're right," and we texted a bit more until I got somno and called it a night.

I figured I didn't have to worry. I didn't have the jewel; I was safe.

But, I realized, as I was about to drop off, the killers don't know that.

*

Well, I didn't get my somno much after *that* (thanks a lot, brain!). I've seen the vids. If big bads think you have something, they never cred you when you say you don't. Especially if they talk bug and I talk normal. The only thing would be to find the missing jewel and give it to them. I would have to retrace everything I did from when I left the hat store—and hope no one saw it and felt sticky about it. I was up for hours searching my room, but it hadn't fallen into any cracks.

I had had enough, so I lay down. The next thing I knew, it was morning and someone was buzzing the door.

The time said mid-morning. The Maahm and the Dodd were off somewhere, trying to negosh whatever they had come here to negosh. Maybe it was Daisy.

It wasn't. I looked at the peeper screen. A giant bug was at the door.

Oh, spirk.

I needed to get out and find the jewel or end up with my head on the floor and the rest of me twitching.

The buzzer burped again. I made like, "Just a minute," nine-one-

oned as fast as I could punch the button.

The squid on my cell-screen started squawking at me. I made like, "Help," but it didn't seem to understand and I caught that it didn't know normal and was speaking bug or squid. I made like, "Just send someone," but the squid gave a very peeved look and shut me off.

Were they coming? I couldn't know, so I grabbed some clothes (old stuff from Earth—no time to look modern), trying to think. Our quarters were small, and there was only one door, unless I wanted to smash a window and see the stars close up.

I tried to stay breezed. The 'rents might think I'm stupid because I make like modern, but I'm not. I began to form a plan.

The bug was still outside. I opened the door quietly and made like, "Yes?" sweet as pears.

It must have learned some normal, since it made like, "You have something."

I made like, "I think you mean someone else."

It didn't work. "You have something." A pause as it consulted its pod (Note to future me: get one so you can learn to talk bug). "Yesterday."

Well, it wasn't going to fall for the stupid act. "If you mean that jewel, I don't have it."

Again it consulted its pod. "You still do. Our probe found it."

So the little flying probe was theirs. It was just like my nightmares, only slower. I had seen the tapes. I made like, "Well, you can come in and search if you like." I held the door open to let it in.

The bug hesitated, then entered.

But I made myself gone, shutting the door behind me and darting away. A second bug was watching, but not close enough: I was down the corridor in a blink.

Maybe it was the grav, and I'm sure it helped that I was on the Lax team back home (and I wish I was there), but bugs don't run very fast. I was in the crowd at the mall before the bugs could even get going, and dodged my way into the store where I had bought the breezy hat. I crouched like a crab and searched the floor for the jewel.

Not there. Of course it wasn't there.

I could see a bug outside. He was scanning the crowd with his beady eyes.

And just as I was about to nine-one-one again—who cared if they didn't understand me; a scream is a scream in any language—I saw they were joined by someone else.

Squids. They were talking up a tornado together, and then the squids started talking on their cells and scanning the crowd, too.

They were coming after me. I couldn't stay there; I knew if they found me they'd turn me over to the bugs. Friendly policeman, my ass.

My cell bleeped out a tone (Denni Deasel, of course) and I switched it on.

It was the Maahm. She made like, "Irene, where are you?"

Nothing gubbed me more than when she used that name. I'm Reeni; who could stand a name as painful as "Irene"?

But I didn't bleet. I made like, "Maahm? Nine-one-one the squids. The bugs are after me."

"I know."

"You know?" It was always a shock if the Maahm knew anything about me.

"One of the Zegazans is here. You're in great danger."

I make like, "I *know*! From the katting bugs!" She doesn't like rough speech like that, but I had cause. "They want to kill me."

"No. They explained it all to me. You're being paranoid."

"Of *course*, I'm being paranoid. Giant *bugs* are after me!"

I punched off the cell. They had gotten to the Maahm. I bet they promised her a trade agreement or something if she sold out her daughter.

I blacked her and the Dodd, too. No calls from them, not while the bugs were telling them what to do.

The bug outside was looking my way. I went behind the rack, then dodged past the storekeeper and into the back. It squawked at me, but I didn't care.

There was a toilet in the back. (Helpful hint: stay away from alien toilets. Spirk city.) I ignored the purple stains and spotted what I was looking for: a hatch in the ceiling. There was one in our toilet, too, and I was going to find out where they led. I climbed onto the toilet (I knew my shoes were ruined the second I thought of it, no matter how clean the thing was. There were probably alien *things* on the seats. Probably, they could jump). It was enough for me to reach the hatch.

It opened easily (now that was creepy, too).

As I suspected, there was a shaft. It was dirtier than a perv's bad dream and smelled of you-name-it, but it was an escape.

I crawled through it for what seemed like days. It was a real maze up there, and I figured the more mazy the better. The space was tight, too, which probably would keep the bugs out. I could feel the metal squeezing me like I was going through a tube of toothpaste.

After too much time to tote up, I reached a spot where I could sit up and feel just a little bit safer. Just let the bugs find me now.

But I couldn't stay here forever. I needed to find the jewel and get the bugs away from me. Maybe I could sneak out later, when they were gone.

If I could ever know when that was.

I felt tired. It's hard work escaping, and I kept wanting to fall asleep. Maybe just a minute.

My cell Denni Deaseled.

I punched up my phone. It was Daisy.

"Reenie? Are you all right?"

And I suddenly felt much better. There was one place I had forgotten about, one place where I could have dropped the jewel. "Daisy? Did you check your place?"

"Look, Reeni, you have to listen to me—"

"Because you're my only hope and I think I dropped the jewel at your place and if you find it, maybe the bugs will leave me alone."

There was a pause. Daisy finally made like, "Reeni, it's not a jewel."

"You didn't see it."

But she made like, "No, Reeni. It's something else. It's an egg."

I made like, "An egg?"

"Yes. From the Zegazans. The police were wrong: the dead one was female. The egg looks like a jewel, but it burrows into the body of a warm-blooded host. Gives off a chemical that makes you paranoid, so you hide away somewhere and then fall asleep. Then ..."

Spirk to that. I had a bug's baby inside me. But I'm no fool. "How did you know this?"

"The Zegazans told me. They're looking for you. It's been a big mistake—"

I shut off the phone. They had gotten to her. She was telling lies for them. To tell the God's honest, I never really trusted her anyway. She may have been working for them in the very beginning.

No. I was safe here.

Or was I?

I stared at the phone. Can they trace it? Can they figure out where I was? And if they did, what would the bugs do to me? Probably that spirky story of Daisy's was what they had planned if they found me: turn me into bug baby food.

Tired. So tired.

I shook it off. The phone was my enemy. They could find me with it. I couldn't take that risk.

I pounded it into the metal of the vent again and again, harder and harder, until the plastic snapped and it was nothing but junk.

I was safe. I could rest.

But, just as I was about to shut my eyes, I looked at the remains of the phone.

"My God," I made like. "She was right."

*

It's a lot easier getting unhidden. I kept feeling I wanted to sleep, and worried that the bugs might get me, but the idea that baby bugs would be eating my insides was spirky enough to keep me going until I found a hatch and crashed through the floor.

So I wake up in an alien hospital with the Maahm and Dodd by the bed. And Daisy.

The Maahm made like, "Don't worry, Irene. You'll be all right."

Like I didn't *know* that. I made like, "Don't call me that. My name's Reeni."

The Dodd smiled and smugly made like, "It looks like she's better."

They filled in the blanks. The bug they killed was putting eggs in warm-blooded hosts. They had tried to keep it quiet—it wasn't allowed off-planet, but I guess this was some sort of perv bug—until they realized they couldn't find me on their own.

The doctor—a cross between a cat and a giraffe—came in and asked me if I wanted to see what they removed.

How spirky was that? I said, no.

I'm better now, and the Maahm and Dodd got me a new phone. A 'plant, so I guess they can really be modern when they want to. Daisy is helping me learn alien by texting me in it. I'm catching on quick.

And the bugs have given me a credit chip. Damages. And I think it's time to go out and see if I can drain it dry.

Oh. And can you believe this? The Maahm actually asked how I realized Daisy was telling the truth about the egg? Come on—only a dorf wouldn't know *something* was wrong when I wrecked my phone.

Text you later.

Learning How to Be a Cat

Jenny Blackford

He's learning how to be a cat,
little by little.

He caught a frog again last night:
a Common Eastern Froglet, small as a baby mouse.
The hunting's in the genes. He'll sit all night
tracking a tricky leaf or savage stick.
Just once, well past his kittenhood,
he caught a moth, a Cabbage White,
and yowled with passion and anxiety
and pride, as he delivered it to me.
Mom was impressed; she'd have been happy
with thousands more of those marauders
gone from the garden, but they've eluded him
since that one time.

He's learning how to be a cat.
He was delivered programmed for the hunt,
but someone failed to install the code
for how to kill his prey.

He brought the froglet to my room last night,
held in his mouth as tenderly as any proud
mouth-brooding frog might carry its own young.

Somehow, he yowled his triumph
around the slimy bundle on his tongue.
He bent his pale-furred head down to the floor,
opened those strong jaws and sharp white teeth,
formidable instruments of death,
and let the froglet plop out of his mouth
onto the carpet. It glistened there, a little stunned
to find itself disgorged on the beige wool,
but each long sticky toe was perfectly unharmed.
It croaked, and hopped under the bed.
He looked at me, and looked where it had gone,
and looked at me again.
The question was quite clear.
What should he do, now that he'd caught the prey?
And would I help him, please?

The froglet's fine. I caught it, gently as I could,
and put it in a bucket overnight, then
walked to where some neighbors have a shady
accidental froglet pond set like a birdbath
on a concrete stalk awkward for cats to climb—
especially a cat who cannot climb much past my knees
before he falls, pretending not to care.

He's learning how to be a cat,
in increments so small that I'll escape
this heavy Earth for Moon or Mars,
before he learns to climb even a shrub.
It's just as well: the lower gravity
will help him chase bright moths,
dusted with Earthlight, across the lunar seas,
or hunt the silver Martian birds that nest
in twisted golden trees beside the dark canals.

Not With You, But With You

Miri Kim

Last night Daphne's dad became a Civil Servant. We all tried so hard not to look like we felt sorry for her and fought over giving her our plate of cake and sitting next to her when she looked tired, which was all the time. But when the memorial was over and only a couple of us were left with her we didn't know what to say—do we tell her we're sorry or don't we?—so none of us really said anything and the room went so quiet we could hear the adults talking downstairs and then all of a sudden we could hear Daphne sniffling in her sad daisy-colored heap at the rained-over window.

From across the room Brynn gave me a look, like: *do we pretend we don't hear her?* Then Mom came up to get me and I jumped up to leave, but she made me go back and give Daphne a hug good-bye. At first she didn't even look up at me, but then, just as my hands were leaving her hair, she wiped at her face and said, "Thank you, Naomi."

I couldn't think of anything at all to say to her because what could you say to a girl with *that* for a father?

*

Tonight Mom and Peter leave me at home with my older sister, Jamie, who promptly goes out at eight with Dickie, who is her new Man, as she calls him. The movie Peter got for me is stupid. I turn it off and sit in silence for a while, but only as long as I can stand the dull thickness in the air, and then I play pick-the-last-digit on my phone to see who I should call. Immediately I think of the number seven, which is no good as Daphne's is the only number that ends in seven. I definitely don't want to call her even if hers is the number I picked and I almost always listen to myself; next I think of the number three, which two girls have, so I call them up in alphabetical order. Lynn picks up on the second ring but tells me she has got a thing at her church, which I know is bunk because I can hear voices in the background and they all sound like boys and they keep calling her name in a weird way. I hang up. Next is Vita but she doesn't even pick up. Then I grow tired of pick-the-last-digit and think of hanging with Brynn, but on second thought I don't want to see her.

That's when my phone rings.

It's Daphne. I hesitate instead of answering right away because I haven't seen her in school all week and in that time I started hanging with Vita, who doesn't get along with Daphne. If I like being with Vita, isn't that a way of choosing her over Daphne?

"Hey, Nomi," she says when I answer. She's calling me by the name she used to call me in elementary school. Her voice sounds thin and sad as a raincloud. "What are you up to?"

"Me? Nothing. How about you?"

"Nothing."

I stretch out on my bed and decide to use *my* old pet name for her in elementary school. If she wants to be lovey, I can be, too. After all, we are still friends, even if I haven't seen her in school all week, even if I almost chose Vita over her. "What's up, Nee?"

I can hear her sniffling. Probably she has been crying all night, maybe all week. "I've just been—thinking."

I make a thoughtful noise. Of course she has been thinking, probably about her dad. I've been thinking about her dad, too, in my own way, and I've had maybe, five conversations with him in my lifetime. More than his voice, though, I mostly remember his face. He looks a bit like a character on TV, a guy who played a cop whose name I can't remember, both the actor and character. It's just as well. Daphne's dad no longer has a name, either. Civil Servants aren't supposed to.

"I found out my dad's CSN," Daphne says suddenly.

I sit up. "How?" For some reason the word *why* bounces around in my head, but something stills me.

"It was easier than I thought it'd be. I didn't have to do anything at all. Somebody called looking for my mom, but they only had my number, and..." she trails off.

"And? Nee?"

"He sounded cool. Sort of nice. And he said—he helps put families back together. Whatever that means."

"Oh." Suddenly the room feels cold, and I'm aware of how empty the house is. Funny how big houses seem when there's only you tucked away in your little corner. I sit up and hug my knees to my chest. "So what else did he say?"

"He said my dad's Civil Servant Number is eighty-four, and he's going to be assigned downtown, instead of far away. He's supposed to be far away. That's what they promised, Nomi, but he said they almost always lie about everything."

"Oh." It comes out in a croak, and I quickly clear my throat.

There's a pause, then she says, "We didn't talk long." Her breath rattles the line. "I was going to call you, before, so I could ask you if you thought it was a bad idea, talking to somebody about my dad like that. I know how much you liked him. My dad, I mean."

I rack my brain, trying to think why Daphne would say that. I think about all the times I slept over at Daphne's, the dinners where I sat on her dad's right and stole glances at him to see how much he looked like the cop on TV whose name I can't remember. I try to remember the five conversations we had together, if we talked about something special or if it was just the same old stuff I talk about with other girls' dads: school and my family and my grades and my plans for whatever. I think everything over and I can't see why Daphne would say I liked her dad, a little or a lot. I can't think of any reason at all. "I don't think it was a bad idea," I tell her. "Anyway, that guy called *you*. You didn't do anything wrong."

"I should've hung up on him, I think. My mom—she never gets the phone anymore, did I tell you that? She has hers turned off and the landline's being rerouted to my aunt's."

"So he called you because he couldn't get to your mom?"

Daphne makes a little mm-hmm sound, but it's muffled like she's covering her mouth.

"When did he call you? Just now?"

"Hmm," she says. "Yeah." I think she has her hand away from her mouth now.

"Do you think he's going to call again?"

"I don't know," Daphne says. "Maybe."

I set my phone on my knees and press my ear against it so our breath on the line sounds hollow and muffled at the same time. "How come your mom doesn't answer the phone anymore?"

"People keep calling," Daphne says. "People who don't like Civil Servants."

*

On our way home from the market Mom and I pass Founders' Square, where people are holding a big rally, and we get stuck in a huge block of traffic. Long lines of people walk past our car holding signs that have nothing written on them, only an X. Occasionally, they thump our hood or the hoods of other cars and shout and whoop and holler. The crowd grows bigger and bigger; Mom doesn't seem to care. She lights up a cigarette and talks on her phone, but she must notice something's wrong because she locks our doors and starts drumming her fingers on the steering wheel.

"And then what'd you tell her?" she says into her phone.

Several minutes pass and the cars don't move forward. In the distance someone starts banging away on a drum and there's fresh chanting but I can't make out any real words, only a sort of mushed up shout. Suddenly there's a sharp shrill whistle, like someone's setting off fireworks, and the people in the car ahead of us get out and look up at the sky. They don't look scared, just excited, so I unlock my door and climb out, too. I don't see any fireworks.

Then there's a loud bang, and a weak little puff of smoke rises into the air. It sounds like a giant water balloon bursting, which is a funny thing to think but it's what comes to mind. A tall dark-skinned girl hanging out on the trunk of the car idling in the next lane looks over at me and says in a bored way, "Just a boob bomb," and I nod and try to look unimpressed.

But I *am* impressed. Nothing ever goes on in Founders' Square, only book fairs and farmers' markets and things like that, never a rally where people yell and throw bombs. I peek in the window at Mom, and I ask her if I can check it out.

"No, get in the car, Naomi," she says, but I tell her I can see up the street and the cars aren't moving and that I'll be right back. Before she can say no again I move away. Out of the corner of my eye I see the tall unimpressed girl and when she sees me she joins me, sort of, and together we move toward the Square.

Closer, at the edge of the crowd, the noise is deafening and there's a pressed-together high buzz in the air, but I still can't see what's happening, surrounded by all these people. The girl's still by my side and suddenly she nudges me and says, "Are you with it?"

I look over at her.

She's older than me, and she smells like cigarettes. She rolls her eyes at me like she can smell me too, and to her great disgust I don't smell like cigarettes. She turns away and slips into the crowd. I give myself one more minute of standing around looking at a wall of people until I have to go back and join Mom and the ice cream melting in the backseat.

That's when I spot him. Daphne's dad. Civil Servant Number Eighty-four. Of course, he doesn't look anything like how I remember him; only the face is familiar to me. The face they left alone, along with his broad shoulders and thick waist, but everything below his gun holster they have pulled off of him.

And then in a weird moment time seems to stand still as his gaze moves over the crowd slowly, slowly. I feel cold and tight all over, but I can't stop looking at him and finally he sees me, too. He looks right at me, as if I've called him by name.

As if he knows me, still.

I can't move. I can't feel anything but the searing sharp chill of his gaze traveling all that space to find me. Fear curls around my throat with icy fingers.

Another high, sharp sound bullets the air. This time thick black smoke mushrooms up into the sky high above us. What was an orderly wall of people starts collapsing around me as everyone tries to press forward and move back, all at once. When the smoke settles, Daphne's dad disappears from view and then I finally feel in my own skin again and I remember how to move; I want to move *away*. I turn and blindly squeeze through the sea of bodies rapidly swelling into a solid mass of claws and panicked faces, ignoring the wailing of sirens, ignoring the choked wild screams all around me, and then I'm running, running, running—

*

I take a taxi out to Hope Plaza to meet Daphne. Hope Plaza was her idea. My sister says you don't go to the Plaza to shop, you go there to meet boys, but since coming here tonight was Daphne's idea I don't know how true that can be. Probably Daphne has neither boys nor shopping on her mind. And neither do I. Lately I have been seeing more and more of Daphne and less of Vita and Brynn and the others. It's not as if I want to keep seeing Daphne; it's more like I have to because every time I see her face, I can see her dad's and then I remember how it felt to be frozen with fear and I can smell the tall girl's cigarettes and hear the warble of police sirens and see the birthmark on Daphne's dad's neck that they didn't bother removing when they took away so much of him and then I remember asking Mom if I can go see the rally and it's like I'm remembering everything backward. It's kind of funny, living this way, funny and kind of exciting.

On the sixteenth floor I find Daphne sitting alone on one of those light-up mood benches that were so cool last year, but now everyone has them in all sorts of places, like bakeries and things, so they're not so neat anymore. Daphne's bench is lit-up green. I've forgotten what that's supposed to mean. Pent up, maybe, or hopeful. I can never remember.

She looks up. I give her a little wave.

"Your mood is green," I tell her.

"We can walk around now if you want."

I sit beside her and lean back. "Wait, I want to see what my mood is."

Daphne sits stiffly beside me while we wait for the bench to read my mood. Instead of her usual purse, she's holding a worn-looking book bag. It's definitely not the premium one she uses at school.

"It used to be my dad's," she says.

My ears grow hot. "Oh."

A few seconds later my side of the bench turns a pale orange.

"Do you remember what this color's supposed to mean?"

Daphne stares down at her fingers, or maybe her bag. "Cross."

"Angry?" I frown. "I'm not angry."

"White-orange means you're upset about something." Daphne shuts her eyes briefly. Her lids are heavy and pink and stretched tight over her eyes, the skin shiny like new scars, but I know it's just pink eye shadow. Daphne is easily the prettiest friend I have, though she's not really popular with the boys at school, and she doesn't even have lots and lots of friends like Brynn, who is easily the most popular friend we have between us and Brynn's not even pretty, just sort of *vibrant*.

"Well," I say, "where do you want to go?"

"I don't know." She chews on her lower lip. "Let's just walk around."

We get up and walk over to the screens, just to look because it's already half past nine and I have to go home before eleven. Daphne says she doesn't have a curfew anymore, but probably she has to get home early, too. As I watch the ads next to the marquee, I notice Daphne isn't doing the same. Instead, she's staring off into space, her big hazel eyes glassy and unfocused.

"They always play the same old stuff on these things," I say just to say something.

Daphne doesn't say anything back.

Then I catch something out of the corner of my eye: a group of boys, and they're watching us. They're older, or at least they're taller than most boys at our school. When one of the group catches me looking he gives me a wink. He's wearing his dark hair partly shaved in the sign of an X. I'm still not sure what the X means; it could mean he's anti-Civil Servants, or that he's doing it to look anti but isn't really. But definitely he's anti-Something enough to do *that* to his hair.

Suddenly I remember what the tall older girl asked me, that day at the rally. *"Are you with it?"* I still don't understand, but the question haunts me.

I turn away from the X-haired boy and try to ignore the fluttery jagged-edged wings scratching at my insides. I don't know how my sister can catch a new Man every week; I can barely look at this one without wanting to puke and run away.

And then, he's here. The boy. Close enough to reach out and touch. He pays attention to me mostly, which is strange as most boys go for Daphne and ignore me completely. This time it's all flipped around. He looks at me and says, "I think I know your sister. You're Naomi, right?"

"Uh-huh, and she's Daphne," I say. Daphne's staring at him, hard, like she knows him, but he's acting like she doesn't even exist.

I never have anything to say to older boys, and neither does Daphne. When the silence between us grows a little too long, the boy turns to give his friends a funny little wave and that's when I see the tattoo on his palm. Probably it's been done with ballpoint or henna but it looks etched in, not smooth and vivid like a fake would be. It's a black X.

He catches me studying his palm and I quickly glance over at the ads on the walls. A new ad starts up, as if on cue: men in a row hoist guns on their shoulders and shoot into the sky. The bang isn't very loud but Daphne gives a little jump.

The boy offers us each a cigarette. He watches us and smirks to himself, like he can see right through our clothes. "Hey, let's get out of here," he says. A warmness flows through me, not quite pleasant: kind of funny and weird and ugly and nice, all at once.

Are you with it?

On impulse, I take one of his cigarettes and tap it against my palm like people do on TV.

"Are you with it?" I ask him suddenly. My heart stops beating for a moment, then pounds away fiercely.

One corner of his pierced mouth lifts into a zigzag smile. "Yeah," he says. "Sure."

Daphne frowns at me. "Nomi."

I take the boy's hand and turn it over palm-up. "Okay," I say, my ears growing hot, "prove it."

"How?"

"Don't you know?"

His expression hardens. Then, just as quickly, he's easy and careless again. "I know where they keep them," he says quietly. "The Civil Servants, when they're not out on rotation."

"What did you say?" Daphne says. Again she gives the boy a long, strange look and again I get that funny feeling that they know each other.

"I can show you," he tells her.

"You're serious?"

"Yeah. Sure."

Daphne doesn't look at me, only at him, and he only has eyes for her when just seconds before it was different. I know how stupid that is. Daphne is lit up by all these ads, and her sadness about her poor ruined father makes her even more appealing. Of course he's into her and not me.

"Show me then," she says.

I won't be the third wheel. "I have to get home," I tell the air. Later

I'm on the light-up mood bench again, alone. My skirt and sweater glow with color. Not white-orange this time, but a pretty shade of lilac. I don't know what this means. I never know what anything means.

*

A few days later I'm with Daphne in Citizenship class. While the teacher has us type out an essay on why it's important to turn in our Body Ownership Conferral Card a year early, before our sixteenth birthdays, Daphne has her head ducked and her hand is a claw gripping her hair. She doesn't write a single thing, not even her name, and then later when we have to turn in our files, she leaves her space in Mrs. Summit's box empty and blinking. From across the room Brynn locks eyes with me and gives me a puzzled look. I shrug my shoulders.

When the bell rings Daphne slips her thin arm through mine, her face pale and her hair a messy bird's nest. "Let's ditch," she says quietly. This is the first thing she's said to me in days, because she's been a walking ghost ever since that boy with the X-ray eyes and his stupid X-hair took her away from me at the Plaza. Brynn is following us expectantly. For some reason I wave her off and she gives me a look like she doesn't know why I'm sticking with Daphne instead of her. She walks out of the room with a flip of her hair.

"Come with me?" Daphne says. There are dark shadows under her eyes and bits of red around her lips like she's been trying to chew her mouth off.

"Where?"

"Anywhere. No, wait. He's coming—he's picking me up." Daphne presses her left hand to her forehead and winces. I grab her hand and inspect it and see that her palm has gotten infected from a tattoo she's gotten. The skin around the legs of the etched black X is bright pink and swollen. She takes back her hand and presses it to her side.

"Oh, Nee," I breathe. "You didn't."

She looks at me, her face drawn and pinched. "It means I'm with it. Against them. Together we're with it. Better to be together against it than alone. That's what he says." Her voice goes soft. "Are you with it, Nomi?"

I frown. Something clicks in my head, but it's not the pieces coming together or anything like that, it's more like a latch sliding across a door.

She chews on her lip. "He wants you to come with us." She sounds like *she* doesn't want me to, but she'll ask because it's what *he* wants. Whoever *he* is—though I think I have an idea.

I feel cold all over.

"Nomi?"

I shouldn't. I'm not. But because she asked, I do.

We go around the arts building over to the old bike rack where there's a small hole in the chain-link fence covered by vines. Daphne goes through first and she holds the opening out for me as I crawl through.

"Where are we going?" I ask her as I straighten and brush the leaves off my sweater.

"Downtown," she says, glancing at her phone.

The word makes my stomach turn painfully. "What, *now*?"

"Come on," she says, leading the way. She has on her dad's book bag; it sits awkwardly on her thin shoulders, too high, too bulky, too big on her delicate frame.

We walk down the block and over the small hilly yard of a large brick house ringed by stinking red roses. Daphne leads the way onto the opposite street, but as soon as we're off the road, she stops me. She pulls me by the arm and forces me against a stop sign. "I changed my mind," she says. "You can't come with us."

I push her away but she's strong, stronger than I she should be looking the way she does. "What's with you?"

"You can't come, Naomi," she says, her dark brows drawn together. She takes a step away, holding her tattooed hand to her chest. Her thin face twists into a mask, an old lady mask. "I changed my mind," she says. "I don't want you with me."

I start to smile, thinking she's playing at something, but her face only goes colder. "Don't follow us," she says.

She jogs away from me and down the street. I watch as she stops beside a silver car glinting in the sunlight. After she climbs in, the boy from the Plaza sticks his head out of the driver's side window. "Nomi!" he says, in a singsong voice. "Nomi, come on! Come with us!"

I lean against the stop sign. I should run out after her, no matter what Daphne said. I don't like the idea of her going off to be alone with that boy, though I know they must've been hanging together all this time that she has been away from me. But I don't. I hang back, my heart beating oddly in my chest, like I'm having some sort of attack. I know I'm not *with it*, I'm thinking, if it means going downtown.

They have too many rallies there now, violent ones. They're not even real protests, just an excuse for lots of anti-people to come together to throw things at the buildings, at cars, at the police, but mostly at the Civil Servants. People have gotten hurt at Founders' Square. Lots of people. "Anti" and regular old people caught in the crossfire.

After a while, I hear a car speed down the road; when I look, they're gone.

Back at school, I join the others at our usual lunch table and tell them Daphne and I aren't friends anymore and Vita looks at me with a little grin and Brynn flips her hair at all of us.

I don't think about Daphne again for the rest of the day, but as soon as I get home her face is all over the TV. Mom and Jamie are all upset and Peter rests his hand on the top of my head and the four of us stand in a V in front of the TV and I watch in a stupid daze as they replay the bomb going off over and over and over. Then Mom goes to answer the phone which must've been ringing for some time and for some reason her soft "Hello?" from the kitchen is like a balm to my right ear. Jamie wipes at her face and sits on the sofa; Peter and I don't move.

At some point the tape of the bomb going off is replaced by a recorded message from a group of masked people wearing big black X's on their bare torsos. One is a woman, and the arms of her black X are faint where they meet the curve of her breasts. They say they're responsible for today's bomb and for each subsequent bomb from now on, each one representing the ninety-three.

"Ninety-three?" Peter says thickly.

"Civil Servants," my sister murmurs, and she explains that she's been reading up about it on the underground news feeds, which talk about things that don't get talked about on TV. After a while I stop listening to Peter and Jamie talk because I'm transfixed by the carved X on one man's body, the one sitting next to the half-nude woman. His X isn't a tattoo, as I first thought, or paint like the others'. His is a scar, jagged and darkened over time. He must've mutilated himself for this cause a long, long time ago.

I move away from Peter and crumple to the floor, right in front of the TV. It's *him*. I'm sure of it. Even with the voice garbled and his face behind a mask I can tell it's him. The X-hair boy. The boy with the X-ray eyes. The boy with the silver car. The boy who took Daphne away from me.

"She died to save Eighty-four from his miserable existence," the half-nude woman with the X on her breasts says, and the video cuts to footage, more poorly shot than the one the news keeps showing but the view is closer, much closer to the fountain where Daphne died.

I can make out her long black hair, the awkward bulk on her shoulders. She's running. Someone turns around, faces her. He's long and gleaming and horrible. She runs and runs and he just stands there, waiting for her, and then there's suddenly without any warning a great big gush of red, like wet goopy fireworks, then black smoke billows out into the air, flames blaze high into the sky, people run everywhere, and then the news feed goes dead. Then Mom comes into the room and tells me there's someone on the phone who wants to talk to me and *why* is my cell turned off? It's dangerous, you know, especially on a day like today.

I take my phone out of my pocket. At the sight of its dark screen something hardens between my ribs, like cold wax, and it's hard to breathe or think or see anything but suddenly I remember the way Daphne looked on the mood bench, her pale skin lit electric green— the color of sickness, not a mood at all, just sickness.

Are you with it?

I was never with it. I even turned off my phone so she wouldn't, couldn't call me, just in case. She was never with it, with me, ever.

As I walk into the kitchen I hear Mom say, "She used to be such a good girl," and I can't tell if she's talking about me or Daphne.

Mom left the receiver facing up; for some reason I don't want to pick it up. Instead I press my ear down onto it.

"Hello?"

I stare at the dull white walls of our kitchen but the only thing I can see is the big gush of red, the terrible bloom of blood where Daphne stood at the fountain for the last time with the ruined reassembled body of her dead father. So much blood, for only one-and-a-half bodies. I shut my eyes but I can still see them. It. Everything.

"Hello?" I say again into the spiral of holes. My voice sounds muffled and hollow. An echo of an echo of an echo.

Powerless

Leah Thomas

When I was born, I was born screaming. There's nothing interesting about that, I guess. It's the same for almost everyone I've ever heard of. If you weren't born screaming then you were born with too much optimism.

My name is Oliver. You don't have to remember it, because you will never meet me.

I think this is a shame, because I'm not boring. I can juggle forks like nobody's business. I'm adept at *kanji* calligraphy and I can whittle a piece of pine into anything—well, anything made of pine. The physician who comes to check on me is impressed that I can lick my elbow. I've read more books than I've got hairs on my head, and I have mastered playing the glockenspiel. An Austrian boy named Moritz has been my pen pal since we were both seven; he gives me strange advice about women, but otherwise he's all right. He's taught me some Deutsch ("*Verdammt! Gib mir eine Zigarette!*").

Most interestingly, I love a girl who makes me ill.

All it took for me to become so interesting was enough boredom to drown in. You'd be surprised how living alone in the woods can warm a kid to the delights of glockenspieling.

*

At first they tried to treat me, but hospitals don't treat me well. Hospitals are home to all kinds of electricity. Every single machine gives off its own brand of stinking energy, and my seizures are triggered by all of them. Anything and everything electric.

45

All the MRI machines are wrapped in scarves of golden light that give me pounding headaches. X-rays emit rich scarlet ringlets. Fluorescent bulbs exude a silver mist that drifts downward like craft glitter. Power sockets? They spit out blue-white confetti curls. Batteries in use are little twists of bronze radiance that shatter to gray when they run low.

I've never looked directly at a television. That would send me tonic-clonic in seconds. Televisions are bursting with inorganic light and organic color, a miasma of noise. I'm told that's all televisions are to anyone.

Motor vehicles are as foreign to me as glockenspieling is to you. Engines are hard, because the smog of energy around them is dark. I can't tell you what color Mom's truck is. Every time I've seen it from my bedroom window, it has been surrounded by a gritty, opaque nebula.

My favorite agonies are the things that people hold closest—things that truly alienate me. Cellphones, music players, computers. When they're switched on, their auras bounce off the skin of their users. Cellphones lend the faces they are pressed against a luminous sheen. Headphones coat ears in minty residue. But laptops are the best. Fingers on keyboards are traced by trails of light, like long strands of grass.

It was at Junkyard Joe's that I saw my first laptop. Joe's cabin was the only place within a few miles of ours. The cars in his yard are the only ones I've seen clearly. Dead, scattered across the lawn like metallic bones in some mechanical elephant graveyard. I used to sneak away to crawl between them. Mom was always frantic, wondering where I'd gone.

The laptop would seem a massive brick of a thing now. The little girl on Joe's porch didn't see me crouching behind an old pickup. Her name was Liz, but I didn't know that yet. She was sitting at the lopsided picnic table and biting her lip, oblivious to the strips of emerald energy that gathered around her fingertips whenever she pressed the keys down. The white light of the screen was reflected in her eyes. It made me think she was staring at a moon. I could not comprehend why that white light captivated her.

Did the screen reflect her like she reflected it?

I knew that if I got closer, my stomach would knot. Veins in my temples would bulge. I would convulse, would fall and hit my head on the wooden steps.

But perhaps seeing whatever she saw would have been worth a seizure.

*

I wasn't supposed to go anywhere alone. Mom was always my shadow. Playing Huntsman in the woods is a lot less fun when your mother's sneaking along behind you, lurking beneath trees with the sort of grace you'd expect from a drunken amputee.

When I was in my room, she checked on me every seven minutes. Sometimes she brought warm food from the woodstove, or cold milk from the freezer in the distant garage. She watched me from my bed while I studied at my desk. Occasionally she spoke. More often, she only peered at me with fingers on her lips. Her smiles were tiny and her laughter halting.

She'd promised not to trap me. Whether my father wanted what was best or worst for me, I don't know. He died and left us enough money to live on, but with one condition: if I ever decided to go, Mom must let me.

I didn't think she could keep that promise.

Maybe that's why I was always trying to leave.

*

I was nine when I finally got the training wheels off my bicycle. Days later, I pulled it from the tangled hoses in the shed. I pedaled down the dirt road that led out of the woods. Tree roots jutted into the path. They looked like nothing so much as outstretched hands. Every time I ran one over, I thought I was running over someone's fingers.

I wasn't running away from Mom. I was running toward all the things I'd read about. I was chasing humidifiers, semi-trucks and cash registers. Stereos and movie theaters. Everything I thought was life.

The first power line on the edge of our woods all but blew me off my bike. Orange electrical tendrils dangled from the overhanging cable. They hung from the wire much like Mom's bangs hang across her forehead. The moment I neared them, my stomach clenched up. A spasm went through my right foot; it slipped from the pedal. It was like the tendrils had grabbed me, had wrapped around my cranium and squeezed. The roots on the path had done nothing, but that silver cable in the sky threw me sidelong into the ferns.

But just as there had been something hypnotic about the laptop, there was something alluring about those tangerine tendrils billowing in an unseen breeze. I was determined to cross them, even if their licks left me twitching.

*

When I returned to the break in the pines, I rode one-handed with a fishbowl lodged under my other arm. I dismounted, let the bike fall, and shoved the bowl over my head. It caught on my ears, but I fought it down. Soon my breath was fogging up my vision. Trying not to tremble beneath my makeshift helmet, I approached the apricot agitators that swung from the power line.

I'd read pamphlets about hazmat and NBC suits, although Mom hated giving me false hope. I'd also read that glass doesn't conduct electricity.

Besides—it worked for spacemen, right?

Liz must have laughed at me. She lived in town, but Junkyard Joe was her uncle. Her father loved blackberry pie and there were lots of berry patches behind the car graveyard. Picking berries wasn't what other kids did on the weekends, but Liz wasn't other kids. I didn't see her standing in the ferns; I just assumed that no one was around because no one ever was.

Liz crept up beside me and pressed her face close to the glass. "GOING DEEP SEA DIVING?"

I fell backward into the leaves.

"What the heck are you wearing?"

I wiped pine needles from my palms and raised my eyes to see my non-electrical assailant. Through the distorted glass, she could have been anyone, anything. I pulled the bowl off of my head.

She was the girl I'd seen with the laptop. Her dark hair was tied back in a ponytail. Her brown face was freckled, completely at odds with my complexion. She was wearing short overalls with pockets full of blackberries. One dirty kneecap had a wet leaf stuck to it.

I didn't love her yet.

"Oh no." Her expression softened. "You aren't developmentally disabled, are you? Do you perhaps suffer from a mental impairment?"

"N-No ..." I was ... embarrassed? Petrified?

"I'm Liz. My parents are both social workers; my mom works crisis. She stops people from killing themselves." Liz smiled. I'm sure she thought it was reassuring, but it was such a wide smile. Compared to Mom's, it was terrifying. "If you have a mental illness, I'm totally cool with it."

"Not mental …" My ears were burning.

"And you are?"

"Sick. Allergic to … to electricity."

Liz raised her eyebrows. "You must be crazy."

"No." I stood up on wobbling legs and pointed at the power line. "Watch."

I ran full tilt at the break in the trees. It was the most reckless thing I'd ever done, and when the tendrils tossed me back and I ended up shaking on the forest floor with a nosebleed, I was amazed that I suffered nothing worse.

"Whoa! That was weird. Almost like you hit an invisible wall or somethin'. Did it hurt?"

I nodded.

"*Cool.*"

My face flushed.

"But that's *not* why I said you were crazy." She became suddenly stern. "I said you're crazy because you said your illness before you said your name. That's like one of my dad's clients." She pointed a reprimanding finger at me. I think my nose started bleeding again. "DO NOT DEFINE YOURSELF BY YOUR ILLNESS, Mr.—?"

"O-Oliver."

She reached a hand out. I thought she was going to help me up, but she proffered juicy, purple berries. "You want some, Ollie? Or do you wanna sit and bleed some more?"

Okay. By then I totally loved her.

*

Liz explained the circumstances to her parents, who were abnormally kind people. Her father wrote Mom a letter that made her cry. She always wanted me to have friends, but it was pretty hard to convince people to send their kids to a cabin in the woods to spend time with what they presumed was a young leper.

Every Wednesday afternoon, Liz's parents dropped her off at the end of our long driveway and she skipped up to our door, usually wearing plaid skirts and white tights coated in mud.

She always shouted: "I'M HERE!"

I was already at the door.

*

"My parents love cripples. Weirdoes, too," Liz informed me during an early visit. We were playing with building blocks in my room. Sticking turrets on ships, constructing floating castles.

"Weirdoes?" My pirate stabbed her tower. It collapsed into her frigate's sail.

Liz twirled the sail between her fingers. "You're the biggest weirdo I've ever met. You don't go to school. You've never used social networks or chat."

"But I can't."

"You're hopeless. You've never texted anyone. You've never seen a hand dryer or a soda pop machine—"

"But—I told you! I *can't*!" I dropped my pirate.

"*Hopeless*. You've never seen an electric razor or a train, or heard music or—"

"Shut up!" I cried. I kicked her frigate over. "I know music! I play the glockenspiel!"

Liz terrified me with her smile again. "You didn't say 'I can't!' that time. That means I can help you."

Her social worker parents had really done a number on her.

*

If Mom had known what Liz and I were up to, she wouldn't have let the girl anywhere near me.

Liz came to my room carrying her dad's book light, which had a tiny electric battery in it. It was the most precious thing I'd ever held—imagine being able to read at night without a lantern! But before she started "helping" me, she began each afternoon by listing off things I'd never done until I was livid.

"You've never sat in a massage chair, or seen a sitcom or even a *lamp*."

"I've seen lamps!"

Once I was riled, she would switch the light on and toss it to me. I shivered when I caught it, my head throbbing, but I wouldn't fall in front of her again. The first time had only been okay because I hadn't loved her yet.

I held it for as long as I could.

She grinned. "See? No biggie."

*

To you it must seem inevitable that this would sour.

Liz lived in a world of motion. My world was one of gathering dust, of stagnation. As we grew older and Liz entered junior high and then high school, she seemed to evolve into another creature—a thing of curves and eyeliner that wouldn't be caught dead in overalls. Though she kept grinning, I could tell I was becoming a chore. She talked more and more about school, about places and people I would never see.

I remained the sick kid. Even Moritz's lewd jokes were old news. I had nothing for her.

We clung to the old game. But there was boredom in her voice, now, when she listed all my nevers, and those nevers changed tense in a way that disturbed me.

"You'll never hear dubstep, or a dentist's drill ... or the bell chime between classes ... or ..." She stared at the old book light and sighed.

What right did *she* have to be bored?

I held my hands up. "Here."

She passed it to me, but for a single moment, there was pity in her eyes. That was something I'd never seen there, and it made me drop what I'd caught.

"Oh, Ollie." She frowned. "If it hurts, let's stop. It's just sorta ... cruel."

I'd only ever held small batteries, and only for seconds. The one time she'd handed me a flashlight my eyes had rolled back into my head. Since then she'd steadily been losing hope and interest. That hurt more than anything I could have held.

When she stopped bringing the book light, my hands ached for it.

*

Mom spent more time with me when she knew I was unhappy, but I began to think she was overdoing it. I mean, Zeus wasn't going to manifest in my bedroom and slap me across the nose with a videogame console.

I became frustrated with her ceaseless attention. I scowled when she came in. I snapped anthologies closed and glared at her if she spoke. Worse still, sometimes I didn't acknowledge her at all; I continued carving or folding origami until she left, as if she had no more presence in my room than the life-sized skeleton that stood in the corner. All the same, every fifteen minutes or so she was there in the doorway.

Once I pushed the telescope against the pinewood door until it jammed shut.

"Oliver? It's … breakfast. Toast and marmalade."

I did not reply. I heard her set the plate down, but she was still standing there.

Thirty minutes later, her knocking became frenzied. There was panic in her voice. "You're scaring me! Just—just open up! Please!" The door rattled. "Do I have to call the police?"

Somewhere in the garage I'd never been inside was a cellphone. I wondered what color its electricity was. But police scare me. They carry saffron-slashing walkie-talkies and they never take them off. If they sent an ambulance it would be like sending my hearse.

"Just—leave me alone!" I said. "Go do something else!"

"Do *what* else?" she shouted, and her voice broke like it never had before.

"Mom?"

No reply.

Maybe she never wanted to live alone in the woods with a convalescent child. Maybe she wanted to start a rock band. Maybe she wanted to study astrophysics. She would have her own life if I hadn't been born the most invalid of invalids. I didn't know her favorite food, her favorite color, what her ambitions were.

I didn't know her at all.

"Mom!"

I knocked the telescope away and opened the door.

She was on her knees on the floor. Tears streaked down her cheeks. But when she saw her sadness mirrored on my face, she wiped them away.

*

When Liz did not come for a month, I thought I was dying. I rode my bike to the power line every day. I wanted to find her, but I couldn't cross those orange bangles.

"Sorry," she said, when she finally turned up. "Driver's training."

"You couldn't schedule another day?" I knew I sounded desperate. I was.

"Nope." But she looked down at her cup of tea. She was lying. I was losing the blackberry girl and there was nothing I could do.

She talked. There was going to be a dance in a week or so, on the next Friday. Halloween-themed, with costumes and everything. It was the first one of her sophomore year. She told me she was going with Tommy Mulligan, a senior who I would absolutely love.

"He's smart, like you; he's going to study computer engineering at State. I should bring him here to meet you sometime."

She had never offered to bring anyone over before. I thought I wouldn't love Tommy Mulligan at all, although I might love kicking him between the legs.

"Dances are juvenile," I said.

For a moment she was angry, and then that terrible look of pity returned along with something even worse - understanding. She pulled her hand from the teacup. It was warm on mine.

"Oh, *Ollie*. You know I would go with you, right? But—Tommy's really nice. And ..." For once, Liz struggled for words.

"I can never dance to electronica," I said, smiling wryly. "I can never attend university or study engineering."

If only she had grinned.

*

I had to do something.

Liz came over on the rainy Wednesday before the dance, apologizing to my mother for her muddiness. In my room, I lit the lantern and cleared model ships from my bed so that we could sit. I waited for her to go to the bathroom. She always did, after school. She hated using public restrooms.

You'll never see a public restroom.

She left her backpack on the floor. It didn't take a lot of digging to find what I was looking for. It was one of the things that people kept closest to themselves, a little square of metal with earbuds dangling from it. I put the earbuds in my ears. My fingers hovered over the triangular button. When I heard the toilet flush, I pressed it.

A viridian, amorphous surge of electricity engulfed me.

When Liz came back, she knew something was wrong. She was probably tipped off by the bulging of my eyes or the way my head kept thrusting itself back and forth, back and forth.

"Ollie!"

"D-Dubstep." I tried to smile, but my words were slurred. Liquid slipped from my bottom lip. More than saliva, because I'd bitten my tongue.

Her eyes widened. She tried to pull the player from me but my fingers tightened around it.

That wasn't the oncoming seizure doing that, I swear. I couldn't tell her that the sounds from the buds were so foreign, so different from anything I'd ever felt that I would have died to hear more. There were … poundings? Bass? And something that must have been a *synthesizer.*

If it hadn't been *her* face, *her* eyes imploring me to stop, I never would have let go. When she yanked the earbuds from my ears there was blood on them. She kept clawing at my hands.

I unclenched my fingers. Blood spewed from my nose as she threw the machine out my window, into the rain. But it still felt like I was holding it, like its vibrations were shaking me. I was trying my hardest not to let the tremors win. But when a seizure takes you, you're powerless.

Mom told me that she came in right then, right when I lost consciousness and started convulsing outright. It didn't take her long to understand what had happened. She told Liz to leave.

Liz went. I wondered if all she had ever wanted was an excuse.

*

It was the night of the dance and Liz wasn't coming back.

"I bought this for you months ago," Mom said, from my doorway.

I was curled up under my blankets with my back to her; I had been lying like that for most of the past two days, since my physician had come by to patch me up. When I said nothing, Mom dragged something into the room and left.

I rolled over and looked. It was another manifestation of her selflessness—an ugly, wonderful thing that sent shivers of hope up my spine. I climbed out of bed, pieced it together, pulled it on and went to the kitchen.

"Where … where did you get it?" My swollen tongue throbbed.

"Online. Auction."

"Will it work?" I said, through the filtered mouth of the gas mask. Sweating, I lifted one heavy arm of the thick rubber-coated canvas suit. I had seen pictures of NBC suits before, had dreamed of them. The one I was wearing was of Soviet Russian make, nicknamed a womble. It must have cost her all of what was left of my father's inheritance.

"I don't know." Moistness in her eyes. "I'll ... I'll get the truck."

*

I could see enough through the goggles and the windshield to know that the electric heat of the engine was propelling us forward at speeds my bike could never achieve. I didn't seize, despite the dizzying bouts of color that assailed me as she drove. Either the womble was working or I had fooled myself. I breathed a sigh of relief into the mask when we passed unhindered under the tendrils of that power line.

We pulled onto the main roads of town. Piercing cobalts and ceruleans swarmed around billboards, jabs of amber lashed out from streetlamps. Coagulated browns overtook us as we passed other drivers.

Mom kept glancing at me, as if looking away might puncture the suit.

When we pulled up in front of the school, I struggled to breathe. There were *people* out there, heading from the darkness to the lighted building.

Mom whimpered. "My god, what are we doing?"

"It's okay."

She helped me out of the truck and threw her arms around me.

"I'll wait here at ten, okay?" I tried to sound confident. I thought I was hallucinating.

Her tears slipped down the canvas on my shoulders.

"I promised I'd let you go."

*

I stumbled into the school alongside other monstrous shapes, flinching away from light bulbs overhead, twitching at the sight of phones in hands and the feel of the beat emanating through the floor. My heartbeat felt spastic. Both my fists were closed; I handed a mummy at the ticket table ten dollars. He gestured to the double doors that said GYM.

That room was sensory murder. The usual pain wasn't there, but I could feel the weight of electricity suffused around me. The colors were unbearable. I could hardly see the dancers and the DJ through the coalescing clouds in the air around them. Individual shades, individual auras were impossible to pluck out. They were tangled and smeared together in a seething mass that circumvented dozens of laughing kids.

It could have been worse. I don't know what people are usually like, and I think it was easier for me to see werewolves, superheroes and vampires through womble eyes than it would have been to see normal teenagers through my own.

Of course I recognized her, even in costume. Liz's dress was black with glow-in-the-dark bones on it; her torso looked like the model skeleton in my room. Her face had been paled with makeup and she'd put shadows under her eyes, beneath her cheekbones.

She looked like me, only beautiful.

But she wasn't standing alone. She was attached to a blond boy dressed as a knight in foil armor. If I kicked him between the legs I'd probably be kicking homemade chainmail.

I trudged to her, pushing against dancers who swore at me. The suit was working, but it wouldn't for long. The perspiration, the flashing from all sides, the din of voices that I was unaccustomed to, the onslaught of light … I was being smothered.

Colors swallowed me as I reached for her.

My glove crushed her corsage. She pulled away. "The heck?"

"Hey," said Tommy Mulligan. He squinted at me, half-smiling. "Who's this? Brian? Great costume, man!"

I unclenched my other fist and pushed Liz's music player into her hand. I'd cleaned the blood and water off. She frowned at it. Then her eyes looked straight into my goggles.

"*Ollie?*"

"Liz!" I said, loudly as I could. The heat was excruciating. I pointed at the DJ. "Electronica?"

"Ollie, what—how—?" Through the haze I think I saw her eyes widen.

"No … biggie." My legs gave out.

Tommy Mulligan used his arms to support me. "Man, you're hyperventilating. Take that thing off!"

"I … can't."

Tommy misunderstood. He thought he was helping me. That was the worst thing—knowing that he really *was* a decent guy.

"No!" cried Liz.

"Here," said Tommy Mulligan, and he yanked my gasmask off.

My head exploded. A barrage of malevolent electricities stabbed me in the eye sockets. It was beyond pain—it was concentrated anguish at the base of my neck, expanding and searing as I waited for my brains to splatter onto my shoes.

I screamed as blood vessels in my eyes burst, as my hands started flapping. I screamed twice as loud as I ever had until the sound reverberated up to the gymnasium rafters. And when I fell to the floor I screamed even louder and my skull threw itself against the wood.

I screamed.

The world ended.

*

It ended for the DJ. All his speakers blew out in the exact instant that his laptop died. The lights above sputtered, went out. Cellphones sparked and people dropped them. All that was electric died with my scream.

For once, I made the world convulse instead.

I was on my back. The sound of stampeding, costumed teenagers shouting in the dark was shaking me to the bones.

"Is he okay?" Tommy Mulligan, my knight? *Verdammt!* "I'll get—get help." His footsteps joined those of the exiting, hollering masses.

I opened my eyes. Liz was leaning over me. I could see her face in the glow of her skeleton dress, although it hurt to stare through the red haze of broken blood vessels.

"I brought the … house down," I said, all stumbling tongue.

"You're crazy," she said. Her relief was almost tangible, another color.

I didn't look away. "You wanna dance?"

"You didn't bring your glockenspiel." She laughed, or choked.

I could see her eyes, just barely. She didn't look bored. I thought her freckles were piercing through the makeup. And when she hugged me in the emptying gym, a current passed between us.

She proffered her hand.

"Do you wanna stand, Ollie?" A hint of that grin. "Or do you wanna lie there and bleed some more?"

I stood.

King and Queen

John Grey

They're up there somewhere,
the light that moves,
that is not a star.
On autopilot I expect,
their rocket cruising unknown space lanes
while they grip hands
and stare out at the galaxies,
the worlds they conquered
by letting them be,
the races they assimilated
by being themselves,
the discoveries they made
from no preconceived notions.

While warriors razed cities
with the flames of indifference,
the king and queen of space romance
rebuilt the future from the rubble.
While warlike peoples,
exported their nightmares,
they recast their findings
at the whims of their dreams.
Out of death, life.
Out of despair, hope.

They're up there somewhere,
the passion that inspires,
the resolution that reminds us.

The Stars Beneath Our Feet

Stephen D. Covey and Sandra McDonald

"Planck," I say. "Please note, for the record, that this is entirely Zack's fault. And when I say 'for the record,' I mean when the rescue party finds our frozen corpses floating like popsicles in this crappy spaceship."

From the other side of the cabin, Zack glares at me and replies, "Planck, for the record, remind your owner that she's the one who wanted to skip school and come along, totally of her own free will. It's not my fault the flight software crashed."

Planck watches us silently, his eyes wide.

I check my skinsuit readouts. It's not actually too cold in here yet. Sure, life support is off, but the tugship is well insulated. We have emergency lighting too, so it's not too dark.

"Planck," I say, "tell Mr. O'Neil that the next time he plans a romantic rendezvous, he should make sure he can send a mayday when his plans go spectacularly wrong."

"Romantic!" Zack sputters. His cheeks turn pink. "Who would want a romantic rendezvous with you?"

Boys. They think you can't see right through them.

"I know why you got me here," I snap. "You're just like the rest of them."

"If by 'rest of them' you mean the people who find you annoying, then yes I am!" Zack fumes and glares out the starboard porthole. Twenty kilometers below us and rapidly spinning out of sight is orbital Moon Colony 5, where we both live with a hundred thousand other colonists. Where my parents, even now, think I'm on a class field trip to the agrofields and not trapped on a one-way death trip.

My name is Min Wan, and I'm never going to live to see my seventeenth birthday.

For the record, neither will Zack O'Neil.

But Planck will survive. He's a mechanical panda with soft fur and big dark eyes, no bigger than my fist. The cutest little panda ever. Right now he's curled up on my shoulder, a warm fuzzy ball of black and white.

"Planck," I say to him quietly, "tell my parents that I did make Zack bring me along. His idea, but I wanted to come. It was stupid and I apologize."

It's not much, but maybe it will make them feel better at my funeral.

*

This whole misadventure began yesterday, when Zack hit me in the head with a volleyball.

"Sorry!" he yelled, kicking to my side with the help of his air fins. "Are you okay?"

Around us, fifty other kids spun and somersaulted in the blue chamber of our zero-g gym. The teachers watched from behind plastiglass windows, glad to let us burn off energy for an hour. I'd floated off to be alone, because all my friends were giggling over boys or gossip. But that didn't mean I wanted a concussion.

"You're such a klutz," I told Zack.

"I was aiming for Chang," he said.

My twin brother, Chang, zipped by us with an evil grin on his face. "Gotta try harder if you're going to hit the Great Chang! The Great Chang sees everything."

Honestly, that's what my brother calls himself. The Great Chang. I say he's the Great Dork. But not as much of a dork as Zack O'Neil, who's always in trouble for unauthorized lab experiments and unauthorized computer access and unauthorized just-about-everything. Whenever a teacher is foolish enough to let Chang and Zack work together in the lab, they all end up in the principal's office. They're the yin and yang of trouble. The sun and moon of irresponsibility.

I, on the other hand, have a perfect disciplinary record.

"I'm sorry for hitting you," Zack said, his eyes downcast. His curly brown hair floated in the zero gravity. "I guess I was distracted about going to Colony Six tomorrow."

I scowled at him. "Don't be silly. No one visits C-Six."

"Huh?" His gaze jerked up. "Oh, what? No. Of course not. Never mind. See you later."

He started to kick away.

"Oh, no," I said, grabbing his sleeve. "What are you scheming now?"

"Nothing." He flashed me an innocent look that would fool no one with half a brain. "I'm completely schemeless."

"If you're going to C-Six, you're stowing away on something," I said suspiciously. "I thought you were still grounded from the last cargo ship you snuck onto."

Indignant, he said, "It wasn't a cargo ship. And I didn't sneak onto it. The robot pilot invited me. He was happy to have company."

Chang zipped by us again, saying, "Zack! Throw the ball."

Zack hurled the volleyball his way. I shook my head in exasperation. "I don't want to know anything more. Go ahead, stow away again, get expelled. Who wants to visit C-Six anyway?"

Then I stopped.

Because, hey, it's the biggest project in the history of space exploration. Totally not ready for habitation yet, but I've seen the specs in Dad's office. The launch bay itself is more than a kilometer long. When they finish building it out, it'll have docking bays and launch ports and construction pods for dozens of different ships. Short-hauls and long-hauls, piloted and drones, ships that'll take us to Jupiter and beyond.

I'm going to be on those ships one day. Captain Min Wan, merchant fleet. Or maybe I'll start in the Space Corps, work my way up through the ranks. My own ship, my own crew, adventure on the horizon and the stars beneath our feet.

"You've got that look in your eye," Zack said, frowning.

"What look?"

"Like when you speed in your mom's transport and then sweet talk security out of giving you a ticket."

I got very close to him. "Listen to me, Zack O'Neil. If you're going to Colony Six tomorrow, I'm coming, too. As long as you can positively, absolutely guarantee we won't get caught."

He looked around to make sure no one was close enough to overhear. "It's an unmanned agro tugship. It launches at oh-nine-hundred and returns at sixteen hundred, regular as rain. I already made the trip once."

"You did not."

"Swear."

"What about the cams and locks?"

"I can get around them," he said confidently. "How do I know you won't tell anyone?"

"Because unlike some people, I can keep my mouth shut."

From a dozen meters away, Chang threw the volleyball straight at Zack's head. Zack spiked it downshaft, making Chang chase after it.

"Be at Docking Station Three at oh-seven-thirty," Zack said. "Wear your skinsuit."

And then he kicked off, upshaft, past a bunch of jocks tousling over triad basketball.

Because Chang's always getting in trouble, people think I'm the responsible one in our family. But I'm no wallflower, sitting home studying flight manuals all night. I get in plenty of trouble when no one's looking.

My specialty is not getting caught.

And I was doing pretty good at it, too, until Zack tried to kiss me on the tugship and doomed us to certain death.

*

Here's a universal rule about spaceships: green lights are good. Red and yellow lights are not so good.

Zack got us onboard, just like he promised. When we launched, all of the indicator lights on the control panels were green. Fuel cells, power supply, radio, auto navigator, stuff like that. All of the cargo containers hooked up in a train behind us were also sending green lights.

But now every light is fiery red. Doomsday red. You're-in-Big-Trouble red.

The flatscreen monitors are all dark. Until the software crashed, we were on a preprogrammed course for Colony 6. Now we have no thrust at all, only momentum, and no idea of our course or speed. There are only two ways out of the cabin: the airlock that leads into space or the access tunnel to the power plant. Down below are three

Vax 4000 fuel cells that usually generate twelve megawatts. They're all offline now, completely useless.

Zack anchors himself to the base of a flight chair and tries to pry open a panel near the floor. "There must be an on/off switch to reboot this monster," he mutters. "You could help me look."

"We've looked and looked," I remind him. "And then we looked some more. Do you remember when we looked? You were here, I promise."

He grumbles something not very nice.

Planck pats my shoulder softly. He doesn't talk. Some models do, and I think that's kind of creepy. He's programmed to comfort me if he detects stress in my voice.

"It's all right," I tell him, stroking his fur. "Zack's just being Zack."

Zack ignores us. Did I mention that he's really tall? The tallest kid at Orbital High. When he was twelve years old, he stowed away on a spaceship and ended up spending six months in low gravity. That would make any kid grow like a beanpole. He's not cute, not really, unless you like curly hair and a narrow freckled face that's usually either grinning or scowling, but rarely in between.

On impulse, I snap a picture of his backside and long legs with my Quicker. I wish I could use the Quicker to call for help, but it's out of range. Between it, my spacesuit, Planck, and Zack's gear, we could maybe scrounge up thirty watts of power. But even if Zack can find an on/off switch, we need two hundred watts to reboot.

"You could be useful and try to analyze our trajectory," he says.

"I already thought of that. My GPS isn't going to work without a line of sight, and I can't see C-Five anymore."

"So go look for C-Six."

"Fine," I say, and float to the port porthole. For several long minutes there's only stars and other stars and more stars. Then Colony 6 edges into view. Just like home, but wider and longer and covered with gantries and cranes. A big spinning tin can for explorers and adventurers, or for people who just can't afford to go back to Earth.

After several seconds of computations, my Quicker offers up its results. The verdict comes in blue letters and makes my stomach knot.

"I have bad news and worse news," I tell Zack.

"Yeah?" He's gotten the panel open and is poking at something he probably shouldn't be poking at. "What is it?"

"We're heading right for C-Six."

"And?"

"We're going to hit the outer cylinder wall."

Zack jerks upward and smacks his head against a ridge of metal. "Ow!"

I wait a moment, but no blood or bone chunks start floating around.

"Hit the cylinder wall?" he asks, rubbing his scalp.

"Which is spinning at ninety meters per second," I remind him. "Forty percent faster than Colony Five because it's so much bigger. Also, the wall is covered with handfasts for the maintenance robots. Those are going to rip through us like a chainsaw through tissue paper."

"Huh," Zack says.

"Huh," I mimic.

He holds up a finger like our science teacher does when she wants our attention. It means he's about to be brilliant. Okay, not brilliant. He's about to have an idea that he *thinks* is brilliant, but is probably crazy and ridiculous. Maybe this time it'll be crazy and ridiculous enough to save our lives.

Instead of a rescue plan he says, "I'm hungry."

"Hungry?" I demand. "We're on a collision course and you're hungry?"

"I can't think when I'm hungry." He starts rummaging through his backpack. He pulls out iced tea, Space-Ade, tofu sandwiches, black bean salad, fruit, and onigiri.

"Since when do you like onigiri?" I ask.

"My stepmom thinks it's good picnic food."

"You told her we were coming here?"

"I told her I needed a picnic lunch for two, not *where* we were going." Zack offers a rice ball. "Here. They're good."

I float over and take it. Dying of hypothermia doesn't mean I have to die hungry.

"Okay, I see two choices," Zack says. "One: we jump out the airlock. It'll be easy to jump fast enough to miss C-Six and avoid the collision, but we'll still have to survive long enough for someone to notice us and rescue us. My suit's good for four hours, tops. I'd guess yours is even less."

"What's wrong with my suit?"

He snorts. "No one's going to take you seriously as an astronaut when you're wearing a pink suit covered with rhinestones."

I smack his arm. "It's not pink, it's sandstone. We don't all go for funeral black like you."

"It's pink."

"It's just as good as yours."

He's not convinced. He brushes an imaginary speck off the sleeve of his all-black suit. Maybe one day he'll buy one that matches his chocolate brown eyes. Not that I think about the color of his eyes much.

"Anyway," he says, "choice number two is we don't jump, but stay onboard and signal for help. Do you happen to have a laser pointer?"

He's so annoying I could scream. "I must have left mine at home."

"How about a mirror?"

"Sure! Because I'm a girl in a pink skinsuit! Maybe I'd want to check my makeup, is that it?"

Zack frowns. "Does that mean you don't have a mirror?"

I point over his shoulder. "We can use that access panel you just removed. Go outside, tether to the ship, try to signal someone. How hard can it be?"

He gulps the way Chang does when he gets spacesick.

"What?" I ask.

"I'm not a big fan of spacewalks."

I stare at him. "All those times you've stowed away on stuff, and you never went outside?"

"Of course I went outside. That doesn't mean I like it."

I reach for my helmet. "I'll go."

"Have you ever done it before?"

"Sure," I say. "In a simulator. How hard can the real thing be?"

It's not until I'm standing alone in the airlock, listening to the atmosphere vent, that my stomach does a funny, uncomfortable flip.

I'm about to step into outer space. All by myself. Me, outer space, and one super-strength tether line. No air fins or thrusters. If the line comes loose, I'll float off to a slow and awful death.

"Are you okay?" Zack asks over the radio.

"Yeah, fine."

The door slides open. Wow. Outer space. The entire amazing

universe, billions of stars and planets. It's like the 3-D planetarium at school, amped up to infinity. I'm a microscopically tiny speck of dust.

Min Wan, spacewalker extraordinaire.

"You actually have to leave the hatch if this is going to work," Zack says.

Taking a deep breath, I triple check the tether, then float out. Just like the gym, I tell myself. The stiff aluminum panel between my gloves is half a meter long and twice as wide. I try to capture the yellow sunlight and aim it toward home, but it's impossible to say if I'm hitting anything anyone would notice.

Zack says, "You should sweep the pattern over several areas."

"You should stop talking and let me do my job."

Several minutes pass. There's no sign anyone on Colony 5 sees my mirror flashes. I turn around and try signaling Colony 6 instead. Maybe some bored technician will look out a porthole at the right moment.

Zack says, "Aim your mirror at the inside edge of the solar power ring. Installation crews might be working there."

I try. C-6 is getting closer and closer.

Zack is watching from inside. "Once we drop into the shadow of the solar power ring, we'll only have ninety seconds before impact. I'll say it again: jump or stay?"

This is the kind of decision that I might have to make one day when I'm a captain. I just didn't plan on making it before I graduated high school.

"Stay," I tell him.

I climb back inside. The control cabin is too close to the tugship hull to risk riding out the impact there, so we retreat down to the access tunnel for the power plant. With our skinsuits and helmets on, we're floating pretty close together. Okay, embarrassingly close together. Zack is white-faced behind his faceplate. I think he's worried. I think I'm even more worried, and not even Planck's soft bleats can calm me down.

"I can't believe you planned all of this," I tell Zack, to keep our minds busy. "Software crash, losing power, slamming into C-Six. All just to impress me."

His shoulders stiffen. "Are you delusional?"

"All for one kiss," I remind him. "Obviously you hit the wrong button when you were trying to suck my face off."

"I didn't hit anything," he says, but he doesn't deny the kiss.

It was actually kind of quick. Kind of sweet. Maybe I ducked away too quickly. It's one thing to have your brother's best friend invite you to stow away on a ship. It's another when he tries to stick his tongue in your mouth.

I should have seen it coming. But I never see it coming. I always think a boy is interested in me because I'm smart and like rocket ships, but it turns out he really likes my long hair or my big breasts or the fact my family's rich. Rich enough that my grandmother sends gifts on every birthday, including this rhinestone skinsuit (which is definitely sandstone and *not* pink!). We go back to Singapore every Christmas to spend time with her, while some kids (like Zack) have never even been to Earth.

Something crunches above our heads. The whole transport ship lurches.

"Hold on!" Zack yells, wrapping one arm around me and hooking the other on a metal grip.

More lurches, and my heart is pounding in my chest, my breathing way too fast. The noise is deafening, like nothing I've ever heard—metal being ripped apart, all those holdfasts slicing right into us.

A moment of silence.

Then the biggest slam of all. Zack's helmet hits mine and we're jerked roughly sideways even as he tries to keep us safe. Gravity kicks in and pushes me against him.

Silence returns.

"Is it over?" I ask. It's barely a whisper.

"I guess," he says.

We both check our suit readouts. I don't feel any puncture wounds or sharp pains, and my indicators are all green.

"Are you okay?" Zack asks.

"Yes. You?"

He hugs me. And laughs like people do when they escape Certain Doom. Maybe I hug back. Maybe I laugh, too.

He says, "We still have standard cabin pressure. No hull breach."

It's kind of nice, feeling his arms around me. "Why do we have gravity?"

"We're either snagged on a holdfast or we got wedged into the solar panel ring," Suddenly, his expression falls. "We might break loose and get flung into space at any minute. We'd better go check."

He lets me go and pulls himself into the main cabin. I'm right behind him. The cabin has crashed off-kilter. With gravity in effect, the airlock is now poised over our heads and the sloping gray flatscreens cover the deck.

"Let's take a look." Zack points to the starboard porthole, which is elevated because of the angle of the cabin. He sticks the toes of his boots into openings never intended for climbing and helps me up. We wedge ourselves side-by-side, peering out into space.

Above us, the wall of Colony 6 is a line separating the stars from black nothingness. The solar power ring is maybe a half-kilometer away, blocking part of our view. In the distance, two cargo containers are tumbling and curving out of sight. Earth drifts into view: blue and green and impossibly far away.

I pull off my helmet. "We're snagged on the wall."

"Yeah."

"Why aren't you happy?"

"The cylinder spin is going to thrust us outward. Eventually it'll hurl us into deep space at ninety meters a second."

I squeeze his arm. "But someone's bound to notice the crash. We made a lot of noise and debris. All we have to do is wait for help and not freeze to death."

"And not suffocate," he says. "Our carbon dioxide's going to build up because the scrubbers are offline. We'll have to vent and refill, if we can access the oxygen supply for the fuel cells."

I raise my eyebrows. "The liquid oxygen supply? The stuff that's too cold and too dry to breathe?"

"We'll have to warm it up," he says. "Let me think about it."

He thinks. I think. Nothing brilliant comes to mind. We watch the Earth spin outside.

"How long before anyone notices you're missing?" I ask him.

"My stepmom will be pissed if I don't show up for dinner."

"My mom will call Security if I'm ten minutes late."

"They'll check all the habitat cams," Zack says. "Maybe track us as far as the docking bays. Someone will figure it out and start searching the debris field for the tugship. Eventually they'll scan the wall and spot us here."

"Eventually." My stomach growls. "Planck, for the official record, please note: next time, don't hang the food on the ceiling."

Zack looks up at his dangling backpack. "Huh. Good point."

We sit around in the cabin and try to think up new plans. If we had magnetic boots, we could hike across the hull. But we don't have magnetic boots and there are none in the storage closet. I could use the panel to try signaling Colony 5 again. But it's fifty kilometers away and the panel's too small to make more than a tiny glint. We could bang on the cylinder wall with something, trying to attract attention from inside, but it's eight inches of solid steel. Even a sledgehammer would be too quiet.

"I'm tired," Zack says. "I can't think when I'm tired."

Planck is already sleeping. Or pretending to sleep, because that's what robots do. I pet his soft fur and his robot ears twitch. "Take a nap, Zack. I'll keep watch for the next calamity."

Like Chang, Zack can fall sleep just about anywhere. He curls up in the corner and within five minutes he's snoring. I watch him, thinking about that kiss again. I guess when you grow up with someone, all those years of pimples and scabby knees and boyish pranks, it's hard to notice when they change into someone different. Someone you might want to kiss, if only he didn't do it so quickly and clumsily.

Outside the porthole, the spin of Colony 6 brings home into view. Out of sight. Into view again. Out of sight. I wonder what the Great Chang is doing right now. My parents are going to be so mad at me. I shiver, but not because of that. According to my skinsuit, it's only five degrees Celsius in here. No wonder my face is tingling. I turn my skinsuit up warmer and shake Zack's shoulder.

"Zack, we're venting heat."

"Huh?" He blinks at me, confused, and then checks his own readings. "No, it's okay. We've been cooling at roughly six degrees an hour. Radiative cooling is proportional to the fourth power of the temperature, so a little change makes a huge difference. I'll bet we won't get much colder than zero."

As if hypothermia is no big deal.

"Maybe," I say, "we could free the ship from the wall. The spin would hurl us off and we'd be back in sunlight."

Zack runs a hand through his hair. "Or fling us farther away from

C-Six so they never find us."

We watch our breath frost.

"We could ..." He starts to say, then stops.

"What?"

His cheeks go pink. "Share body heat. Hug each other."

"In skinsuits," I remind him.

"Still, your back and my front," he says. "It's better than nothing."

This has got to be a plan to grope me. Then again, I'm not a fan of turning into a frozen hunk of meat. He sits up and I sit back against him. It's awkward. He's tall enough that his head rests on top of mine, though, and after a few minutes it's kind of okay. From where we sit we can watch the porthole where, any minute now, a rescue ship will appear.

Any minute now.

"I'm sorry," he says, his voice low. "I just wanted to impress you, not get us killed."

"So you planned the software failure?" I tease.

"Of course not. This whole trip."

"How about hitting me in the head with a volleyball?"

He sounds sheepish. "Okay, that part, yes."

"Planck," I call out. "Please note, for the official record, that Zack will do anything for a date."

The panda climbs up my leg and nestles in my lap.

"It's not a date," Zack says. "More like a ... trip."

"A date."

"Hmmph," he says.

We watch the stars and wait.

*

I don't remember falling asleep, but I wake up with a headache: CO_2 poisoning.

"Zack, we forgot!" I lurch upright. "The carbon dioxide's killing us!"

He grumbles something and goes right back to sleep. In the dim emergency lighting I can see his lips have a bluish tinge. I slip my helmet on, then pull his on too. Within a few moments he's blinking up at me. I check our readouts.

"We have to try to get to the liquid oxygen," I say.

The oxygen is stored down in the power plant. There must be

pipes and valves to feed the fuel cells, but the panels are welded shut and there's no way to open them.

We have only three hours of oxygen left in each of our suits.

"Okay, plan B," Zack says behind his faceplate.

"What's plan B?"

"I don't know."

He stares at me. I stare back. I know what he's thinking because I'm thinking it, too. We're really going to die. Here, in this ship, before any help can come.

My Quicker sings out my favorite song.

"Hey!" I say, heart jumping. "They found us."

"Who is it?" Zack asks.

I stare at the screen, elation quickly fading. "Nothing. My alarm. My mom programmed it to remind me to take my vitamins."

Zack turns away.

I put the Quicker away. I don't want to cry in front of Zack, but I feel absolutely wrung out and ready to curl up in defeat.

Then I take my Quicker out again. It glows blue.

"Wifi," I say.

His voice is dull. "What about it?"

"What's the wifi range on these things?"

"I don't know. A kilometer, probably," he says. "You'd need an open signal. Colony Six doesn't have any of those yet."

"But Colony Five does, right?"

"Sure. Dozens of them along the hull for departing and arriving ships."

"So if we get within one kilometer of C-Five, our Quickers could send messages."

"How?" he asks wearily. "We're fifty kilometers away and we can't get the ship unstuck."

I take his hand and make him look at me. "We don't need the ship. We jump on our own."

Zack swallows so hard his teeth click.

"That's not a good idea," he says.

"It's a perfect idea," I tell him. "But first we have to send a signal."

We spend the next twenty minutes ripping free any large panels and grates that aren't welded to the ship. Then we have to rig a way to climb up to the airlock. I have to stand on Zack's shoulders, definitely not fun, and he has to shimmy up the emergency cable, even less fun, and then we have to haul up our stash.

"It's as easy as bowling," I tell Zack once we're in place. "Come on, you can do this."

Colony 5 rises below us. I drop the first panel. It falls away at ninety meters per second, just as the laws of physics say it will. If we're right, it should pass within a half-kilometer of C-5's wall.

A minute later, Zack drops a metal grate. It trails the first one like a silver raindrop.

Three, four, five, six items, timed at one minute intervals. We're making things that will reflect radar. Soon, if not already, meteor alarms across the colony will start blaring. Radar and visual telescopes will turn our way. Even Chang might notice. Mom and Dad got him a nice setup for his birthday this year.

"Okay, Zack," I say. "Now us."

Zack grips the hull so hard I can almost hear his knuckles pop. "I think I'll stay here. You know how I feel about spacewalks."

Planck is nestled up in my helmet. He makes a noise like he agrees with Zack. Silly robot.

Ten seconds until Colony 5 rises above our horizon again.

"If you come with me right now," I promise, "I'll give you a kiss you'll never forget. Take my hand, Zack."

He does. I pry his other hand off the edge of the tugship.

We leap.

For ten long seconds we somersault through the shadows. Ninety meters per second is just about two hundred miles an hour on those old computer games Chang likes to play. But it doesn't feel fast. It feels like we're sailing along in one enormous dark zero-g gym. Then sunlight blasts over us. My face instantly warms. It'll take a little longer for the rays to penetrate my suit, but I've never been more thankful for that burning ball of hydrogen and helium at the center of our solar system.

I peer through Zack's visor. His eyes are screwed shut.

"Just tell me when we land," he croaks.

I turn on my helmet light and emergency red strobe. Then I turn his on, too. We tumble together, head-over-heels, about one turn every twenty seconds. Earth rolls into view and then out again. Colony 6 recedes behind us. The giant cylinder of Colony 5 gets closer. On any given day it'll never win an award for aesthetics, but right now I've never seen anything prettier in my whole life.

"If we hit it, we'll die on impact," Zack says unhelpfully. "If we miss, good, but we're going to keep overshooting it. They'll have to chase us and pick us up before our oxygen gives out."

"I know, thanks!" I say, and turn on our Quickers. We rigged them to our suits before jumping. They blast out our mayday messages. Hopefully someone will pick up...

It's ridiculously hard to judge distances in space, especially when you're hurtling through it. One minute C-5 is right in front of us, and the next it's already behind us and getting smaller.

Panic seizes me. That looked a lot farther than one kilometer.

"I don't think we got within range!" I say.

"Sure we did!"

"How would *you* know? Your eyes are closed!"

"I have confidence in physics!"

As we tumble around, I can see blue green Earth. And Colony 5, and Colony 6, and of course our big fat moon of gray rock. I can see that I might never get to be a space captain at all, and that's pretty awful. But maybe Zack's right. Physics and science and a nice dose of good luck might still save us after all.

Just in case, in my mayday message on my Quicker, I told my parents that I loved them. That if I die, it's only because a piece of software failed. I hope they forgive me one day and by the way, Chang can have all my stuff except my diary, which they can send to Grandma. She was an astronaut once.

I guess maybe I'm an astronaut now, too.

I wish I wasn't so tired.

I wish I could keep my eyes open to take pictures of it all.

I wish …

*

Static blasts through my helmet.

"Min Wan, if you don't answer me right now you are grounded for life," my father says.

"Oh, no," I groan. It just figures Dad would commandeer a rescue shuttle and come racing after us. Even now, a silver ship is zooming our way. "Zack," I say. "Wake up."

"I'm awake." He stares past my helmet. "Wow, look at that."

There's a space net ahead of us. And another rescue ship. No, make that three. A fleet of ships, and oh boy, this is embarrassing. I'm never going to live it down at school. One day I'll be a hundred years old and my parents will be a hundred and thirty and they'll *still* be nagging me about this.

I guess my perfect record is perfectly spoiled.

"You can only ground me until I'm eighteen," I tell Dad over the radio.

He laughs. "Try me, kiddo."

It's not easy to catch two people hurtling along in space. But the crew does it anyway, and we get tugged inside the best airlock in the whole world, and once we're inside Zack starts laughing with relief.

"I never had any doubt," he says.

I yank off my helmet and pull Planck down to my lap. He's fine, of course. We're all fine. The white inner door hisses open and a crowd of people peer down at us. My father, of course, and maybe the ship's captain, and a medic, and some random crewmembers who just want to see what these crazy kids have done to themselves.

"Min Wan," my father says, shaking his head. "You are in an unbelievable amount of trouble. You too, Zack O'Neil."

Zack isn't laughing now. He knows my father has a temper. I hold up a finger to Dad, asking him to wait, and I help Zack get his helmet off.

"I promised you a kiss," I tell him.

His eyes widen but he doesn't protest.

I bend close. Try not to bump his nose, or worry about how bad my breath might smell. I press my mouth to his and taste salt and sweetness both. We did it. Survived. He cups my head with his gloved hand and leans in closer and oh … it's like falling into sunshine after being in the shadows. This is what the girls at school are always hoping to find. Someone who looks at you and sees you not as the rich girl, or the girl in a sandstone (pink) skinsuit, but as someone smart and strong and kissable.

And for the official record, I see him, too. Not just as some reckless kid who's always in trouble. He's smart and brave and he's going to have a lot of adventures in his life. Maybe one day I'll even hire him to be on my crew.

My father clears his throat. I break away, my face warm from everybody watching.

Zack smiles at everyone, the Big Dork.

"Best date, ever," he says.

"I agree." I say, and kiss him again.

Out of the Silent Sea

Dale Lucas

Private Owen Mboku saw the column of flame rushing down the corridor to meet him and leapt through the nearest hull breach. Everything was ablaze and roaring as the steel skin of the warship buckled and exploded. Mboku reeled into the void, end over end, tucking his extremities as he'd been taught in jump school to make himself a smaller target for shrapnel. In zero-g, a stray fragment could take off his head, a limb, or even punch a hole in his EVC suit and depressurize him. He was only eighteen and in no hurry to die.

Vacuum stole the last of the ruptured warship's atmosphere, smothering the flames. Then there was only velocity: a zooming, tumbling madness of rent metal, debris, and wheeling stars.

Nanosensors in Mboku's EVC suit locked onto what had been center mass for the warship only moments ago and his deceleration jets fired, first to arrest his spin, then his forward motion. Within moments he slowed and came to a sort of stop. Pieces of the warship whizzed around him.

First general order: in case of hull breach or ejection, arrest one's motion and avoid being slagged by supersonic flak.

Check.

Second general order: secure position and activate personal data transmitter for retrieval.

Mboku scanned the debris field before him. If his calculations were right, he was floating near the space where, only minutes earlier, their jump frigate, the *Timurlane*, had been positioned. Now there were only the stars and the tumbling remnants of the Kharmuz warship, all plummeting away from him into the emptiness. Vertigo set in, courtesy of zero-g and the bottomless black of deep space all around him. He thought he'd beaten it with hypno-therapies and psych counseling, but now it came roaring back: a hollowness in his gut, spreading cold waves of nausea through him. He switched on his com.

"Private First Class Owen Mboku, number four-one-four-eight-six-zero-seven-zero-four. Adrift. Repeat: adrift. Reply."

Static intermingled with a few garbled signals.

He tried again. There was no answer.

Owen Mboku closed his eyes and began to count in Zulu—the tongue his grandfather taught him in childhood. *When frightened,* grandfather had said, *consider your troubles in the tongue of your ancestors. Wherever you are, they shall come to your aid.*

Even twenty thousand light years from the world that bore them? Mboku wondered.

He reached one hundred in his count, took a deep breath, and began to count backward.

*

He dreamt of home: him and his childhood friends hiking and camping in the foothills outside Neopraetoria with his grandfather. They were all so young, the blue sky above them, the green hills to one side, the indigo ocean to the other, rippling fiery gold in the gloaming.

They were leaping from the rocks into the sea below. Owen was afraid.

Zapata went first. Brett followed. Jake lingered on the rocks beside Owen. The girls bobbed in the gently seething tide below them, their young bodies glistening in the dusk, their dark hair slick against their heads and shoulders. Knowing that Owen was afraid, they beckoned him with open arms. Still he stood frozen on the edge of the precipice, unable to jump.

Then Zapata opened her arms and called out to him, her voice hard and unforgiving. "No fear, Owen!" she commanded. "Now, jump!"

Terrified, but eager to please her, Owen Mboku jumped.

The sea rose to meet him.

From that vision, Mboku opened his eyes to a field of stars. According to his chronometer, he'd been adrift for eight hours.

Where were his friends now? Zapata, Jake, and Brett? Mboku checked the casualty rosters each day as word came in from the far fronts of the war. He sent them messages when he could—usually in the aftermath of an operation to let them know he was alive and well—but they rarely responded and those responses were brief, bearing the same polite wonder as his own: Here I am, alive. Hope you're well.

He imagined Zapata again, treading water beneath him as he stood on a precipice, afraid to jump. This time, however, they were not children, but as they were now: barely eighteen. Owen was a compact, well-made young man of Bantu-Nicon extraction, ebon and handsome, Zapata a lithe Anglospan beauty with a strain of old Iberian blood.

No fear, Owen, she said. *Now, jump!*

He would jump now but there was nothing to jump from, and nowhere to jump to. What could he do, now that all his choices had been taken from him?

*

Thirty-six hours ago, the company had gathered in the holo-room. The company CO, Captain Reik, gave them the rundown: they were moving through a loose asteroid belt, ships leap-frogging from rock to rock, trying to stay out of range of Kharmuz scans to catch a small war-party unaware. This was their first opportunity to go head-to-head, at close range, with a Kharmuz warship and its destroyer escorts. Thus, it would be the first large-scale combat exercise for the three legions of the 84th UTF Ranger Corps.

Jumpers.

Human torpedoes.

It went like this: each soldier slipped into a quarter-ton extravehicular combat suit of titanium-aluminum alloy and carbon-reinforced Kevlar derivative, with a nuclear-powered microfusion unit built into its back and numerous nanotech gadgets and gizmos distributed throughout its bulk for the purpose of making a fragile flesh-and-blood soldier into a self-contained engine of nuclear-powered destruction. Standard issue firepower included a medium weight plasma pulse rifle, a dozen PEP-charge microgrenades, a focused laser torch for cutting (or close combat), and a plasma sidearm, almost as powerful as the blaster rifle, but with only half the effective range. A few soldiers in each platoon carried heavier artillery but, by and large, the armaments were uniform.

In g, powered and supported by their hydraulic armatures, the suits were fairly easy to manage. In vacuum, they were almost graceful. A young woman in Mboku's unit once demonstrated this by dancing in one of the blasted things.

Suited and armed, they gathered in the jump chute—a long corridor in the belly of their frigate, below the ship's gravity well, barely wide enough for two of them to stand abreast. A light magnetic field kept their feet anchored as they waited for first bell.

First bell—a whoop-whoop-whooping claxon that sounded their approach to a hostile target—and each soldier turned his or her back to the soldier beside them, facing the outer walls. Below them lay a bank of hatches. *Second bell*—the hatches popped and each soldier slid into the jump chamber, feet first. The chambers were small and, inside them, they hunkered with bent legs and tucked arms, steel infants in an iron womb, waiting to be blasted out of the all-too-short birth canal into the cold vacuum beyond.

Once loaded, they would often wait for some time. In training, instructors kept them in their jump chambers for six hours, no word from command or the company leader. Mboku had thought he'd go crazy on that exercise. The waiting nearly brought on a panic attack. To hold his fear at bay he thought of Zapata. She became his coach, thoughts of her settling him when panic rose in his throat and his heart trembled in his chest.

He thought of those moments on the high rock above the Uhlangan Ocean, Zapata playing siren to his reticent Ulysses.

Jump! she commanded.

As always, Owen jumped.

When the hostiles were in sight, a new claxon sounded: *third bell*. The hatches shot open on pneumatic hinges and the soldiers hung, suspended in their chambers, human torpedoes staring down at their target adrift in the void a few hundred, or even a thousand kilometers distant in the star-strewn gulf. As third bell squalled its last, they hunkered in their snug steel wombs—praying, mumbling, sweating—transfixed by the sound of their own breath inside their helmets.

Then the alarm went silent and they were launched.

They left their jump chambers, traveling at one hundred meters a second. Their frigate shrank away behind them and the jump target filled their forward vision, expanding at a terrifying rate.

This was the short and terrifying portion of the journey when the jump troopers had no control. Velocity drove them. A laser guidance system installed in their chest plates kept them moving toward a preprogrammed point on the target craft. At a certain point, automated jets would fire to decelerate them and set them down gently on the target's hull without smashing them flat.

But nothing could save them from the hail of anti-boarding fire. In the sixty-to-ninety-second interval between launch and touchdown, they could only fall, and hope, and pray.

*

Something bumped lightly against Mboku. He punched his attitude jets and turned 180 degrees, face-to-face with the object of collision.

It was a Kharmuz soldier in EVC armor. One arm was torn away, cauterized at the bicep, probably by flak. Something larger had torn through his midsection and nearly bisected him. He drifted, frozen blood forming a strange, crystalline bloom where his rent abdomen gaped.

Mboku studied the corpse: the sharp angles and strange textures of the suit plates, the alien markings on the pauldrons, breastplate, and helmet. Rank, insignia, ID—who knew?

The faceplate was down: smooth, black, and reflective. Drawing a deep breath, Mboku reached out, grasped the edge of the soldier's breastplate in one hand and the faceplate in the other. He tugged. The faceplate broke away.

Like everyone else, Mboku had heard of the Kharmuz predilection for self-mutilation and body piercing—a ritual carried to self-decorative extremes beyond any of the varied cultural norms found throughout human space. According to reports, the Kharmuz pierced any patch of soft flesh they could find, wrapped themselves in wire, even sunk hooks and barbs into their flesh. Nonetheless, hearing of a thing and seeing it up close were two entirely different matters.

Small hooks drew this Kharmuz's eyelids back, revealing eyes covered by a black nictating membrane, like a pair of massive black pearls, hooded above and beneath with slivers of dark blue underflesh pierced with golden wires. Another pair of hooks pinned the corners of the soldier's mouth, drawing his lips into a terrible, wide rictus. Pins fanned out from the Kharmuz's earlobes, nailing them flat to his skull. More pins stretched in a double row up and over his head like a crown. Thin, curved pieces of metal—pale crescents in the vague starlight—were threaded into the flesh of his protruding cheeks. Mboku refused to think about what pins, barbs, wires, and hooks still lay hidden beneath the soldier's suit.

Mboku stared at his lifeless companion. Pity and fear and disgust all vied in him, but disgust won. Gently, he pushed the corpse. It tumbled away, swallowed by the darkness. He hit his jets to arrest his drift.

Mboku checked his chronometer. Seventy-three hours adrift.

Zapata's voice echoed in the chambers of his mind: *You lucky bastard, Mboku. Seventy-three hours alone. Just you and your thoughts without a soul in sight.*

He imagined she would smile crookedly as she said it, then lower her eyes.

Zapata's presence in his mind helped to quell his fear in the face of mortal terror but, ironically, he had always feared telling her how he truly felt. He knew she hurt—deeply, horribly. He had wanted to tell her that he would listen to her whenever she saw fit to share that hurt. He wanted to tell her that he would hold her and, if need be, wipe away her tears.

He was a fool, drifting alone in the void, with only the knowledge of his foolishness to accompany him. He wore a hundred kilograms of Kevlar-aluminum-titanium compound armor, a small nuclear fusion reactor on his body, and he felt more naked and exposed than he'd felt in his entire life. The darkness molested him. The stars tittered and winked their derision.

If he survived this, he would find Zapata. He would tell her everything and fear nothing. She would accept his confession and share her heart in return, or she would shake her head and assure him that she just never saw him *that way*.

But he would never remain silent again.

He checked his chronometer, watching as the seconds changed, breath-by-breath.

*

Command had thought that a massive force of extravehicular combat troops could take a whole warship by slipping through its defenses: micro soldiers circumventing macro weaponry.

The theory was sound but training hadn't prepared them. How could anything prepare a human being—a fragile, carbon-based life form unable to survive its own home world without clothing and shelter—to become a ballistic missile, blasted into the void at a hundred meters a second, plummeting through a hail of photon cannon fire and light-yield nukes, zooming closer and closer to the great steel hull of a spacecraft nearly a kilometer long, its surface crawling with hostile, armored troops just waiting to get their hands on the newcomers falling out of the boundless vacuum?

Mboku had thought he was dead more than once during this last jump. Not in danger: just plain dead. Hit, blasted, vaporized. Only the sick knot of fear coiled in his belly and the thumping of his pulse in his temples reminded him each time he missed a fission flare or dodged a white-hot photon beam that he had emerged, miraculously, alive.

Hundreds of his fellow soldiers were not so lucky. He saw Fain Brady ram into a fission flare, swallowed instantaneously by its flower of light.

Ana Padarak lost her head to photon fire.

Mizo Izeki collided with another jump trooper. Their seals ruptured and rapid depressurization killed them both.

Another trooper lost a leg to the photons. His heat seals managed to keep him from depressurizing, but he fell toward the rally point like a lame bird—crushed on impact when his decel jets didn't fire.

Mboku thought he would be crushed as well. A moment before the zero-braking point, his decel sensors flashed, his belly lurched, and touchdown was imminent. Fear remained but his training took over. Mboku raised his rifle and prepared to land.

Contact. Mboku's legs buckled and stiffened, the impact absorbed by hydraulic shocks. Blindly, he raised his rifle and blasted away. The plasma rifle pulsed silently and he spun on his heels, strafing a full 360 before ducking behind a spidery antenna array.

Plasma fire filled the vacuum above his head. He couldn't tell which was hostile and which was friendly. Rallying points and troop formations were forgotten. Every so often, a flailing form would go tumbling upward into the void, blasted from the warship's hull. When seals were compromised and pressure lost, the magnets in the soles of their boots released. Bodies did not fly free so much as float, drifting slowly, up and away from the pandemonium on the surface of the warship.

Mboku laid down more fire, blasting nasty holes in a trio of Kharmuz soldiers and smashing a pair of antennae. Gradually, the din of his own ragged breathing subsided and he heard his platoon leader crackling over the com, ordering all who could hear him to follow his beacon to the rally point: a trough in the warship's surface, not forty meters from where Mboku hunkered down.

Mboku saw a gap in the Kharmuz soldiers and went for it.

*

They broke into four squads and squared up around the trough where Sergeant Monaghan was busy setting PEP charges. When the triggers blinked and the countdown meter flashed, all four squads took cover behind the nearest antenna arrays or scan plates. There was a muffled explosion followed by a gale wind. When they raised their heads, they found a three-meter hole in the warship's side. Glittering debris, frozen coolant, and bursts of fetid air streamed into the void.

Mboku didn't know what to expect on the other side of the hull. Bedlam? Hell itself?

He said a prayer to his ancestors, raised his rifle, and followed his companions through the breach.

Inside, they were under the sway of the ship's gravity. Gravity bred mass, and the suits relied more on their hydraulics for movement. Without the grace of zero-g, their two-by-two leapfrogging up the passage was an awkward ballet.

Mboku thought vaguely of the data merchants back on the *Timurlane*, watching the vid feed in the ready room, dictating play-by-plays into their digirecorders, tweaking the signals when electromagnetic noise scrambled them. Mboku and his platoon, most of them just kids like him, rushed head-on into the belly of the beast, while in the comfort of a crew cabin just a hundred klicks away, the information junkies were watching and recording, all the while ingesting kaff and methamphetamines to take the edge off.

The Kharmuz spared no thought for comfort. The walls were hex-steel plating, the floors grated, gangways running over bundles of snaking cable and fat conduit. More cable and conduit snaked along the ceiling, and wan yellow arclights lit the dim passage in jaundiced pools bordered by deep shadows. Every rivet and bolt and welded scar was visible.

The platoon neared the bulkhead and the sealed pressure hatch. Monaghan ordered Harris up to point again. Harris obliged, pulled another PEP charge from his ordnance belt—this one weaker than the charge that opened the hull—and pressed it flat against the seal of the bulkhead.

All down the line of the corridor the troops planted feet, hugged walls, and prepared for the wind-tunnel effect of explosive decompression.

Harris turned back to his charge. Before he could activate it, the bulkhead door split open and a column of Kharmuz in EVC suits barreled forward, three abreast, blasting away.

Harris was hit and trampled. Monaghan tried to fall back, took down a single soldier in the advancing column, then lost his head to plasma fire. Rada Sinclair, across the hall from Mboku, took a hit to her breastplate. The blast didn't punch through, but the force and the incidental heat blew her shoulder seals. She had time for a short, sharp cry before she depressurized. Mboku watched as her eyes sunk and her flesh drew taut over her skull. She died in seconds—every blood vessel bursting.

Then came the explosion that tore the ship in two. The ship's gravity failed. Everyone not rooted with boot magnets stumbled upward and bounced around the long, narrow confines of the corridor. The dead, Terran and Kharmuz alike, bobbed like fish in a red tide.

In the next instant, a column of air—drawn toward the hull by a compromised bulkhead blew everyone back toward the breach: toward the vacuum and the void beyond. Mboku caught himself on a blasted conduit, gripping it hard as friends and foes alike were ejected. Then came the column of flame roaring up the passage toward him.

He let go. The flames screamed down the passage, filling his world for an instant before blowing him into the void. He tumbled away from the warship, a dismantled casualty riding its own fiery wake to oblivion.

*

One hundred-sixty-three hours, four minutes, seventeen seconds.

Mboku didn't know what had happened and he didn't care. Maybe one of the other platoons had gotten close to the ship's command deck and the Kharmuz blew their ship rather than have any intimate knowledge of it fall into enemy hands. It would certainly fit the paradigm established.

All that mattered was that he was adrift—almost seven days and counting—and more than likely he would die before anyone would retrieve him. He was one soldier—one lousy private—from a battalion numbering twelve hundred people sent to breach the Kharmuz warship.

That ship, now the vast sea of drifting debris surrounding him.

That battalion, now decimated.

They didn't talk about this part in training.

The suit could run on low power for weeks. It recycled his sweat and urine, made jet fuel from the leftovers, and gave him regular protein and vitamin injections.

But his survival systems wouldn't last.

And before they gave out, he might go crazy.

Choices. He had to make choices.

One: hang in there. Breathe. Sing songs. Count in Zulu. Run backward through the names of his ancestors. Count stars. Just keep on keeping on until someone came to collect him—or until he went loopy and gave up his ghost.

Two: end it fast. Blow his seals and give his last breath to the vacuum. If he had his rifle, he could shoot himself, but that was long gone.

He still had his sidearm. A head shot would end it quick. Quicker than the vacuum. The vacuum was fast. A few seconds, no more—but who knew what one felt or thought or sensed in those last moments? Blood boiled, lungs sucked dry, body moisture flash-frozen.

But what if his extremities numbed to the vacuum and something kept flickering—warm and alive—deep in the center of his brain? He might linger for a full five or ten seconds, breathless, cold, in agony.

His grandfather once said that all choice was an illusion. *All living things are subject to the whims of unseen powers, the great spirits of the land and sea and sky, and some even greater, beyond the elements, conducting the heavens themselves.*

Zapata would have none of that. *You always have a choice*, she'd said since they were children.

But sometimes, nothing you do can change what's to come, Owen would argue.

Doing it anyway is a choice, isn't it? Sometimes, all you have is the choice to do or not do, whether it gets you somewhere or not. Mboku found himself torn between their voices. He wanted to take strength from Zapata's determination, yet in his present state, he felt more like the citizen of the universe his grandfather had described: a speck of sentient dust, floating alone in the boundless void of all creation. He would never be found, never find his way home, and now he would never see Zapata again.

Private Owen Mboku closed his eyes and prayed in the tongue of his forebears: *Strength*, he begged. *Courage. I shall stare into this silent sea, and before the darkness swallows me, I shall know my slayer or be damned for my ignorance.*

He opened his eyes, stared into the void.

The void stared back, gaping and hungry.

*

Where was Zapata now? Mboku's heart ached, thinking of her as he last saw her: embracing him, squeezing his hand, then moving slowly but surely away from him, into the arms of the UTF Celestial Expeditionary Forces.

Quit looking at me like that, she had said, and then offered her last bit of advice. *No fear, Mboku. I mean it.*

Lazing on the beach of his childhood, drifting through the debris of the great, abortive battle surrounding him—Owen Mboku realized that he loved Zapata Triste, had loved her since their childhood. He found his love had deepened with time, with distance, with awareness.

Where was she now? If the jump troops were engaged here near the outskirts of the Orion Arm then greater Kharmuz legions were probably massing near galactic center. Wherever the conflict was deepest and deadliest, there was Zapata, probably a squadron leader by now, having made a name for herself.

If she wasn't already dead.

Mboku thought of Rada Sinclair, the terrible animal sound of her last, shocked cry. He imagined Zapata making the same sound as stray flak cracked her fighter canopy, or blaster fire punched through the sides of her craft, or she lost power in her photon thrusters and kamikazed into the nearest warship …

Com static. An indicator on his gauntlet blinked, went out. Mboku's heart froze.

Faintly, he heard the scratch of a human voice—then static returned and the light died. Sweepers, searching the debris field for salvage?

Mboku identified himself, his voice alien in his own ears, rasping and jittery.

Static and silence answered him.

He could boost his range, but that would mean powering his suit. Even if he increased to one-third power, whipping the reactor into gear would use a great deal of his reserves. What if he was wrong? What if the voice in his ear was an auditory hallucination?

No fear, Zapata said in his ear.

He broadcast again.

A tiny burst of static made him twitch, but it might as well have been a sunspot from the nearest visible star.

He fired his attitude jets, slowly spinning, scanning the vast debris field around him.

Something flashed briefly above and to his right. He thought of firing another attitude burst but let it go and waited as he revolved again toward that small, bright light that had caught his eye. As he came around and scanned the field, he saw nothing but debris.

He spun four more times, each time staring in that direction, memorizing the debris pattern and disbursement, seeking any sign of movement.

Nothing.

He couldn't drift any longer. He'd been floating for two hundred and forty hours—more than a week. It was time to move, even if it took him nowhere.

He punched his reactor controls, ordering a power-up. The indicators on the LED screens inside his helmet pulsed and came to life. The running lights and headlamps on his suit came alight. He felt the air scrubbers kick in, quickly sucking the staleness out of his suit atmosphere and replenishing it with fresh air. He was revitalized in moments. When one-third power was attained and confirmed, he hit his jump jets.

He accelerated through the debris field, allowing only a moderate burn but gaining velocity fast in the vacuum. After five seconds, he switched off, riding his newfound velocity, swift, but not so swift as to risk a damaging collision.

As he sped along, he saw the flash again, higher, but still on his right. He fired his attitude jets again and shot upward toward it. His stomach lurched with the sudden vector change but he didn't care. Something was up there.

He activated his com again and repeated his distress call. Static replied.

Again, the flash, now moving, passing just out of his field of vision, over his right shoulder. Mboku fired his deceleration jets, fell into a gut-wrenching spin, then fired his accelerators again. He was still deep in the midst of the wreckage.

Where was that light? Where was it coming from?

Then he saw a dark fragment of ballast come tumbling toward him.

Mboku's heart leapt even as his mind cried out for action. It was moving fast. If he wasn't careful, it would plow right into him, burst his seals, shatter his faceplate—

Right behind the hurtling piece of debris a suited Kharmuz bore down on Mboku with incredible speed. Mboku hit his decelerators. The Kharmuz matched, slowing, but still tumbling toward him, arms out, ready to grapple.

Mboku drew his sidearm, got off one good blast that flashed wide, and the Kharmuz trooper slammed into him. Mboku lost his bearings, the debris field and the stars, awhirl in his vision, blocked by his shadowy, clanking adversary. For an awful moment, Mboku caught a glimpse of the Kharmuz's face through their visors: a toothy, snarling countenance with split nostrils and a forked, pierced, flapping tongue. As Mboku struggled with his com assembly, the Kharmuz's gauntlet slammed into his helmet.

Mboku punched the Kharmuz hard in the solar plexus, his fists pounding like pile drivers. The Kharmuz's gauntleted fingers drew back and a moment later struck Mboku with a rabbit-punch to his crown.

They went spinning off in opposite directions. Wheeling, Mboku hit his attitude thrusters and decelerated just in time to avoid slamming into a huge, riblike girder from the warship. He wheeled around, planted his feet, and shoved off when they touched the girder.

The Kharmuz's spin was arrested. Already it adjusted its vector and readied for another attack.

Pointless, Mboku thought. *We're adrift, helpless, and this fool wants to fight.*

The Kharmuz came hurtling toward him.

Mboku raised his fist, froze. His sidearm was gone, lost in their grappling.

But he still had a few PEP grenades.

They plunged toward one another. The Kharmuz pinwheeled its arms like a desperate swimmer. Mboku reached for his belt and drew a single grenade.

They collided. The Kharmuz got one hand on Mboku's breastplate and drew back the other for a strike.

Mboku shoved the PEP charge against the Kharmuz's breastplate and stabbed the trigger.

He blocked the Kharmuz's strike, raised his legs, and shoved off, launching away just as the charge detonated. The Kharmuz's torso vaporized. It's limbs and head went spinning off into space, flesh and metal and insulator fragments tumbling this way and that among the drifting debris.

Then Owen Mboku was tumbling heels-over-head, the debris field spinning around him, the stars dancing in a terrible, feverish waltz before his eyes. Something hit him. Vaguely, he realized he couldn't feel his left leg. There was a coldness, a tightening in his throat, then warmth invaded the cold region beneath his knee and all was well. An indicator flashed on his LED screen, but he was beyond caring.

*

He woke from the darkness into a terrible cold and realized that someone had stripped away his clothing.

The world was zooming by around him, white and bright and incredibly loud. He lay immobile on a cold table, carried along on a column of electromagnetic resonance. His armor was gone. A blinding light filled his vision. He could not feel his left leg.

I've fallen into a star, he thought.

Voices spoke, calling his name. Ghostly faces filled his vision. Warmth and agony and panic swept through him, top to toe and back again. He was shaking, crying, flailing his arms, begging for silence, begging for the abyssal reprieve of the vacuum.

Then he was nothing at all.

*

His debriefing was short but the therapy required to gain use of his new prosthetic leg was long. He learned that sweeper scouts creeping through the debris field had seen the flash from his PEP grenade. A routine scan locked them onto his homing beacon. They arrested his spin with a mag sail and one of the sweepers went EVA on a tether to draw him back in.

He'd lost his leg in that spin, probably slamming into a sharp piece of debris at just the wrong angle. Luckily, his suit seals held and saved him from depressurization.

In a way, the time he spent on the medical frigate was longer and lonelier than the time he'd spent drifting. There was the noise of the world around him now: the gentle, subsonic hum of the medical frigate's antimatter reactor, the chatter of certain loquacious patients, the insistent silence of others.

He was polite, and he shared smiles and warm wishes with the therapists and the nurses, but by and large he kept to himself during his six weeks of recovery. Once the debriefing was done, he put in for a post-trauma furlough before being recycled to active duty. Company command waited four more weeks before denying him.

UTF Celestial forces had routed a massive offensive near the Lagoon Nebula, just inside the Orion Arm. The Kharmuz fleet splintered and scattered. The smaller arms of those scattered forces were overtaken and captured by jump troops. The offensives culminating in Mboku's drift bore up a great deal of vital info about the UTF's new enemies, but there was still more to gather and it could only be taken by force.

It was just as this information reached him that he received a flash from Zapata Triste. Her location was listed simply as UTF Celestial Fighter Carrier *Cuauhtemoc*. It was not a real-time message, but a recording, indicating that it had probably been relayed from some distance.

Zapata stared into the flash camera. She looked as beautiful and weary and unaffected as ever. "You gave me a fright, Mboku," she said. "I didn't sleep for days after I saw your name on the MIA rosters.

Glad to see they fished you out of the big black."

Tears burned Owen Mboku's eyes. How old was this message? For all he knew, she could have gone into action again since recording it. Once more, he could have lost his chance to say something to her—something real that could never be taken back.

"I'm due for some shore leave in the next quarter," Zapata said, then specified, knowing that they would be in different time zones. "Fourth quarter, that is. I was thinking Ngaroto. I hear the mountains are nice. If you can get away …"

She let that invitation hang in the empty air and vast cosmic distances that separated them.

"Anyway, I'm glad you're still with us, Owen. Drop me a line sometime. And *no fear*. I mean it."

She smiled in that sad, beautiful, heart-breaking way that she always had, and her flash ended.

Mboku didn't know how long he sat there at the com station, mulling his next course of action. He only knew that the inevitable moment came when his finger stabbed the REPLY button on the control panel and the small, red RECORD light indicated that he was on-camera, creating a flash to send back to Zapata.

In less than a week, Corporal Owen Mboku would be hunkered in his jump chamber, waiting for the third bell. The chamber door would open and he would stare into the gaping maw of the silent deep—the hungry vacuum that once had swallowed him and, by some strange fortune, hurled him up again onto the shores of life. The stars would be waiting, numerous and distant as the ancestors to whom he prayed and a warship would drift far beneath him, an invitation to oblivion.

But right now, he was in a fleet station com lounge, recording a flash for his childhood friend, the woman he loved, another warrior at another front in the war.

Staring into the flash camera, Corporal Owen Mboku jumped.

The Blue Hour

Brittany Warman

We have carved our heart out of the sky—
Hands clasped, the beach darkening around us,
A cool blanket over summer.

We talk about how
There might be shadows in space,
If the sun is in the right position,
And the planets agree.

We talk about the loneliness
Of lightspeed,
The vanity of Cassiopeia,
And the gravitational pull between us—
I think about how nothing lasts
Not our lives, not this moment,
Not the trails of the stars.

BRITTANY WARMAN

The moon over the ocean
Watches our small selves
For a moment
And forgets us.

We are earth-bound black holes,
Drawn into each other
In the hush of twilight—
Nothing to the sun.

I bring my mouth to your ear and say—
Tell me about how
We used to spell out our names in the stars,

About advances in telescopes,
About love in the darkness.

Another Prison

Rahul Kanakia

Cheyenne spent her first thirteen years on seven hundred acres of abandoned suburb that surrounded a defunct lottery plaza. The original residents had been relocated long before Cheyenne and her parents arrived.

For Cheyenne, the outside world didn't exist. Her mom was afraid that the state would take her daughter away, so she never let the girl accompany her on trips outside for work and supplies. Cheyenne spent her childhood wandering through the collapsed houses and the knee-high grass that'd worked its way through the asphalt. Her favorite place was the plaza that'd once printed the tickets that could make your dreams come true. She spent hours splashing around in the puddles of ever-dripping sap that fell from the quiescent circuits of the wish-fulfillment machinery. She lay ensconced in those subterranean workings and dreamt of how she was gonna fix up all these machines someday.

When she got home, her mother would berate her, and tell her to never ever mess around with those lottery machines: wishing and hoping was what ruined people's lives; their family got along perfectly fine without having any part of that.

In her thirteenth year, Cheyenne fainted in front of her house. Her mother tried to call her an ambulance, but ambulances would not come to the wasteland. Instead, her parents drove her to the county hospital. When the state got ahold of Cheyenne, they slit her open and found a half-dozen tumors lined up around her ovaries and uterus. They gave her a hysterectomy and a few rounds of chemo and a place in the foster care system. Her mother went to prison for negligence. Her father skipped bail and moved North.

An aunt claimed Cheyenne. The girl came to the city, where she lived in the east wing of her aunt's mansion. She ate from wafer-thin diamond plates and wore single-use dresses. For weeks after arriving, she couldn't sleep: the nighttime streets were too alive with screams and moans.

Her cousins taught her to line up in front of the little lottery booth at the corner and compare wishes with the relo kids. Even at that young age, the kids had split up into camps. Some—mostly city kids—wished for interesting, unlikely things: weird adventures or the ability to achieve amazing things. Others—mostly relo kids—wished for life-changing, more-probable things: usually love, or wealth. But Cheyenne's wishes angered both groups: she wished for boring, unlikely things or minor, probable things, like a cat with two tails or a bag that perfectly matched her new dress. Many of the other kids were on the cusp of figuring out their real wish—the one they'd spend their whole life buying tickets for—and for a while they thought that Cheyenne was mocking their search, but eventually they figured out that Cheyenne had grown up without the lottery. She was a primitive, and she just didn't know any better. On lottery days, when everyone anxiously watched everyone else, people felt safe around Cheyenne, because they knew that she never wished for anything dangerous or life-changing.

Whenever she was willing to ride the bus all day, Cheyenne could see her mother. During one of her last visits, Cheyenne's mom asked, "How's the old homestead?"

"It's what made me sick," Cheyenne said. "At the hospital they told me that no one's allowed to live there."

"Don't you believe it!" her mother said. "I bought that land, and I signed all the forms to go and give it to you. That place is yours. You can't let them take it from you!"

When Cheyenne was fifteen, her aunt's second son won his lottery. He was only nineteen years old. He would never say what his wish had been, but the day after his number came up, he hooked up with the prettiest girl on the block and they started robbing banks. Cash flowed freely. No one worked. There were lottery tickets scattered all over the house. Some said that the boy won too early, and that it would be the ruination of him. He seemed happy, though. Everyone seemed happy.

Still, Cheyenne couldn't quite come up with a mature wish. Whenever her cousins coerced her into buying a few tickets, she would wish to be left alone. That wish had terribly bad odds, which is how she knew it was a special wish: a daring wish. But it also scared her. What would it mean to be alone?

A few days after her sixteenth birthday, Cheyenne strolled out of her aunt's house. Until the moment she leapt onto the boxcar, she wasn't sure whether she was actually going or not. She rode the freights until she got to a place she remembered. Then she started walking.

It was a dry, sunny day, but her home smelled like rain. There was a plate on the table holding the mold-blackened outline of what'd been a slice of bread. There were two cups of dehydrated grit that'd once been coffee.

The couch was damp and warm, as if it'd been fermenting. She lay back on it and stared at the long scars running through the plaster of the ceiling. A ray of light, springing from the corner of the roof, illuminated the swirling motes of dust stirred up by her passage. She raised a hand and let it play through the air, catching the light. Then she let it fall onto the scar on her abdomen. Maybe the cancers would grow back, but what did that matter? She was finally alone.

*

Cheyenne woke up with the tattered remnants of her childhood blankets piled up over her. She threw them off. It was so quiet. She'd slept on the same bed as when she was a kid: a green cot set up behind the couch.

Then she sat straight up. Something was beeping. The kitchen door opened. People were talking.

"It's just how they left it," said a boy's voice. "Look, there's even a little note stuck onto this table: 'buy more beans.'"

"So eerie," said a girl's voice. "Why is this house in so much better shape than the other ones?"

"I don't know. Just luck, I guess. They must have all been perfect like this, once. These people had to evacuate on a moment's notice when the plaza started outgassing."

"This is beeping *a lot.*"

"Don't worry. We'll only stay inside for fifteen minutes. We'll be fine."

"Oh my god, this note ends with 'I love you.'"

Cheyenne dressed quickly. She hadn't grown much; most of her old clothes still fit. Then she strode into the kitchen and interrupted the two tourists as they ran their hands across her countertops.

"Don't touch that," Cheyenne said. "That's my pa's writing."

The two of them wore shimmery plastic suits that covered up their whole bodies.

After a moment of silence, the girl said, "You're … you're not wearing a suit." A wisp of hair had wriggled down and was visible through the woman's faceplate: it was dyed pink.

"You're on my land," Cheyenne said.

"No one's allowed to live here," said the boy. His beard was a wispy thing; even though he'd probably gone without shaving for a few days, there was still a bare patch under his chin.

The girl tugged on the boy's shoulder. Cheyenne backed away and then turned. She burst into her parents' room and looked through the dresser drawer. The revolver was still there, wrapped in an oily rag.

But by the time she reached the kitchen, the two tourists were gone. From the porch, she watched them bicycling away through the tall grass. Cheyenne inhaled the summer air. She sat on the rickety rocking chair that'd once been her mother's summer roost. She rocked once, experimentally, and then went back and forth rhythmically, gun in lap, as the shadows of the houses steadily darkened the cracked asphalt and rusty rows of parked cars. The wasteland was silent, except for the weak, occasional chirp of the crickets that hadn't yet died.

That night, Cheyenne pulled a can of baked beans out of a cabinet and ate it cold, with a plastic spoon. Before going to bed she scrubbed the grimy mirror in the bathroom and then stood in front of it while she felt all over herself for cancers. None today.

*

The girl bicycled up around noon the next day. Cheyenne was in her backyard, looking at the wild tomatoes.

"You're not going to eat those, are you?" the girl said.

Cheyenne plucked the largest one and took a bite out of it. Red juice ran down one corner of her mouth. She did not wipe it off.

"I brought you your own suit," the girl said. "Everyone at the camp was saying that you must be the daughter of the folks who used to live here once upon a time ..."

She lay the package down on the patio table.

Cheyenne sat down on one of the wrought-iron chairs. Hundreds of ants boiled out of the soggy cushion and ran across Cheyenne's legs. She sat up, threw the cushion into the grass, and swept the ants off her hips with rapid pats. When she looked up, the girl was giggling.

"A suit would've helped with something like that," the girl said.

"You're from town?" Cheyenne said.

"Not really. I was relocated here nine months ago." The girl gestured over her shoulder. "I live in the camp, you know."

"Where you from originally, then?"

"I was born in San Diego."

"Oh, I hear it used to be warm there."

"That's what my mom said. I don't remember it."

"My aunt told me it was always best to stay away from Californians on lottery day. She said you all hadn't seen enough winter and that you weren't practical enough to wish for ordinary stuff like money or love."

"Do you play? There's a dispensary right inside the camp. I could get you a ticket sometime if you want."

Cheyenne didn't say anything. There was a bee skimming the top of the grass. It alighted on one flower and scuttled up inside the bud and waved its tiny legs for a little while, then buzzed upward and tumbled onto a neighboring flower. As she watched, it inspected a third, fourth, and fifth flower. The bee was so methodical. It made Cheyenne feel lazy. But after the fifth flower, the bee dropped down into the grass and never rose up again.

"It's so quiet here," the girl said. "I guess your aunt was right about some things. I don't like to be around people—especially relocated people—on lottery day. You never know what's going to happen. When someone wins ... it can be stressful sometimes. But there's nowhere to go. In the camp, there are people everywhere. Even when my door is closed, I can always hear them in the halls, with their chatting and yelling and gossiping. But it's worse outside. The farms have a putrid stench that I can't stand. I took a bus to a park, once, but it was so full of people. I couldn't breathe."

Cheyenne bit into the tomato again, just to see the girl wince. After a few more moments of silence, the girl propped her bicycle against the rotting fence. She flattened down a tussock of grass and sat down atop it. She watched Cheyenne for a while and then began plaiting the grass into wide circlets that quickly fell apart under the fumbling of her gloved fingers. Eventually, with a covert glance at Cheyenne, she unzipped the gloves of her hazard suit and ran her bare fingers through the grass.

Cheyenne barely moved. At times, she managed to regain the sense—dimly remembered from her childhood—that time had stopped and the world had become utterly still, but then she would exhale and the sensation would fade.

As the sky turned red, the girl said, "Well, I guess the drawing has been over for a while by now. Maybe I won." She smiled. "I guess I'll find out soon."

"What about your friend?" Cheyenne said. "Will he be bothering me again?"

"Oh, Monroe? He comes here all the time, just to dig around and take pictures. I think you scared him yesterday."

"If you come back, bring food. Otherwise you'll be trespassing."

"Sounds good. I'll hide out here again next Wednesday." She grabbed her bicycle. "My name's Julie, by the way."

"Take this with you." Cheyenne threw the bundled-up suit at her. "My papa tried to wear one for a while, but you can't see or feel anything when you're inside them. Besides, it's perfectly safe here. I've lived here all my life, and I'm fine."

Julie nodded, and then got on her bicycle and wobbled off through the grass.

*

Julie visited faithfully. Sometimes she even came when it wasn't a lottery day, just to sit on a hillside and breathe in the scenery. After a few weeks, Monroe started coming with her. He'd putter about the edges of the wasteland with his shovel and his backpack, and Julie would always keep one ear cocked to track his location. They still wore suits most of the time, but often their gloves were off and their faceplates were open.

It took a while before Monroe was willing to spill more than a few words in front of Cheyenne, but once he relaxed, he became positively chatty. Eventually, he took her aside as if he was asking her about some big secret, and, in a whisper, asked Cheyenne if she would deign to show him the lottery plaza. She laughed and promised to take them there next Wednesday.

The lottery plaza had displaced the town's center. It rose up for five stories, presenting a blank marble face to the outside. Inside, it was a place of sunny balconies and nested courtyards. Cheyenne and her two visitors were sitting on the mezzanine, looking down on the rain-filled fountains and the tangles of flood-borne stairways, kiosks, and tables that had dammed up the narrow places of the ground level. On the surface, everything was still, but if Cheyenne put her ear to any surface, she could hear the distant hum of machinery.

"Look over there," Monroe said. "These little grottoes are where they went to discuss matters of the heart with the lottery providers. See how the water would have run through the fountains and drowned out their voices so no one else could hear?"

Cheyenne nodded. She didn't like to hear about how thousands of people had once played around in *her* plaza. She bounced a pebble off the brass railing. The impact resounded through the vast amphitheater.

Julie was riding her bike in slow circles around the edges of the tiled balcony. It was lottery day again. Cheyenne had noticed her pressing her hand to her hip pocket underneath the suit, where she kept her lottery tickets.

"What do you wish for?" Cheyenne said.

For a moment Monroe was put off by this unexpected interruption to his monologue. "Well, that's ummm ... that's not a very polite question, but I usually wish for ... well ... for the ability to discover something new. Something *really* exciting."

"That's a lie. I know at least that much."

"What do you mean?"

"That's not your wish. That's okay, though."

Julie had disappeared into one of the corners. Cheyenne went to find her. Monroe hefted his pack and talked about going down into the shopping levels to see if any unclaimed lottery prizes were still lying around somewhere.

Cheyenne came upon Julie in one of the grottoes. She was standing close to a wall, shining a pen light over it, and running her fingers over the faded inscriptions: hundreds of crudely chiseled hearts. The letters were indecipherable, but the shapes were still clear.

"Every one of these was a dream come true," Julie said. She ran her fingers across the length of the wall.

A harsh beep startled them. Julie had accidentally touched the wishing panel. The terminal was just a blank black spot on the wall, now, but something, somehow, still lived within it.

"Can it still print tickets?" Julie said

"I don't think you'd want them, even if it could."

Julie had a hand on her lottery ticket now. She looked at the time on her phone.

"You must think I'm so silly," Julie said. "Here I am, afraid of winning and afraid of losing."

"Then don't play."

"I knew you'd say that. I wish I were like you. You're exactly the sort of person who'd win in a second, if you ever bothered to play."

"Am I?"

"Sure. I mean, well, I know that the odds are *supposed* to be random. They're printed up so neatly on my ticket and everything. And, for my wish … well, the odds are okay. It's a good wish. An easy, simple wish. But, still, I'm not the sort of person who wins. The people who win are people like you: the ones who already have everything."

"What's your wish?"

"The most popular one: to fall in love. Well, and to be loved in return. That part means worse odds, but it can't be left out."

"Anyone in particular?" Cheyenne said, wondering whether Julie would end up robbing banks soon.

"I found a good enough person. Not … not so in demand … but still not bad, if I looked into his eyes and really loved him and knew he loved me, then that's all I'd need, right?"

"Not Monroe?"

"And why not? He's fine. I enjoy spending time with him."

"Does he know?"

"Of course not. What's the point of bothering him? I looked up the odds I'd get for lots of men in the camp. Monroe's were good."

Cheyenne couldn't help but laugh. Julie slapped a palm against the wall and then pushed away. She stormed onto the balcony and shouted for Monroe. After a quick, indistinguishable, conversation, their voices faded. Cheyenne lay on the ground in that darkening grotto. She wanted to go after them. Once, she even got up. She'd introduced them to her sacred place, and now, even though she barely liked them, she felt like she had some sort of duty to them. But ... they were such simpletons. How could she put her faith in them? She put her ear to the tile and let the comforting hum of the machinery coax her back into a solitary frame of mind.

*

Still, they came back the following week, and from then they were around even more often. Julie started spending more and more time in the wasteland. Although when Monroe was around Julie talked on and on and on, Julie and Cheyenne rarely spoke to each other. They allowed the hours to elapse in silence. Once, Julie tried to hook the television up to a portable battery she'd charged at the relo camp.

"What do you want that for?" Cheyenne said.

"So we can have something to look at."

"Oh." Cheyenne went back to staring at the ceiling. The cracks were growing wider, like the ceiling was an egg that was close to hatching.

Julie abandoned her effort with the battery, just like she'd abandoned trying to clean up the place. Cheyenne was a ghost inside her own home. She'd been there half a year and she hadn't yet moved the moldy plate on the table or the note on the counter. Aside from the bedding on her cot, she disturbed nothing. Sometimes she'd stand just inside the door of the bathroom and spend hours looking at the arrangement of her parents' toiletries on the sink, but she never went further than that. And though she'd slept on her parents' bed a few times, she'd come to regret even those intrusions. To make up for it, she'd sealed the place off and sworn never to go back inside.

One Wednesday night, they were watching a meteor shower from a hill at the southern border of Cheyenne's land. Behind them, the wasteland was utterly dark: a gently sighing sea. In front, long ribbons of light knotted in the hard, tight cluster of the relocation camp where Julie and Monroe lived.

The two visitors were sitting slightly ahead of Cheyenne. Something made her look down. Julie's hand was pressed tightly to her pocket. She and Monroe were looking tentatively at each other. Their shoulders were touching infinitesimally. One was murmuring to the other. Cheyenne could make out neither the words nor the speaker. A few moments later, they made some excuse. Their headlamps cut through the night as they bicycled away. In a brief flash of reflected light, something fell from Monroe's bicycle.

When they were gone, Cheyenne scrambled over to where the object had fallen and looked for the piece of paper. With her hands and knees in the grass, she finally pulled up the damp lottery ticket.

It was Monroe's ticket. She spread it out on the kitchen counter, next to her father's note. Monroe had wished that Cheyenne would fall in love with him. Cheyenne felt a pain in her chest. His odds hadn't been great, but they'd been okay.

Monroe had almost snatched up Cheyenne's whole life.

When they walked into her house the next day, they were holding hands. At midday, Julie took Cheyenne aside and whispered, "I won!"

Cheyenne displayed the hint of a smile as Julie burbled on, then they embraced. When Cheyenne had a moment, she slipped Monroe's lottery ticket into his hand. He turned white. After that day, she never saw him again.

Julie still came sometimes. She didn't need to hide from lottery day anymore, but she still wanted to see her friend. Then they quarreled over Cheyenne's unwillingness to come visit her in the camps. Julie said that she couldn't afford to subject her eggs to any more toxic exposure. She said she was never coming again. A part of Cheyenne was glad. Every time Julie had come around, Cheyenne remembered Monroe's wish.

The night after the fight, Cheyenne went into the bathroom and put her lantern on top of the toilet lid. She inspected herself in the mirror, then put a hand on her abdominal scar. For a moment she felt faint, and thought, "Oh god, this is it." Then she recovered her footing. No, that was nothing. Just a little scare. It wasn't her time yet. Thank god, not yet. Then she cleared her parent's toiletries off the sink and threw them, one by one, into a garbage bag. After she'd finished cleaning the bathroom, she headed for the kitchen. She cleared away everything but that note on the counter.

A few months later she was cooking stew on a camp-stove set up on the kitchen counter, and some of the liquid dripped onto the note. The brown liquid stained the words beyond recognition. For the rest of her life Cheyenne would be sad about that accident, but first, for a brief moment, she was relieved.

Market Day

Anna Della Zazzera

Saturday—market day
it used to be my favorite day,
before the dust blew like whooping cough
and the rain stuck like spit in my hair

Before the caustic storms,
before Second Phase Diet Simplification,
when famine was a word for the "world" news pages and
you could still buy honey and wheat

When I was little
my mother owned a flower shop
Each Saturday, at sunrise
we would fill buckets with armfuls
of delicate freesias, decadent orchids
and park our cart amid tables laden with crops

I remember meandering through the fruit and fragrance
like Demeter in her crown of braided corn
taken in by beauty and abundance

And the bustle was blissful,
while today it is rank
The crowds writhe under spoiled skies
the gaunt glow of daylight
a mockery of dawn

I push pitilessly through bony bodies
hungering for a past where
pumpkins were my sentinels and
cherries were my riches
in my palace of opulent eggplant
chamomile grew lush through my toes

I settle for a bag of dried beans, a bulb of garlic
and add it to the miserable turnips in my basket

Saturdays are not what they used to be,
and I haven't seen fresh flowers in years.

Driven Out

Steve Alguire

The wind shrieked and fell, shrieked and fell, rattling grit against the windows. All Seth could see outside were the clouds of sand, sometimes brown, sometimes gray, swirling furiously around the little clapboard schoolhouse as if they were trying to uproot and devour it.

"Open to Genesis two:eight," Mrs. Abel called from the front of the room. She was looking out the windows as well, twisting her fingers together. Inside the classroom, there were thirteen children in rough, gray homespun clothes. They opened their bibles as one. Seth elbowed Matthew and hissed, "Where's Ephraim?"

"Cut it out!" said Matthew, shoving back. "How should I know?"

"Does *she* know?" said Seth.

"She's his mother. She oughta."

"'And the Lord God planted a garden eastward in Eden,'" recited Mrs. Abel.

"Friggin' idiot," said Seth. "He promised me he wasn't going to try it again."

"You don't know he tried again," said Matthew.

"Everybody knows! Look at 'em!"

None of the children were looking at their bibles. They were stealing worried glances at Mrs. Abel, at the windows, at each other, at Ephraim's empty seat.

"'And out of the ground made the Lord God to grow every tree,'" said Mrs. Abel, "'that is pleasant to the sight, and good for food …'"

"Did you help him?" asked Seth.

"No."

"So he did try again?"

"Shut up!"

"'And the Lord God took the man, and put him into the Garden of Eden to dress it and to keep it ...'" recited Mrs. Abel.

"Does he really think he can get away with it?" said Seth.

"I'm not sayin' anything," replied Matthew.

"'And out of the ground the Lord God formed every beast of the field, and every fowl of the air ...'" recited Mrs. Abel.

"It's his father's fault," muttered Seth. "My dad says that idiot tried fifteen times before they lost patience and ... you know. Ephraim's an idiot too, so he's following in his father's footsteps."

"'But thou hast wasted thy inheritance, and endangered my garden, and proven thyself unworthy, and evil ...'" recited Mrs. Abel.

"Does he really think he can get to the port at all, through this?" muttered Seth, snapping a nod at the windows.

"'Cursed is the ground for thy sake; in sorrow shalt thou eat of it all the days of thy life,'" recited Mrs. Abel, pacing back and forth in front of the blackboard; "'Thorns also and thistles shall it bring forth to thee ...'"

"Even if he got in, how does he think he can get on any ship at all, let alone the right one?"

"Mrs. Abel, I can see something!" cried little Sarah, jumping up. All the children except Seth and Matthew rushed to the windows.

"'Therefore the Lord God sent him forth from the Garden of Eden,'" moaned Mrs. Abel, staring at the door.

"It's cherubim," whispered Sarah.

"Sit down, everybody!" shouted Seth. "Hands on your desks, eyes on your hands! Not a word! Do not look at them!"

The children scrambled back and did as they were told. The littlest ones screwed their eyes tight shut.

"'So he drove out the man; and he placed at the east of the Garden of Eden cherubim, and a flaming sword which turned every way ...'"

The door crashed open. Dust howled into the room and blanketed everyone. The door slammed. One cherub stood at the back. A second came slowly up the aisle. The floorboards sagged under its weight. Hands clenched in front of him, Seth squinted sideways at the glittering armor as it passed. It was dragging the body of Ephraim in one massive, three-fingered claw. It stopped in front of Mrs. Abel and dropped her son at her feet.

"Attempted illegal passage," slurred the cherub with a tongue unused to human words; "Suspected destination, Earth." It turned to face the class.

"What is the crime?" it asked.

"Imperiling the garden," catechized the children.

The cherub started back down the aisle.

"Who is guilty?"

"Man and his children."

"Who saved the garden?"

"The cherubim."

"How?"

"By taking man away."

The cherub stopped. Seth knew that if he looked up, he would see himself reflected in the glittering visor.

"When will man see the garden again?" it asked.

"Never," Seth answered.

The door opened, the cherubim swept out, the door slammed. The wind howled and Mrs. Abel sobbed beside her child.

Pennies

Irving

No one knows
who started the tradition
of putting silver dollars
on the eyes of bodies
in their suspension containers.

When I asked Uncle Lapham about it,
just before we shoved Dad's crate
into the transporter chamber,
he said it was because
pennies weren't big enough
to cover them anymore.

Then he said
the part I don't believe:
That when they materialize
on the other side,
to be thawed out someday,
the coins are gone.

A Voice in the Night

Jack McDevitt

—For Jean Shepherd

Alex Benedict first encountered the voice while playing a board game on a friend's porch. The parents were inside listening to a recording of a guy reminiscing about what he'd gone through trying to summon the nerve to ask a girl to go out with him. Her name was Peggy and she was the girl of his dreams. The guy had been in the sixth grade at the time. "My problem," he said, "was that whenever I got close to her, I froze, completely and absolutely. Then I saw an advertisement for a self-hypnosis package that guaranteed you could persuade yourself that *you* were the ultimate prize. Good-looking, smart, funny." He laughed at the sheer stupidity of the idea. "*Any* girl could be yours. That was what they guaranteed." He laughed again and they cut in with some music. The show's theme, growing louder, indicated they were drawing to a close. "I'm still trying to get it to work," he continued. "Maybe I don't have the mirror set right."

The theme, Alex learned later, was Shefski's *Liftoff*. It suggested a musical rocket, soaring into the stratosphere.

It was a great voice, and Alex realized he'd been paying more attention to the recording than to the game.

"Who *is* that guy?" he asked the father.

"He's Horace Baker, son. A radio comedian from, I don't know, thirty or forty years ago."

Jake had never heard of him. He did a search and discovered his program had been three hours long, broadcast on Sunday evenings to an impassioned audience across the North American continent. North America and Earth were a long way from where Alex lived, but he and Horace had connected. He downloaded some of his stuff, and became an overnight addict. Horace was the funniest guy he'd ever heard, while simultaneously describing a life Alex knew quite well. He talked about his misadventures trying to "become one of the gang." And collecting superhero memorabilia. "My favorite," he said "was Captain Chaos. Her special power was that wherever she went, she sowed utter confusion. Her abilities derived," Horace explained, "from the fact that she came from a long line of politicians."

Alex listened to the recordings whenever he had time. Over a span of about two years, Horace provided him with a sense of what it meant to be human, why he should be skeptical of people's opinions, especially his own, and how easy it was to laugh at most of life's misfortunes. He loved the guy.

*

Alex lived with his uncle Gabe, an archeologist. While most of the other kids went swimming and played ball, he spent his summers in various dig sites. It was the twelfth millennium, and the human race was by then spread across the stars. It had left its mark on a thousand worlds. And there were evenings when Alex and Gabe sat together in a tent under the triple moons, listening to and laughing with Horace. "He was one of a kind," said Gabe. "I grew up listening to him."

"Where is he now? Did he retire?"

"He died a long time ago, Alex. Forty years, I guess."

"I'm sorry to hear it."

Gabe was tall, easy-going, dressed in the khakis he always wore on the job. It had been a long day at a site that he suspected held the remains of Gustofalo II, the beloved founder of the Karim Republic. But that had been six thousand years in the past. The area had been rife with earthquakes. The original settlers had gotten unlucky.

The better part of what had once been a city had been buried. They looked through the scanners and saw porticoes, dormers, a ruined temple, sheets of concrete that had once been sidewalks. Eventually the area had been abandoned altogether. There was no easy way to know which, if any, of the structures contained the remains of the great man.

Local authorities were on the scene to ensure that Gabe's team didn't attempt to make off with anything. He was glad they took the precaution because they also kept idle visitors away. Gabe was working in league with the Holcomb Museum. But funds were limited. They couldn't afford to dig up everything. In fact, the museum representative, after looking at the progress reports, had suggested to him that it would probably be best to call a halt.

Gabe hated to give up. But he was grateful for Alex's interest in Baker, which gave him the opportunity to think about something else. "Did you know he had his own yacht?" he asked.

"Yes," said Alex. "The *Rover*. He was in love with the stars. He talks about them a lot. About other worlds and stuff."

Gabe nodded. "He enjoyed riding in the *Rover*. Sometimes he went alone, sometimes with friends. Anyhow he was alone when he took off on one of those flights and never came back. For almost twenty-five years nobody knew what had happened to him."

"I don't understand that, Uncle Gabe. You mean nobody knew where he was going?"

"Oh, no. He had to file a flight plan just like everybody else. He went to Zeta Leporis. It was one of those places nobody had ever bothered with. It didn't have any life-bearing planets or anything particularly exciting. Hardly anyone had been there. I guess that's what attracted him." Gabe took a deep breath. "When he didn't come back, they sent a rescue mission out. But they couldn't find any sign of him. What had happened was a big mystery for a long time. Eventually, years later, somebody came across the *Rover*."

"What *did* happen, Uncle Gabe?"

Gabe closed his eyes for a moment. "One of the engines blew. Took out his subspace comm system so he couldn't even send an appeal for help."

"And he died out there?" Alex asked.

"Yes. The people who examined the damage said it couldn't have taken more than a couple of hours. The *Rover* was leaking air."

*

Alex was sixteen, not yet ready for existential reality. He became haunted by the images of a terrified Baker, the guy who saw humor in everything, trapped in a narrow space while the air runs out. Alone, and with no hope of rescue. If something like that could happen to him, it could happen to anyone.

What had those last few hours been like?

Gabe saw the reaction. "It's okay, Alex," he said. "I can't believe he wouldn't have been able to deal with it. He was a smart guy. He knew he was taking a chance when he went out there. Let it go, kid."

That evening there was reason to celebrate: The scanners picked up a structure that resembled a crypt. "It might be what we're looking for," Gabe said. "We can't be positive yet."

"How can you tell?" asked Alex. "It's just a rock dome."

"It's concrete. And we can't tell for sure until we go down and look into it. It might just be a cenotaph."

"What's that?"

"A memorial. Sometimes they'll erect one but bury the body somewhere else. You get more security that way from grave robbers. But even that would be progress."

"That's good."

"You're still upset about Horace, aren't you?"

"I'm okay." People should die quietly. In bed, surrounded by their family. He'd never really thought about it before. He didn't much care about Gustofalo. But he didn't want Gabe to see that. "So why do you think that dome might be where he's buried?"

"There's an inscription." He pointed at a string of engraved characters. They didn't look like anything Alex had seen before.

"That's his name?"

"No. It's a quote. It's from *The Achea*. His book of commentary. Which, by the way, people still read today. It's a classic. You should try it sometime."

"What's the inscription say?"

"One chance at life."

"So he's saying what? Have a big time while you can?"

"More or less, Alex. If we're right, it's his farewell message. The way he wanted to be remembered."

Alex smiled. "I think I'd have liked the guy."

*

That evening, clouds rolled in, lightning rattled around the darkened skies, and rain began to fall. Gabe took a call on his link, talked for a few minutes, and then told Alex there was more good news. "We cleared the data with the museum," he said. "Tomorrow, if the weather gives us a break, we'll start the excavation."

"They said okay?"

"Yes."

"Good." Alex looked uncertain.

"Something wrong, champ?"

"Horace didn't leave a farewell message."

Gabe's mind had been elsewhere, and he needed a few moments to catch up. "Alex, he didn't have any way to leave a message. He was stuck inside a ship with nobody around."

"He had an AI. For that matter he could have left something in writing. I looked it up. There was nothing."

"He probably thought he'd never be found."

"Maybe. But I can't imagine Horace Baker going away quietly."

"Apparently he did."

Alex looked at Gabe. "The radio was still working."

"What radio, Alex? What are we talking about?"

A thunderclap erupted overhead. They both ducked. "Big one," said Alex when the rumbling had subsided. "I was talking about the radio on the *Rover*."

"I'm sure that's not correct, Alex. It *wasn't* working."

"No. I found it in the reports. I don't mean the subspace system, but just the radio."

"Okay. So what's the difference? He was light-years from anyone who could have come to the rescue. Why would he bother with the radio?"

"Because that was the way he communicated. He was a radio guy."

"But what would have been the point? There wouldn't have been anybody listening."

"Sure there was, Uncle Gabe. He had the same audience he always did."

"I don't think I understand, Alex."

"He could have aimed the broadcast back home. To Earth."

"Alex, you can't *aim* a broadcast. A broadcast just throws the radio signal all over the sky."

"He could send directional transmissions. Everybody can do that. And it would be juiced enough to make it to Earth."

Gabe wished Horace Baker would go away. "That's true," he said. "And yes, you're right, a transmission like that probably would have had enough power to get back to Earth, but it would have taken eighty years for it to happen. Why bother? He'd be dead long before it arrived."

"I don't know," said Alex. "*One chance at life.* Do you suppose that message was aimed at us?"

"Among others. Sure." He paused. "Oh."

"Uncle Gabe, if he did send a signal, we could pinpoint where it would be at any given time, and we could be there waiting for it when it arrived. We could listen to his final broadcast."

"Radio archeology," said Gabe.

"Yes. Can we do it? When we're done here?"

*

Gabe did not see any point in such an effort. But it was his earnest hope that Alex would follow in his footsteps and become an archeologist. There was no more rewarding profession. For all its frustrations, it provided an opportunity to put history on stage, to contribute to the sense of who we are. So maybe this was a time to give in. Maybe it would light a fire in his nephew. "You'd really like to go after the transmission, wouldn't you?"

Alex lit up. "Yes, I would. Does that mean you'll do it?"

"How do we find it?"

"No problem, Uncle Gabe. I'll do the research and the math."

*

They did not find Gustofalo. But that was okay. Gabe knew that success in his field was often matched with failure. They hadn't actually located the tomb, but they did come away with a few artifacts, which he turned over to the Holcomb Museum. They duly thanked him with a certificate of achievement. And meantime, Alex did his homework.

The date and time of the *Rover*'s departure from the solar system was on record, so he could estimate within a few hours when it had arrived at Zeta Leporis. The drive engine had blown during its arrival. The analysts maintained that Baker could have survived no more than four hours maximum after the explosion. That made it possible to know within at most a ten-hour time period when the transmission would have been sent. So he could calculate within about seven billion miles where the signal would be at any given time.

"You really think you can do that?" said Gabe, for whom mathematics was not a strong suit.

"Absolutely," said Alex. "When do we leave?"

*

Andiquar University owed Gabe a few favors, so they were willing to smile quietly, pretend he was proposing a serious mission, and grant him access to their interstellar carrier, the *Tracker*. They also included their pilot, Tori Kolpath, in the package. Gabe and Tori had flown a number of joint missions over the past decade. She was tall and quiet, absolutely unflappable, with gray eyes and black hair. Exactly the person you'd want on the bridge if you ran into a meteor storm. When he explained the mission to her, Tori let him see she was amused. But otherwise she played it straight.

"Do you think there's a problem?" Gabe asked her.

"No. Not at all."

"Then why the smile?"

"Who is this guy Baker again?"

*

Alex had to provide a specific destination. "That depends on the time we get there," he said. "The signal's moving at 186,282.7 miles per second." Tori rolled her eyes, and he realized immediately that she didn't need that kind of explanation. Of course she knew the velocity of radio signals.

"The transmission will be about halfway to the solar system," she said. "Is that right?"

"Yes, Tori."

"I can get us into the area in about four days. Since we don't know the precise location of the signal, let's arrive a few hours early so it doesn't get by us. Okay?"

They rode up to the space station, boarded the *Tracker* and, without delay, launched.

Alex spent the first few hours on the bridge, watching her operate. He'd once considered the possibility of a career as a pilot. There was a problem, though. Alex tended to get ill when they made jumps into and out of transcendental space. He didn't know yet what he wanted to do with his life. Hanging around Uncle Gabe had left him with a fascination for history, but there was so much of it, thousands of years and hundreds of worlds. What you had to do if you became a historian was to concentrate on a specific culture, and a specific era. He thought how much simpler life must have been when the human race was confined to a single world.

He knew that Gabe hoped he'd become an archeologist, but Alex didn't think he'd want to spend his life digging holes.

*

It was a four-day flight. They spent their time watching shows, arguing about history, and talking about how exciting it would be to pick up a forty-year-old radio signal. But it was clear to Alex that Uncle Gabe and Tori were faking it. They were humoring him. It didn't matter. He wanted to bring home that last transmission. He wanted to know that Baker had been at peace with the way things turned out. And he also believed that capturing the transmission would be something he could one day brag about.

That was the problem with Gabe. He thought of archeology as the science of recovering physical artifacts. Jewels, weapons, agricultural instruments. Stuff like that. But the Baker Signal could open up a whole new era. And one day Gabe would thank him.

That first night, when he'd retired to his cabin and the ship grew quiet, he found himself thinking again about Horace, trapped on the *Rover* with his air running out. And he wondered whether, even if there had been a final broadcast, he really wanted to hear it.

He tried to hide his feelings. He spent progressively more time reading. He played electronic games with the AI. And he worked out a lot. But he could not get Horace out of his mind. And he began to hope there would be no signal.

Finally, after four days of flight, Tori arrived at breakfast and made her announcement: "We're here. We have fifteen minutes to finish. And then belt down."

Alex hurried through his French toast, and Tori invited him onto the bridge for the jump. He sat down beside her and drew the harness down over his shoulders. "Ready?" she said.

"Absolutely." *And please don't get sick.*

He came through it okay, and they glided out under a sky full of stars. They were in the middle of nowhere. The nearest planetary system was three light-years away. Tori checked their location and nodded. "We're right where we want to be, Alex. And we're about four hours early. If you have the numbers right, we're not likely to hear anything until after lunch. The signal should arrive sometime between two o'clock and midnight." She aimed the antennas in the direction from which the signal would be coming, and they settled in to wait.

Tori and Gabe looked through the ship's library for a show they could relax with. They invited Alex to help, but he declined. "Whatever you guys want is okay with me," he said.

They decided on something from twenty years ago, a comedy featuring actors who, to Alex, just seemed dumb. Eventually he excused himself and went back onto the bridge to wait for the signal to come in. It was the first time he'd seen a sky so dark. The stars were bright, but somehow it didn't matter. You needed a sun somewhere.

He sat in the captain's chair. He knew Tori wouldn't approve, but he'd hear her if she got up, and that would give him plenty of time to get out of the seat. When the signal arrived, a green lamp on the instrument panel would flash. And the AI would inform the rest of the ship.

Gabe and Tori were laughing back in the cabin. They didn't seem to understand what this was really about. Somehow that didn't surprise him. Even the brightest adults could be relied on to miss the point.

He'd brought some of Horace's broadcasts along. He hadn't listened to any of them because he didn't want to do it alone. Neither Tori nor Gabe had shown any interest in listening. But on this day, he needed that familiar voice. He checked the titles and set it to play.

First came the *Liftoff* theme. Then Horace's voice.

"I hate birthdays. We all do, of course, after we pass seventeen, but no one wants to admit it. Back on the day when I turned twenty-two I spent the afternoon at a ball game. There was no woman in my life. I didn't have a job. My folks were throwing a party for me that evening, I didn't have a date, and all I could think of was that the years were rolling past and I wasn't getting anything done. My life was getting away from me.

"That same day I came across an ad for a supplement whose makers insisted it would keep me young. The price was a little out of reach, but if I cut some corners I'd be able to manage it. And I began thinking how life would be if we all started living forever. Bosses would never retire. Politicians would never go away. The funeral directors and pallbearers unions would go on strike. And people would be asked to do the patriotic thing, go down to the dock, and throw themselves into the river—"

*

Alex rarely skipped a meal. But on that evening, while they waited, he passed. Uncle Gabe tried to reassure him. "Sometimes you just have to be patient," he said.

They sat in the cabin, trying to find things to say as the final hours wore away. Alex mostly spent his time staring out a portal at the distant stars or listening for the AI to say something. Gabe began telling stories about times when he'd thought he had nothing for his efforts and then it had all turned around. Like finding the secret diaries of Vernon Persechetti, the brilliant composer who'd had inside knowledge of all the scandals of the Leichmann Era. And the Maroni statue of *The Last Virgin*, which had vanished from its place in the offices of the Brocchian attorney general who'd been offended by its lack of clothing. "Sometimes," he said, "the pleasure is just in the hunt. Even if you don't find something, you've eliminated a possibility."

"Okay," said Alex, who didn't buy it.

"Just hang on," Gabe said.

By eleven o'clock, Alex was sure they would not pick up the signal. Maybe Horace hadn't sat down at the mike after all. Or maybe the distance was just too much and the transmission had dissipated. Or— Or what?

Midnight came and went. Thankfully, it was over.

*

Tori got out of her seat. "Let me check something." She went up onto the bridge.

Alex started to follow but Gabe shook his head. "Let her be," he said.

He heard her talking with the AI, but he couldn't make out what the conversation was about. Then she delivered a final adamant "Okay," and came back wearing an embarrassed smile. "I should have thought of this earlier," she said.

"Thought of what?" asked Alex.

"There's a black hole along the line of sight. It was close enough to divert the signal." She shook her head. "What were the odds of something like that happening?"

"So it's lost?" asked Gabe.

"Not necessarily. It's just diverted. We might still be able to find it."

Alex smiled. As if he wanted to pursue it.

*

They got it on the first try. It opened with the familiar musical theme, Shefski's *Liftoff*, and soared into space. Then Horace was laughing and talking about how sometimes things don't go the way you'd like them too.

"*Blew out my engines,*" he said. "*You do something over and over and after a while you get used to the way things are supposed to go. And then you get a surprise.*"

Alex raised a fist. "Yay," he said. "He's okay."

Horace continued in his usual self-mocking tone, describing his situation, air running out, not long to go. "*Sometimes stuff happens. You're listening to this, and I'm a long time gone. I'd like to say thanks to the people who've supported me all these years. But most of them, like me, have probably moved on. And it's not likely anybody out there will ever have heard of me, unless someone didn't have much to do and decided to chase down the signal. But what I want to say is that nobody should miss the chance to come out here. Even if you only do it once. There's too much to see and you don't want to miss it. And believe me, the virtual stuff doesn't hold a candle to sailing through a set of planetary rings. Or tracking a comet. I'll tell you something else, if I'd had the opportunity to pick my location when it was time to check out, this would have been the kind of place I'd've chosen. This is where I'd have wanted to make my exit.*"

"I just don't know how he does it," said Alex. "He's incredible."

"*I've only one real regret,*" said Horace. "*I'd hoped to live long enough to hear that we'd made contact with somebody in Andromeda. Don't know why, but I like places that are really far. Guess I'll have to put that on hold.*"

*

"You did a good job, Alex," said Tori, embracing him.

Gabe smiled. "I think we have a budding archeologist here."

Alex shrugged. "I really like him." He paused. "He talked for, what, an hour? And I didn't hear a word that suggested he was feeling sorry for himself. Hard to believe, considering what was happening."

"I agree," said Gabe.

"I was afraid he might have broken down."

"Apparently not that guy."

"He was just doing what he always did, I guess," said Tori. "A last show, and then good-bye."

"I'm not so sure," Gabe said.

"About what?" asked Alex.

"That it was his last show."

Alex was puzzled. "You think there's more coming?"

"No. Not for us, anyhow. But I think he wanted to do one more before he signed off. I think he wanted to say hello to somebody. I'll bet there's a second transmission."

Alex looked at Tori to see whether she understood. She was frowning. "Uncle Gabe," he said, "you're not making sense. Who would he say hello to?"

"He told us. Weren't you listening, Alex?"

"Oh." A wide smile brightened his features. "Sure."

"Who?" asked Tori. She was getting annoyed.

Gabe signaled his nephew to respond.

"Andromeda," said Alex.

Unwritten in Green

Alex Dally MacFarlane

The outside of the caravan was painted pale brown, with a single line of script running just above the base on all four sides: the names and deeds of past inhabitants.

Lar-teri, who single-handedly defended the group without leaving his caravan.

Tal-seq couldn't see the words from inside. The shutters only flexed to admit light and a breeze.

Those on the side facing northeast were closed, snicked fast, hiding the orange smear that spread across the sky like a bruise.

Abel-uvi, who became leader of her group while unmarried, and for a long year made many important decisions while inside her caravan, until finding a wife and taking the name Fula.

Tal-seq had been inside the caravan for two and a half years. He wanted to whip the befil pulling it, make the creature bear him faster to the place where he would meet his wife. What seventeen-year-old remained in confinement? Instead he reached for his unit, which lay on a cushion: sleek, dark square on bright blue fabric like the sky.

There was nothing to do but reread the weeks-old piece of news on a hub he had been watching for months: *"Unconfirmed: two dead individuals of the Tuvicen (nomadic people) on Krak-vi have been brought to Cai Nu for examination into the cause of their deaths."* No recent reports—or even rumors—confirmed or denied the theft of two people, taken from their proper burials under the sky, and no one had answered Tal-seq's questions about it. A handful of other Tuvicen intermittently looked at interplanetary hubs, as well as the people in the few steppe towns, and some far-off people knew surprising amounts. He'd hoped to get something.

He threw aside the unit, wincing when it landed loudly on the caravan's floor.

Nothing. Nothing at all. How was he going to find out any more about the orange sky?

*

As the group approached the town Gold Walls, farmers prepared their sacks of rice for trade.

A popular children's story among several groups told of rice grown directly in gold, producing grains that turned their eaters' skin into shining wealth. The variants in reality were much plainer.

Tal-seq watched through the shutters as his mother and two others opened the sacks to check the rice's quality. They poured grains into bowls: brown, sticky, blue—all species modified to flourish in arid land. In return his mother offered gold, atiqi cloth and several spices and medicinal plants that only grew in the Elpeca Mountains, away to the east, where the group traded with other Tuvicen.

Town-noises started to drown out the bargaining. People were gathering at the edge of the town, watching the caravans, talking to people they knew.

Through different shutters, Tal-seq looked for his sister Dona. She stood by her family's caravan, holding her two-year-old son and talking to a town-person. Tal-seq clicked his tongue loudly against the roof of his mouth four times, then waited, tapping his fingers on the shutter's frame, as Dona ended the conversation and walked to the unmarried adults' caravan, which was currently his alone.

Dona stepped inside, letting her son down to jump on Tal-seq's cushions. "Do you want something from the town?" she asked.

The shadowy interior made her brown skin darker and dulled the gleam of her wealth hanging around her neck. Outside, her chest shone like the town's few gold walls.

"I have a favor to ask."

"Oh?" In one sound, she conveyed their mother's disapproval and her own willingness to hear him out.

"Could you go to the bar Burnished Root and ask for a man

called Zhelti? Apparently he's been trying to find out what's causing the orange sky—could you specifically ask about any Cai Nu involvement?"

"Cai Nu people." Dona shuddered. "We really do need to get as far from here as possible."

So their mother had said, too.

"I'd like to know what Zhelti knows."

A brief lift of her eyebrow indicated Dona's opinion of his interest. "That place will be full of people who want to touch my tattoos and ask if I really don't have headware. They're simple out here, you know."

"I know." People were even worse on the hubs, but at least they weren't in the same room. "I'll owe you."

Soon, so soon, he'd be free to ask questions himself—and help with trade, and hunt, and walk under the sky again.

"I'll do it," Dona said. "They have a new fig drink there, we've already been told. I'll bring you one back."

"Thank you."

Sunlight caught on her necklaces as she left. Tal-seq watched her walk past the rice, exchange a few words with her wife and deposit their son on her hip, and go on, disappearing between bare walls at a pace that bounced her braids against her back.

*

"Rumors," Dona said.

They sat facing each other, with a pot of spicy nuts and several skewers of grilled meat in-between them. The fig drink lay unfinished to one side: too bitter with the town-people's alcohol. "Zhelti and a group of others go out hunting, quite far afield—looking for equ. They've seen investigators of some kind, kitted out in fancy protection suits, heading toward the orange sky and later coming back. Zhelti spoke to one of them, who reported that the source isn't visible on the surface, only its after-effects: the land there is entirely dead, all brown and orange. These people reckon the extent of the dead land is spreading, although not in any consistent manner. Apparently it's receded in a couple of spots, but mostly it's expanding, slowly, sometimes less slowly. Any recording equipment the investigators leave behind—evidently they've been here before—doesn't last long in that environment. Zhelti says they're not really sure what it is— it's not radiation, or any kind of pollution encountered elsewhere.

They think it will get worse, but can't give specifics. As for the Cai Nu people, one of Zhelti's group thought that some of the investigators were from Cai Nu. Judging by the way they spoke Krak-vi. But others were definitely Krak-vi." On finishing her recital, Dona reached for more meat.

"Why would Krak-vi and Cai Nu people be working together?"

Dona shrugged, uninterested.

It annoyed Tal-seq, how little he knew of interworlds politics. Perhaps some factions did work together. Perhaps the orange sky and dead land concerned everyone enough to neutralize long-standing conflicts.

"I don't think this changes anything," Dona added. "Even Zhelti, who's stuck out here and hunts for his livelihood, isn't panicking. Just concerned. *We're* leaving, once you're formally betrothed—going far away."

"But what if that's not enough?"

"You've said this before."

"If the main governments on Cai Nu and Krak-vi are getting involved and working together this is a lot more serious than everyone thinks. And the stolen bodies—were you told about that?"

"Yes." Dona spoke like spears: hard and sharp. "It is serious. What makes you think we don't understand that? We are leaving this land, our home—would we do that for nothing?" Then she stuck her hand deep into the pot of nuts, so that when she withdrew it her brown skin was flecked with yellow, orange, red, and green powders. "There are different flavors at the bottom," she explained, showing him a palmful of mostly red-covered nuts. "I also bought a *big* bag of figs, without any of that terrible alcohol in them. Do you want one?"

"Sure."

*

The two groups met by old stacks of stones on harsh, bare land. Flowers the rich dark pink of tongues grew only at the stones' base, fuelled by the excrement of small flighted birds that landed there. The Elpeca Mountains faintly contoured the eastern horizon. The sky loomed orange.

The twelve pale brown caravans of Tal-seq's group and the seven dark blue ones of the other group made two halves of a circle, all facing out. Tal-seq stood at the rear shutters of his caravan, across the circle from the other group's unwed adults' caravan where Mar-teri no doubt stood.

The other group's leader, Nalco, stepped into the circle. The rest arranged themselves in front of their caravans. Compared to Tal-seq's group, their numbers were few.

In the last attack, Tal-seq had thrown a spear through his shutters, like Lar-teri, and wounded a woman. One of his sisters had struck the fatal blow moments later. One of his brothers had been killed.

His mother joined Nalco in the middle of the circle to put an end to that violence.

"We've spent months imagining your head on one of our befil's horns or dragged on the ground by the nose," Tala began. "I know you've wanted to do the same with mine. Now our interests are different. That—" she waved a hand in the direction of the orange sky, which dominated the blue in this place "—has killed ten of your group. That has wasted the land beneath it and killed the game. Our two groups need to move far from here, claim new land that is healthy and bountiful. Together, we will be strong enough to overcome any megafauna we find there. I propose a peace. Any violence between us will be mediated as if we were a single group. To demonstrate our unity, two of our children will wed: my son Tal-seq and your daughter Mar-teri."

Tal-seq glanced at the opposite caravan. What did Mar-teri think of this betrothal?

But Nalco, spitting on the ground at Tala's feet, stole those thoughts. "I don't intend to walk by your side unless you're dangling from my befil's horns," he said, rock-rough.

The circle went silent. Not a person fidgeted or muttered, though their eyes moved: looking from Nalco to Tala, encompassing the people standing in front of the caravans. Assessing the outcome of another fight.

It should have been an easy agreement. Reports from other members of Nalco's group had indicated a desire to make peace. Ten adults and children whose caravans had gone under the orange sky in a temporary splitting of the group had returned to healthy lands, only to waste away over weeks; another, a child, had been lost the first night under that starless sky. The group kept good diagnostic units and medicine, the same as used in the big cities on the other side of the planet, but it hadn't helped. It hadn't even been able to explain the deaths.

Had the Cai Nu scientists learned something from their autopsies and analyses? Tal-seq wanted to spit in their faces and cut off their fingers for stealing the dead, yet their potential results interested him.

"You have made a mistake," Tala said quietly.

Nalco reached for his knife.

A spear flew between the shutters of the dark blue unweds' caravan and buried in Nalco's neck.

"As the oldest surviving child of Nalco, I take charge of this group," a woman said, in a voice that carried despite her concealment. "I agree to Tala's terms, including the offer of marriage with her son Tal-seq. If anyone from my group wishes to dispute this, they may enter my caravan and fight me now."

After only a short silence, the people of her group raised a raucous show of support. Nalco bled onto the dirt. Tala approached the caravan and bowed. Inside, Mar-teri would be doing the same.

Tal-seq liked her already.

"I am glad," Tala said. "We have much to discuss."

*

The discussion continued within the quieted circle. It did not take long. The groups planned a route far south and west to lands where no other people lived, via Gold Walls and Viqa to trade for the kind of supplies they might not have access to for a long time: medical, mostly, as well as spare solar panels and fuel cells. At Viqa, the young man sharing Mar-teri's caravan would find a partner and they would swap some of the children to ensure their group's genetic diversity.

Next they agreed on wedding details. Tal-seq suggested that they first move away from the orange sky. "I want to get married under blue sky."

"Likewise," Mar-teri said. "I want to get away from here as quickly as possible."

"Then we will celebrate your betrothal tonight," Tala said, "and wait until we are on our journey to have the wedding."

Finally.

Mar-teri called for two people to remove Nalco's body and bury it in an appropriate place. Tal-seq pitied the man this burial, so near to where the sky turned orange—to where the investigators probably still worked. Not even Nalco deserved that.

The other people of the circle ended their respectful quietness. Feet stamped and voices raised in song. Instruments were taken from their hooks, fire-bricks were turned on and pots positioned above them. A betrothal required a small celebration, before they moved away from the poisoned sky and land.

The two unwed adults' caravans were moved together, door to door, so that they could meet one another.

Tal-seq stood behind his curtain, dressed in red trousers with half the group's wealth hanging around his neck, dangling from his ears and covering his wrists and ankles.

At a murmured word from his mother, who stood on the narrow piece of ground between the two caravans, he and Mar-teri lifted aside their curtains.

Mar-teri was small and muscular, already scarred across her chin and already tattooed, as Tal-seq was, for defending her people in combat. For killing or injuring people of his group. This was going to be stranger than he'd anticipated. But, like him, Mar-teri bared her chest—a sign of trust—with only her wealth in gold covering her skin. As was common among her group, she only braided some of her hair. The rest hung in brown curls almost to her hips.

Her careful expression revealed none of her thoughts.

"I have a gift for you," Tal-seq said, and took one of the bands from around his left wrist. It was his broadest and engraved with mountains and running birds and words—stories—hanging above the land. Mar-teri's dark brown eyes widened in appreciation: not everyone gave their partner one of their most valuable pieces, especially in an arranged betrothal.

"And I for you."

The band Mar-teri took from her wrist was four-sided. Tal-seq turned it over in his hands, surprised by the detail: like on his cushions, its lines and circles represented the land and routes across it, good water-sources, hunting grounds and bountiful lands, but its scale was so minute that it must encompass their entire year's movement and settling.

"Thank you," he managed, and unhinged it to slip it on his wrist.

"Will you share Tal-seq's caravan until the marriage?" Tala said from the ground.

"Yes," Mar-teri said. "Could it become mine and Tal-seq's? When we repaint the caravans, we will put the stories of your unmarried adults alongside ours."

A bold request, so soon in their alliance. Tala said only, "And Nalco's caravan?"

"Several of our families are getting big. I'm sure one of them would be able to look after it." Mar-teri's voice was as cold as a mountain wind, strong with hatred for her dead father.

To that, Tala nodded. "That will work."

"I will gather my possessions."

When Mar-teri was hidden again by the curtain, Tala looked up at Tal-seq with unconcealed happiness on her face. "Thank you."

"It's important." He found that he meant it, truly. What if this did work: one big group, journeying south, away from the unknown threat? What if he was wrong to fear that moving wouldn't be enough?

In his caravan, he and Mar-teri heated pieces of metal in a small brazier and tattooed each other: two circles on each cheek, to show their intent to marry. Now they could walk freely wherever they chose.

Now Tal-seq could investigate the orange sky in person, if he wanted to, as long as it was along the groups' route. The group's, he thought. Soon they would repaint their caravans.

He took Mar-teri's offered hand and together they stepped out of the caravan and into the circle, where they were met with even louder cheers, louder songs, bowls of rice and meat and thick clusters of chives. The songs and smells—and the endless sky over his head—got into him, filled him better than a hundred meals and shutter-framed glimpses of the steppe. He feasted. He talked to Mar-teri. He stared at the stars, unhidden by a caravan's roof, and admired the rise of bright Venus IV—and barely thought of the starless northeast where the sky was orange by day.

*

Only a day later, he checked the hub, expecting to find nothing. The update there sent him back into fear.

He sought out Mar-teri among the fires of the group.

Back in their caravan, she frowned at the unit. "None of us have these."

"Not many of us do either. I just got one because I was confined in here longer than usual." Two and a half years, compared to Mar-teri's more typical half a year.

"That makes sense," she admitted, yet distaste hung in her words.

Tal-seq gritted his teeth, not wanting another round of the old argument: should he use a nonessential unit, should he not, over and over like the phases of the moon. It had been bad enough convincing his mother that he deserved one—compensation for her refusal to let him marry any of the men or women in other groups they'd passed, because none of those people came with treaties. He hated being her youngest child. No one else to save, just in case.

None of that mattered.

"Mar-teri, there's something I need to show you. Tap it on."

Frowning, she did so.

He showed her the accusations of theft, possibly confirmed by a man who identified as Bhar—one of the better-informed and thoughtful far-off people paying attention to the orange sky. "*Three bodies were certainly brought under high security to Jin Centre. Although I personally cannot confirm their identities, I trust my source's assertion that all three are Tuvicen. There is a discrepancy between only two Tuvicen bodies reported as taken from their sky burials, and the three now confirmed in Jin Centre, that especially concerns me. I fear that the third is the child who went missing before the other ten members of her group died. I cannot imagine these people just getting lost in the middle of the night, even the children.*"

"We saw them!" Mar-teri's face twisted with anger and her fingers clenched around the unit. "We saw them in their white clothes, journeying toward the dead lands, when we had just left our people under the sky four months ago."

"I'm sorry I had to tell you this," Tal-seq said quietly, aware that he trod on her grief: her sisters might have been the two bodies stolen from the burial.

"No. It's better to know." She threw the unit onto the nearest cushion and wiped her eyes. "We thought a wild animal took El-qaro," she said, hard-voiced. "This person is right. None of us would wander off in the night. What animal, in those dead lands? We will go far from the orange sky and these people and their killing."

"It won't be enough."

"They'll follow us?" She looked at the unit, alarmed. "Why?"

"No. I don't think so. But the orange sky is going to get worse. What I've read on these hubs makes it clear that these people have no idea what they're doing. They're taking your dead to find out why they died! And now it looks like they took one of your living. Maybe they *will* follow us, to take more people." More likely, he immediately thought, that they would steal from other groups who remained in this area. "Major governments here on Krak-vi and on Cai Nu are involved."

"What can we do?" she said—not fearfully, not with curiosity. Dismissively. Like his mother. "We are just two small groups—now one normal-sized group. We can't stop them. If they're causing the orange sky like a child knocking over a pot, they won't be able to harm us when we go far from them."

He didn't know how to explain his fear—not to Dona, not to their mother, and now not to Mar-teri. "Perhaps," he said, willing himself to share her confidence. He had, only an hour ago.

*

The caravans journeyed south: first pale brown and dark blue, mixed like rice grains, then green, symbolizing new growth. Tal-seq repainted the unwed adults' stories of his group across the bottom of the caravan that had been the other group's.

He enjoyed the feel of the sun and the wind on his skin, he hunted, he talked to people familiar and new. He talked to Mar-teri. It was far too soon to tell whether their marriage would be a simple partnership—a safe unit of two, more likely to survive if the group splintered—or grow into a friendship or a sexual partnership or love. It was too soon, still, for them to be comfortable with each other.

He couldn't stop reading the hubs, looking for information. Nothing told him more about the cause of the sky or the intent of the Krak-vi and Cai Nu people—or what it might mean for the Tuvicen.

And then his father and several others returned from a hunt, brandishing broken-necked equ and a report of human waste found: poorly buried excrement, food leavings, and a small metal object stuck into the ground. Recording equipment, they guessed. The tracks indicated that the people had journeyed on toward the orange sky.

"The investigators," Mar-teri said, her anger carrying to the assembled group.

"Leave them," Tala said. "I hope that they too will die under that sky—while we are safe in the south."

"No. My group has revenge to get."

Shouts of agreement leapt up behind her, not just from her group. Tal-seq joined them. "We could follow them," he called out above the on-going noise. "Most likely they'll see harmless locals approaching, and let us walk right up to them—which we'll need to do, as they'll all have ranged energy weapons." Then he could ask about their work. "And then we'll have some revenge for El-qaro and the others." He wanted both.

"Yes!" said a girl, far too young for confinement: El-qaro's sister. El-uvi. "We will do this."

Tala was frowning. "This is dangerous. What happens if they do shoot before you get close enough?"

"A little group of us riding up," Tal-seq said, "with our weapons hidden, with children." He grinned at El-uvi, who bared her teeth back. "I don't think they'll fear us."

"We will go," Mar-teri said. "A small group. Tal-seq and me, El-uvi, Valiqa and Tema, and Cani." All people from her group. Tal-seq knew what an honor she was doing by letting him join them.

"We will continue south," Tala said. "Hunt well."

*

They left the caravans behind, riding two to a befil with reins tangled around the creatures' horns. Strong enough to pull multiple caravans when necessary, the befil raced at the weight of only two people.

Tal-seq rode behind Mar-teri. Following them rode Tema and Valiqa. At their side, Cani let El-uvi take their shared befil's reins, and the girl's face was grim with the prospect of avenging her stolen sister and sky-wasted family. The wind turned all their braids into whips. El-uvi's hair wanted bones. Judging by her face, so did Tema's. So did Mar-teri's. Tal-seq's anger rose with theirs as the orange sky grew large again, as snapped reins encouraged the befil on—as a small white dome came into view.

They slowed the befil and waved, calling out a greeting in the main language of Krak-vi. Two people emerged from the dome. Neither reached for a weapon.

They didn't know that Tuvicen only rode without caravans for one reason.

"Such a small group of you!" Tal-seq said, jumping down from his befil a short distance from the two white-garbed people. They stood out so brightly against the orange sky. "Aren't you lonely?"

He felt powerful, standing under the wide sky and *doing* something. For all that he'd recited Abel-uvi's story, it had never been his. He felt angry, he felt curious. Now, finally, he could learn something useful.

The investigators eyed him warily. "We're used to it," one of them said. "What brings you to us? We don't have anything to trade."

Another person walked out of the dome, and her eyes widened at the sight of befil and Tuvicen.

"Why are you here?" Tal-seq asked.

"To study the discolorations of the sky," said the same man, "a situation that concerns us as greatly as it no doubt concerns you."

"And what have you learned?" he asked.

At the same time, El-uvi pulled her spear from her befil's harness and pointed it at the man, shouting, "Why did you take my sister?"

The man stepped back in alarm. "I don't know what you're talking about!"

Perhaps the other man and the woman thought their movements subtle. All six Tuvicen saw them start sliding their hands to the weapons holstered at their hips.

"Three of our people were taken to Cai Nu," Tal-seq said. Were these people from Cai Nu? "Ten of our people died under that sky. We'd like to know what you learnt."

El-uvi hissed and hurled her spear at the silent man, who had partially drawn his weapon—which clattered to the ground. He fell after it, with El-uvi's spear pointing from between his collarbones like an especially slim marker stone. Blood bloomed. The remaining man cried out; the woman drew her weapon, but Cani and Valiqa seized her arms and pressed a knife to her throat, and she went entirely still except for the rapid rise and fall of her chest.

"You people killed my sister," El-uvi said, with hatred sharper than any weapon.

"I don't … I don't know! We weren't told that!" The man shook like fabric in the wind.

Soon there would be no more time for questions, only blood on stone. "What were you told?" Tal-seq demanded, desperate for *something*. "What do you know about that orange sky?"

"Nothing!"

"When you've got all this equipment?" With the man being so useless, he made sure he looked at the woman when he said, "You must have ideas by now. After slicing our people apart."

"This is tiresome," Mar-teri said in Tuvicen, "and reinforcements could be traveling toward us on something faster than a befil. Let's kill these two and be finished."

"Yes," El-uvi said, and walked toward her spear.

"We could find out what's happening!" The intensity of his own voice surprised Tal-seq.

"They won't tell us quickly," Mar-teri said, "or do you propose trying to interpret their equipment?"

Tal-seq ignored the sting in her words, because the idea hadn't even occurred to him: take their raw data, share it on the hub, invite everyone to join him in interpreting it. "We could ..." he murmured.

"Let someone else deal with it! We can't."

"What makes you think *they* will? They don't care about us. We're just a few quirky nomads who leave our bodies conveniently out in the open for them to take."

That made her flinch. Everyone else looked at him.

The two investigators shared nervous glances.

He probably could have worded that better.

"They won't let this get out of control," Mar-teri said, almost as angry as El-uvi. "Think about it. Otherwise the people living in cities on the other side of the planet will start to die. All *we* have to do is kill these people and get away from here."

"They'll fight to keep the city people safe, but what will be left for us? Assuming they can even control what they're doing—"

"In that case, we had better just sit here and wait for the orange sky to stretch over our heads, because there's no point trying to survive."

"Yes, that's exactly what I said."

"So, what? What do we do? Become scientists? Figure it out for ourselves? Or shall we go fight their governments? I want to go south to new lands, far from these people, and ensure a good life for everyone in the group."

"I want that too," Tal-seq said. Why did she think otherwise? "I just want to *know*. What if we go to new lands and it's not enough? What if we—" What *could* they do? He'd lain awake at night, stuck on that same question like a wheel on an awkward stone. "We might need to do something."

"This sounds like a well-thought-out plan," Mar-teri said, and with a wave of her hand, ordered the remaining investigators' deaths. Their blood splashed on the ground. "We will survive. We will." To the others, she shouted, "Destroy their things and then let's go!"

Tal-seq could only watch as El-uvi, Cani, Valiqa, Tema, and Mar-teri threw shattered pieces of equipment onto the ground. When the bodies were almost concealed by the shards of white and gray, everyone turned back to the befil. Mar-teri mounted hers and slapped its rump without even looking at Tal-seq: *get up here.* Wordlessly he did.

*

"I don't understand," Mar-teri said, when they finally stepped into their caravan.

"I want us to be safe."

Mar-teri nodded. The wealth at her ears chimed. "You don't need to waste your time finding out what these far-off people are doing. There's so much else: going south, making our two groups work well together, and everything we'll encounter on the way."

Tal-seq bit back the retort that burned on his tongue: maybe, just maybe, the sky turning orange was a bigger problem than they thought. He'd already, on the long, silent ride from the ruined camp to the caravans, made his decision.

*

As she slept, he crouched at the other end of the caravan with possible words tangling in his mind like broken belts. Mar-teri wouldn't understand. He considered leaving the wristband she'd given him. He considered taking it.

"I hope you're right," he murmured.

It was too easy to imagine staying: forever feeling the gust of steppe winds against his skin, the thrill of hunting, the taste of chives cut from the ground and stirred in befil milk. The sky. The conversations around an evening fire. No other place would offer him this life. The thought of leaving his group hurt in ways he didn't even want to think about.

The thought of them dying under an orange sky or an investigator's tools hurt far more.

He kept the wristband. He wrote a letter for Mar-teri and his family.

I'm leaving. I'm still convinced that we'll be in danger, no matter how far south we go. But I'm not going back to the orange sky. I'm going as far away as I need to find out what the orange sky really means for us. I don't know where that is yet. Perhaps I'll be proved wrong after all. I doubt it, though I hope so. I do. I mean no disrespect to Mar-teri. I want to go south with her, but I want this too; it wasn't an easy decision, it hurts, but I have to.

He hadn't intended to write that much, but he left the words—an offering to them, Mar-teri and Tala and Dona and everyone else, in the hope that they understood after all.

In the darkest hour of the night, he mounted his befil and rode north.

*

One of the stories not written on any caravan played through his thoughts, like a repeating clip: *Fal-tuo, who left the Tuvicen for five years but, on his return, was welcomed by his family.*

He repeated the story like a ritual as each day took him further from what he knew.

The End of Callie V

Jennifer Moore

Callie had always imagined Death as a dark, hooded figure with a skeletal frame and a deep, low whisper of a voice. She couldn't have been more wrong. The plump little man who stood waiting on the doorstep was blond and smiley. If it weren't for the big clock in his hands and the name badge pinned to his chest, she'd never have picked him out as an authorized collector of spent lives. She couldn't help feeling a bit disappointed.

"Hello," he beamed. "I don't believe we've met. Mind you, it's only my first week on the job so I've barely met anyone yet. You must be Callie."

"That's me," she agreed. "I've been expecting you. Would you like to come in?"

"Thank you," he said, stepping lightly through the doorway. "It's funny, you're not at all like I imagined. For some reason I pictured you much taller with long dark curls."

"My parents didn't have enough credits left for decent hair," explained Callie. "Which is why I ended up with this." She tugged her fingers through her spiky white tufts. "They skimped a little on the height as well so they could buy me another few months." Fifteen years—that was all her Mum and Dad had been able to afford on their paltry Service Worker wages. And now Callie's fifteen years were up.

She led him into the primary room, apologizing as she did so for its odd appearance. It had jammed on its dining room setting three weeks ago and they were still waiting for the engineer to come and fix it. The sideboard had completely disappeared beneath the porto-kitchen kit that had become their makeshift food preparation area. A king-sized insta-bed stuck out from underneath one of the chairs and Callie skirted around it, motioning Death to do the same. It was funny how quickly you got used to things. Moving the heavy wooden table to create enough room for her parents to sleep had become something of a nightly ritual. She'd missed the comfy sofas and the viewing screens at first but had quickly come to appreciate the evenings spent around the dining table, long after the camping dishes had been cleared away, just talking. Somehow it seemed like a fitting end to her life.

"Can I get you a drink of something?" she asked. In truth the last thing she felt like doing was making small talk over a cup of tea. But she had promised her parents she would be polite and welcoming. They had repeatedly petitioned the local Service Team Leader for the day off but their requests had been denied. It would take more than the termination of their only child to warrant the loss of a day's labor. So they had said their last, weeping good-byes before they left that morning, together with a few final instructions: *Be brave. Be ready. Be polite.*

"No, I'm fine thanks," said Death. "They don't really like us drinking on the job. But don't let me stop you ..." He checked the clock in his hands. "You've got time for a quick one. My next appointment isn't until eleven."

"I'd rather just get on with it, if that's OK."

"Of course. I take it you're familiar with the process? You've read the terms and conditions?"

Callie nodded. She practically knew them off by heart. At the end of the allotted time span she would be decommissioned with immediate effect. The procedure would be instant and painless, her body reverting back to its constituent base parts ready for recycling. Her memories, her essence, everything that had made her Callie for the last fifteen years, would be wiped clean. It would be as if she had never existed. Like Anka, her best friend, whose contract had been up two months before. One day she'd been there, laughing and joking and mooning over Paulo, the new boy with the dark curls and matching eyes, like a regular flesh-and-blood teenager, and the next she'd been gone. *Shwoop.* Just like that.

Callie's class had shrunk considerably over the last few years. Theirs was a relatively poor neighborhood and not many Service Workers could afford more than thirteen to fourteen years on their contract. She was lucky her parents had managed to stretch hers out to fifteen, even if did mean that she was ridiculously short for her age and saddled with the kind of white hedgehog hair that meant the likes of Paulo wouldn't look twice at her.

"Any last requests?" Death asked. "You're entitled to one extrasensory experience of up to three minutes." He smiled. "All part of the service."

Callie bit her lip. She had given the matter a lot of thought over the last few weeks. Anka, she knew, had opted for three minutes kissing a virtual Paulo. It was certainly a tempting proposition. At least then she wouldn't die without knowing what it felt like. But it wouldn't be real would it? Another girl she knew had chosen to spend her allotted time in Park Paradiso, surrounded by real life trees and vegetation—or at least a virtual copy of them. Another opted to meet the grandmother she had never known. Everyone had their own dreams and unfulfilled desires. But how to pick just one longed-for experience out of a whole unlived life? Fifteen years hadn't been nearly long enough to do all of the things Callie had fantasized about. She had never seen the sea. Never touched a flower. Never heard birdsong. Never traveled beyond the city of her "birth." She had never mastered the piano. Never learned to speak more than three languages. Never met anyone from another planet. Never tasted honey. Never been kissed. In the end though she had decided against all of them.

"There was one thing I wanted to experience," she said hesitantly. "But I don't even know if it's possible."

"We can do most things these days," smiled Death, his eyes crinkling like tiny black caterpillars. Callie knew all about caterpillars and butterflies from history lessons. It was her favorite subject and she'd been top of her class every year. Her parents might have skimped a little on her appearance but there'd been no corner-cutting when it came to intelligence and learning aptitude. It was funny to think that all that information—every last bit of knowledge currently stored in her brain—would soon disappear along with the rest of her thoughts and memories. Though maybe "funny" wasn't quite the right word.

"Go on," said Death. "Try me. I'll see what I can do."

Callie took a deep breath. "I'd like to see my parents afterward. I mean after I'm gone." She was slightly concerned about how they were going to cope without her. Every day it seemed there was a new story about someone who'd gone to pieces after their child's contract had expired. It was understandable really. Parents these days were becoming as attached to their geno-kids as previous generations had been to their human offspring. And with low wages and rising living costs it might take a grieving couple years to be able to afford a replacement. Callie just wanted to see that they'd be okay without her—to witness them coping for herself. Even though she knew full well it would only be a virtual approximation of the future, it would still be some comfort.

Death was quiet for a moment as if he was thinking something through. "Well, they never mentioned that one at training college," he said at last. "You're a funny one aren't you?"

Callie blushed. "Can you do it?"

"Well," he said. "Hmmm ... it's just a hunch ..." He gestured to the nearest dining room chair. "Please. Sit down."

She did as she was told.

He set the clock down on the table in front of him and retrieved a thin silver disk from his jacket pocket. He held it up to his right eye for a few moments and then smiled. "Yes," he said. "I think we're in business." He slotted the disk into a discreet panel at the back of the clock.

"Okay," he said, his face tense with concentration. "Now I want you to close your eyes and relax. I'm going to count slowly down from ten and then ..." He started to count. "Ten ... Nine ..." Already Callie's eyes felt heavy behind their lids. "Seven ... Six ..." Her body was sinking deeper into the chair under its own immense weight. "Four ... Three ..." She was drifting into a light, silvery nothingness. "... One."

Callie opened her eyes. The dining table and chairs had vanished and the room had reverted back to its lounge setting. Her parents must have gotten it fixed at last. And there they were, sitting side by side on the sofa, eyes glued to the central viewing screen. Her Mum looked happy and excited; her face seemed to have lost some of the weariness and stress-lines that had gathered around her eyes in the

last few months. Her hair was different as well—shorter and darker—
it made her look much younger. Callie noticed that her Dad's face
was less lined and frowny too. She felt a momentary pang to see them
looking so relaxed and happy without her and had to remind herself
that this was exactly what she wanted for them. Just because they'd
moved on with their lives it didn't mean they hadn't loved her.

Her gaze shifted towards the viewing screen, with its large blue
menu and the Geno-Kids logo flashing in the top left hand corner.
With a jolt of recognition Callie realized what she was looking at—
this was the selection screen for a new Geno-kid. Her Mum and Dad
were choosing her replacement.

"I can't find the right hair," her Mum said, scrolling remotely to
the next screen with her finger. "We don't want long glossy curls.
Where have the white spikes got to?"

"Are you sure you wouldn't rather have something different this
time?" asked her Dad.

"No. Callie has white spikes," said her mother firmly. "She always
has and she always will."

Her Dad grinned. "She won't thank you for it. You know how
much she hates them."

"Oh, girls never like their hair. It's just one of those things. Besides
it's less credits, which means we can stretch to the full fifteen years
again."

"Or we can wait another few years while we save up and then
keep her for a bit longer this time."

Her Mum shook her head. "I'm sorry. I can't wait. I don't think
you can either. Every time she goes it's like a huge hole in our lives and
neither one of us will be happy until we fill it. We need our Callie."

"You're right," agreed her Dad. He pointed to the screen. "Look,
there's the white spikes option. Oh and don't forget to put in that
birthmark by her left ear. I love that birthmark …"

Callie closed her eyes, just for a moment, and when she opened
them again she was back in the dining room, opposite the smiling
face of Death. She smiled right back at him.

"Thank you," she said. "That was a far nicer future than I could
ever have imagined on my own."

"You're very welcome," he told her. "But between you and me, that
wasn't the future."

"Oh I know it wasn't the *exact* future," Callie said. "I realize that no one can be one hundred percent sure of that until it actually happens. But it's the future I'd wish for them." She paused. "And for me, come to that. It's like I'll still be here even after I've gone."

"No, I mean it wasn't the future," explained Death. "It was the past."

Callie's mouth dropped open as she tried to take in what he was saying. "So you mean I'm not the first Callie they've had ...?"

"And I very much doubt you'll be the last," he agreed.

"And they always make me just the same every time?"

"So it would seem. They must love you very much."

Callie nodded. "You're right. They do." She took a deep breath. *Be brave. Be ready. Be polite.* "Thank you again," she said, running her fingers across the birthmark by her left ear, for luck. "I think I'm ready to go now. After all, it's not like it's forever."

"Very good," said Death with a little bow. "If you'd just close your eyes one last time then. Don't worry, this won't hurt a bit."

Speech Lessons

by Alicia Cole

My mandibles will not make
the necessary sounds. Take
polyglot for example.
The consonants between O's
are ample cause for error.

The teacher
reinforces mouth shapes, her
jaws alien.

Mother taught
me not to bite. Her main thought:
first born of new land, hold the
thirst for knowledge heavier
than hunger.

My thorax
rustles as my chest expands,
elytra at rest

BY ALICIA COLE

until I flex my wings. My forearms
sharp as knives, I mouth the forms
the teacher feeds me. We both
tire of this game of syllable
and phoneme.

She wipes her face.
The sun in harsh rays through
the window
lights her gray hair. Like mother,
she is always exclaiming
on the momentousness
of our work. I shift, ache
to fly.

Speak, but do not listen.

The Myriad Dangers

Lavie Tidhar

1.

The aliens invaded at 2:57 in the afternoon, three minutes exactly to three. Which was a good tactical choice—most adults were asleep, taking a well-deserved afternoon nap in dark rooms where the only sound was the soft burr of the air conditioner or the gentle hum of a fan as it turned this way and that.

It was hot.

The heat felt like the aliens' laser beams. It lay over the sea and blasted the sand and made the grass sweat. When you blinked the sweat got in your eyes and everything looked hazy and distant and impossible.

The aliens were small and green and wore purple. Their blasters looked like toys and the aliens looked like wizened children dressed for a Purim party. Hardly anyone saw them. Their flying saucers hovered silently above the white buildings of Tel Aviv. There were hundreds of them. Thousands. The saucers came from the sky and some hovered over the city and some hovered over the sea and some blasted cars as they came along the Ayalon Highway, but not like they were being mean. Like they were just a little bored, and maybe wanting to break things.

Danny was alone when the aliens came. His parents were asleep in the room upstairs and he was outside, despite the heat, standing by himself next to the swings, waiting for someone, anyone, to come along so he could play with them.

It was Rosh Hashanah, or would be in the evening. They'd welcome the New Year as they always did, by going to see his grandparents. They'd go in the car, and his father would hum along with the radio and make up his own words to songs, and when they'd get there Danny's uncles and aunts and cousins and everyone would be there, and there'd be some singing, and not-so-good food, and the television would be on for the news, and it would be one of those long summer evenings that seem never to end without quite leading anywhere, and suddenly he wanted very badly not to go, which was at exactly 2:57 in the afternoon, when the aliens came.

The aliens came marching down the street, like ants, or Israeli Defense Force soldiers. They marched in lines and their hands moved in rhythm but they didn't make a sound. The whole city seemed to be asleep, its defense systems down, its awareness diminished, a whole city dreaming, restlessly, of other white cities, and coolness, and matzo ball soup.

Danny watched the aliens go past. They ignored him, but one of the saucers, hovering overhead, shot out a laser beam that made the swing melt and hiss on the ground.

"Cool …" said Danny.

The word, small and alone, hung in the hot, humid air of the invasion before fading softly. Danny watched the melted metal on the dry ground.

After a while he saw that there were now alien soldiers in front of every door that he could see. There must have been millions of small alien soldiers all throughout the city, standing before every doorway and in apartment block hallways throughout the city. They still hadn't made a sound.

"What are they going to do now?" said Danny, but there was no one there to answer him, so he just watched instead.

At 3:16, in the hot afternoon, the aliens approached each of the doors they were watching and opened them. If they couldn't open them they used their blasters to melt the locks and then they went inside. Every house and every apartment, even Danny's, and you had to get in through a locked courtyard first.

Then they started carrying people out.

Danny watched. He was the only one awake, in the whole wide city. In the whole world, maybe. He watched the strange little aliens carry his mum out. It took four of them to hold her up. She was asleep, and her eyes were closed, and there was a little bit of drool at the corner of her mouth. Two more aliens carried out his dad and three were bringing out the neighbor, Shula, who wore a flower patterned dress and dyed her hair blue and had false teeth that she kept in a tea glass on her bedside table. The teeth floated there in the murky liquid and grinned at nothing. He had seen them once, when he had to go and borrow a cup of sugar for his mum.

The aliens carried people out of their homes. There were old people and little babies and plumbers and schoolteachers on their summer holidays. There were computer programmers and belly dancers and bakers and cinema ushers and homeless people (but the aliens picked them up in the street, gently, the way you would a baby). There were fat hairy men in big white underpants and women with curlers in their hair and men in blue overalls spattered with paint and old people with catheters and a kid in a wheelchair and a couple still entwined, in sleep, in each other's arms.

"I wonder where they're taking them," said Danny, but there was no one there to answer him, by the silent swings. He watched the aliens take all the people out of their houses and apartments and then they stopped, and stood motionless in the silent street.

"Mum isn't going to be happy when she wakes up, you know," said Danny, but the aliens didn't hear him or, if they did, they chose to ignore him. Or perhaps they just didn't understand. No one expects aliens to speak Hebrew. So Danny just watched and then all the flying saucers, at once, shot out a sort of blue light and the alien soldiers and their cargo were lifted slowly up in the air, floating there in the blue with the sun beating down, untold thousands of sleeping people held in alien arms.

Then they all disappeared inside the flying saucers and the blue light vanished and, at 3:46 in the afternoon they, too, disappeared, just like that.

The city was silent and empty and the only sound he could hear, if he tried really hard, was that of the sea, the sound of small waves lapping against the shore. It was a sound both like and unlike the one of small feet padding along, clad in worn-out trainers. The city lay there, in the hot sun of a summer afternoon, on Rosh Hashanah: entombed, empty, free.

"I wonder where they all went," said Danny. But of course, there was no one there to answer him: not even aliens.

2.

"That was strange," said Danny's dad the next day.

"What was?" said Danny's mum.

"I had the strangest dream," said Danny's dad. "That funny little aliens came and took us all away in their ships."

"That *is* weird," said Danny's mum.

Danny wanted to tell them it hadn't been a dream, but didn't. It really happened! He saw it!

The problem was, these weren't his real mum and dad. His real mum and dad were stored on board a spaceship, with thousands and thousands of other human bodies, all floating side by side and in stacks, going somewhere.

When the aliens left, Danny had been left alone by the ruined swing. After a while he went back home, but when he turned on the television there was nothing on, so he turned it off again and went out. He didn't lock the door. There didn't seem to be much point.

It was still Rosh Hashanah, though maybe for his parents it wasn't. Did you have Rosh Hashanah in space?

He wandered the streets. The sun was getting lower in the sky, sinking toward the sea, and it was very slightly cooler. There was no one around.

There were cats, though. But the cats ignored him. And there were dogs, and some of them barked at him, but mostly they just looked confused. There were a lot of pets in Tel Aviv and, like Danny, they expected to be fed.

He felt hungry so he went into an empty mini-market and took a packet of *bisli*, grill flavor, and ate it. Then he wandered back outside.

"What do you think you're doing, kid?"

He turned when he heard the voice. Inside the mini-market the air shimmered, and for a moment he saw, through a membrane of air, a shifting blue light and an amorphous shape and then, like something hatching out of an egg, the amorphous blob became a person and stepped out onto the mini-market floor.

It looked—it looked exactly like Shufra, the checkout woman who was always there when he went to the store with his mum. She was in her mid-fifties, with a blue blouse and a name-tag that said SHUFRA on it in big black letters, and she had long nails painted red that she used to punch the numbers on the till with. In fact, it looked exactly like Shufra but for the eyes. The eyes were empty, and behind them was the same blue emptiness, like the sky.

"I was—" said Danny, and then stopped, because he didn't know what to say.

"You need to pay for that!"

"But—"

But there was no one there, he wanted to say, but instead he went over to the creature that looked just like Shufra, and gave it five shekels, and then shuffled his feet when she—it—ruffled his hair briefly and then told him to get back home, his mum would be waiting.

So he went home. As he walked along the empty streets, with the sun slowly setting beyond the sea, more and more human simulacra materialized all around him.

They looked like everyday people—builders and policewomen, bus drivers and cable technicians, a homeless guy and the two weird old ladies with the runny makeup who always pushed a shopping trolley between them down the road, ignoring the outraged drivers—but their eyes were windows, and beyond them was a clear and empty blue sky, with no clouds or life.

The dogs, he noticed, were growling at the simulacra. But the cats rubbed themselves against them, and their fur stood on end, as if they had come in touch with static electricity.

"Where have you been?"

A simulacrum stood in the kitchen. It looked just like his mum.

"I was playing on the swings."

The simulacra mum looked out of the window. "Someone ruined one of the swings," she said.

"It was the aliens," said Danny.

"Go to your room," his simulacra-mum said.

3.

Luckily they didn't have to go to the Rosh Hashanah dinner after all, because of the zombie invasion.

The zombies came from the north, from the direction of the old cities, of Haifa and Acre and Safed, and they came from the south, from the mountains of Jerusalem, and there were lots and lots of them.

The zombies appeared by lunchtime. Danny was playing by the swings again, because it was still a holiday and there was no school until Monday. The zombies looked just like normal people but they had green skin and bits were falling off them and they smelled bad. The zombies shambled down the street and whenever they saw a person they moaned and groaned and reached for them with green flaking fingers, and when they caught them they bit them, bit them everywhere, on the neck and the head and the ears, on the arms and the fingers, on the belly and on the legs.

And then the people who got bitten, or what was left of them by then, also became zombies.

Danny hid. He'd abandoned the swings for a makeshift castle, climbing high on the playhouse's network of ladders, swings and rope bridges until he made it to the very top. He felt safe there.

He watched his mum and dad. His dad was standing in the street outside, sneaking a cigarette. "What the—?" Danny's dad said. He dropped the cigarette on the ground and by the time it hit the zombies were on him. There were more than ten of them—old ladies with false teeth, a baby that made no sound, a fat man with a hairy back, two school girls, the butcher from down the street and a couple of people who had wandered off the bus at the nearby bus stop. They tore at Danny's simulacra-dad's arms and bit him, like a pack of dogs fighting over a meal. Danny's dad screamed, once, and then he gurgled.

When Danny's dad stood up again he was no longer Danny's dad. He had bits missing everywhere—big chunks on the arms, both ears, an eye, most of a thigh. His clothes were torn and his short hair was matted with green-gray goo.

"Grrrrrr," said Danny's dad.

"Arrrrrgh," said the people who came off the bus.

Danny saw his mum step out of the door, pause, take in the scene, and scream. The scream was long and high and piercing and was the only other sound in the quiet street.

Then she ran back inside and, when she came back out, she was carrying an UZI that Danny's dad kept in the house in readiness for his reserve military service, which took place at least once a year.

"Take that, zombie scum!" Danny's mum screamed, and pulled the trigger.

Bullets flew, cutting through brains and throats and chests and arms. Danny's dad fell back, his arms rising in the air as he sank to his knees, hit by multiple bullets. "I always knew this day would come," Danny's mum said, still shooting. Danny could hear gunfire everywhere now. The city of Tel Aviv had erupted in a desperate war, residents and zombies, guns against teeth. "But where is the government when you need it?"

She emptied the entire magazine and there was a momentary lull. Zombie corpses lay everywhere, broken, twitching, leaking green puss and blood.

From the neighboring apartment their neighbor, Shula, stepped out in her flowery dress and an AK-47 in her arms. "It's started," she said.

And now, from across the street, stay-at-home mums and elderly ladies and young school girls all came marching up toward them. They were all carrying guns. A couple of them, Danny noticed, were smoking cigars. When they came to the apartment—one elderly lady stepping over Danny's dad's corpse—they all stopped, and saluted as one.

"At ease," said Danny's mum.

"Supreme Commander," said one of the women, who was holding a Desert Eagle .50 in one hand and a butcher's knife in the other, "we are ready at your command."

"Troops!" said Danny's mum. "The zombie invasion has started. The moment we have been waiting for has come. We must make for the mountains! Leave no corpse unturned! Kill everything in your path! Who is with me?"

"We are!" cried her troops.

"Who is with me?"

"*We are!*"

"Then let's go!"

And, firing in the air, she led them back up the street, only looking back once, to shout, "I'll be back when I can, Danny! Keep out of sight and remember to wash behind the ears! Love you!"

Danny, perched on his aerie, watched her go. After a while what was left of his dad got up from the pavement. It looked pretty bad.

"Grrrr?" it said, plaintively.

Danny wondered if there was any food left in the fridge.

4.

"Vampires? Really?" said Danny.

5.

It was 2:57 in the afternoon, and it was hot. It was Rosh Hashanah, or would be in the evening. They'd welcome the New Year as they always did, by going to see his grandparents. They'd go in the car, and his father would hum along with the radio and make up his own words to songs, and when they'd get there Danny's uncles and aunts and cousins and everyone would be there, and there'd be some singing, and not-so-good food, and the television would be on for the news, and it would be one of those long summer evenings that seem never to end without quite leading anywhere, and then they'd go home.

But right now, the Rosh Hashanah dinner was far away, light years away in the distant future, and the city of Tel Aviv, *his* city, lay all about Danny as he played by the swings. The city lay quiet and peaceful and empty, in silence, its residents asleep in darkened rooms, like the dormant pupae of an alien species, patiently waiting to hatch.

For now, for just this afternoon, this hot summer day, this holiday, the city was his, Danny's, to do with as he pleased. Anything could happen, a multitude of threats posed for invasion, set and ready to stop the New Year from coming, the tedious Rosh Hashanah dinner, his aunt's cheek-pinching, his uncle's school-Latin phrases aimed like missiles at Danny and the other children, the too-sweet food and the boring television news turned on too loud.

There were aliens and zombies and weird transdimensional simulacra people. Even as he was watching the city was being transformed. Giant, hungry, carnivorous plants spread through rooftops and yards, twining themselves into chained bicycles and parked cars, giant hungry mouths opening, dripping saliva, grinning in the hot Mediterranean sun as they waited to devour the sleeping city.

"Cool …" said Danny.

Danny climbed on top of the swings, and smiled. He surveyed his domain. For just this afternoon, in that twilight moment between the old year and the new, while the city, unaware of the myriad dangers it faced, slept, he, Danny, was free.

The Fall of Stile City

William John Watkins

"You're only young once," Beendohj always said, "and it don't last long!"

If you were an Upper and lived in the plush placings at the top of the central column of the Peristyle, being young could last a lifetime, but Beendohj was right if you were a Squat and lived packed like wafers in the nine flat stories of the Base. Just about everything got shorter as you went from the point of the Peristyle down the gradually widening columns to the Base. Beendohj called it "vertical justice." If you lived at the bottom of that mile high column of columns, you lived at the bottom of everything.

And you worked even lower down. The Countershaft of the main column of Peristyle City, or Stile City as those of us at the bottom called it, went down into the bedrock almost half as far as it went up, and everything that made the city work went on there: lights, ventilation, power, everything from the air columns that lifted and lowered Risers up and down the Shaft to the preparation of the five hundred fun foods the Uppers consumed to eat away their boredom.

In the Base, there were only two kinds of food: bad and worse. It didn't matter: everybody knew Squats had no taste anyway. Generations of inbreeding inferior stock was supposed to have left us on the level of intelligent monkeys. It was common knowledge that Squats had no higher motivations than getting their brains lathered and their glands exercised as often as possible. You couldn't find an Upper from the top quarter of the Peristyle or a Mid from the rest of the Shaft who would have contradicted it.

Squats worked six grueling hours in the Countershaft and then spent fourteen of the next eighteen hours distorting their intellects and stimulating their senses with Sparkle. Everybody knew it and the truth was, they were right, at least if you were young. Not that we had many Olders to look up to. Sparkle runs your mind at half speed and your heart at double time, so you burn out long before you hit fifty as a general rule. Not that we cared. We all said, "Live fast, feel funny, leave a laughing corpse."

Every time we put our heads in the Mesh and let a bit of Stile City's power grid tickle our pleasure centers for a while, we knew we were paying for it with hours we hadn't lived yet and never would, but it's easy to borrow from a future you don't expect to have. All anybody in the Squats had to look forward to was the next shift. Work never stops in the Countershaft.

Anywhere on the Shaft you might, with a little skill and/or a lot of larceny, move a couple levels higher than you started. Maybe in a generation you could visit your Youngers a couple steps higher in the Uprise. But you couldn't rise from the Base to the Shaft. We had only one change of location to make: from the Base, down to the Countershaft, and we all knew it.

And if the Sparkle made us forget it for a few short hours, there was always the Jolt, that reset our brain patterns and got us ready to do our daily part to keep Stile City running. Nobody complained about the chance to work every day. The only way to pay for getting your head stuck in the Mesh was to log some hours in the Countershaft. No work, no Sparkle. It was simple as that. And nobody wanted to give up Sparkle. Except Beendohj.

As far as the Uppers were concerned, Sparkle was the perfect tool. It had no after effects; when the current stopped tickling your brain, your capacities were as intact as they were before you started. You could en-Mesh yourself right up until it was time to sink into the Countershaft to complete a shift, and that's what we did, every day, until the day about six months after we'd been moved up to Minor Repairs when somebody made the mistake of sending me and Beendohj into The Ball Room to unstick a door.

The Ball Room was where The Ball was, and The Ball was the heart of everything that went on in Stile City. Nobody but a few

Uppers really knew how it worked, but everybody knew the basics. Stile City worked because Stile City was built around plasma energy in Dynamic Equilibrium. The energy that ran Stile City was a closed System in continual motion. Motion, in ways a Squat would never understand, created more energy. Dynamic Equilibrium meant making sure the energy used and the energy created were equal. That's where The Ball came in, even its slightest movements changed the shifting balance of energy as it flowed through the Mesh and maintained the Dynamic Equilibrium.

The door we were supposed to fix was a sliding sheet of curved glass in the wall of a round glass room that measured maybe ten feet across. The Ball was in the center, and we stood outside looking at it through the glass walls. It wasn't that big really; the outer, transparent sphere, was about three feet across and the metal inner ball was maybe a foot in diameter. What was impressive, and what made us stop and stare at it until Security warned us to stop Lingering, was that it floated about waist high, bobbing and wobbling in the middle of the room with nothing holding it up. I always thought there was a brilliant shaft of golden energy flowing from floor to ceiling, but there was nothing.

I said, "Where's the Golden Shaft?"

Beendohj looked at me like he thought I was Sparkling. "There is no Golden Shaft," he said.

I was disappointed. "It's in all the holos," I said. I might only be seventeen, but they'd been showing me images of The Ball since I was big enough to walk and every one of them had the Golden Shaft with The Ball floating in the middle of it.

"Squats are stupid," he said, "You have to give them pictures they can understand." I knew he didn't really think Squats were stupid, he was just saying what an Upper would say. Beendohj certainly wasn't stupid. He was the only Squat I knew who actually used the Access. When we were ten or so, they stopped forcing us to use the Access, and most Squats never went near it again, except for something to look at while you were Sparkling. But Beendohj was always using it, just trying to find out things he didn't already know. He knew a lot more than *I* ever wanted to know, but he was always looking for more.

"Where is the Golden Shaft then?" I asked.

Beendohj shook his head in disgust. "Nowhere," he said, "it's not like that. The changes are too delicate. The System's always on the brink of Chaos. The littlest tremor can cause a change of state. Look at the way that thing is dancing around. You couldn't have that right in the middle of things."

"Why not?" The Ball didn't look like it was dancing to me, it looked like it was hardly moving. "You have a glass of water filled up so full you can't put any more in it," Beendohj said. "You add a drop of water, what happens?"

"It flows over."

"Change of state," he agreed. "One drop between full and overflowing. Only sometimes the glass is so full, if you add one molecule to the mist that rises off the top of it as it evaporates, it will overflow. That's the way the System is. This room is full of mist. The Ball is like a lever, you push a little on it here, and it's so long it lifts a mountain on the other end."

It made sense, more or less. I looked at The Ball again. "Where's the energy?"

"It's there," Beendohj said, "it's just in a mist too thin for you to see."

"Next to The Ball?"

"No. In the whole room."

I looked at the door. "We're going to have to stand in the room to fix this."

"It won't hurt you. Just like the Mesh, only thinner."

"And we get to stand in it!?" I asked. Beendohj nodded. That sounded good to me. Light duty and a free Sparkle besides.

"Why do you think they sent Squats?" Beendohj asked. "We're used to it. An Upper would be staggering giddy in a minute. We have a high tolerance."

I didn't like the sound of that. "And it's not dangerous?"

"Would they have sent us if it was?" Beendohj always had a gift for sarcasm.

I might have argued the point but somebody shouted, "Stop Lingering!" It was Security, of course. They watched everybody to make sure you were working the whole time. The voice came from all around us. They did it that way on purpose so you felt like they were everywhere. Beendohj had told me that. He loved subtlety.

There wasn't any arguing with Security. They could keep you out of the Mesh if they wanted, so we went right to work on the door. We had to stand inside the room most of the time and the door took us about ten minutes to fix, but if we went back to Minor Repairs, they'd just find something else for us to do, probably heavy lifting, so we took turns pushing at it and looking busy so Security wouldn't pull us up for Lingering.

But you couldn't keep that up forever without arousing suspicion, so Beendohj got the idea of cross-wiring the door and freezing it shut for a while. He didn't say that was what he was going to do, he just showed me the two energy conduits and smiled.

I looked at the Security camera. He knew they'd find out we did it on purpose. "Squats are stupid," he said.

And I realized he was right. Some Mid would come down and figure out what we'd done after a while, but even if he suspected we'd done it on purpose, he'd have to pull us up in front of a committee of Uppers and all we had to do was shrug and act Sparkled and they'd let us off with a Stern Warning to Think and shake their heads because they would be certain that thinking was the one thing we couldn't do.

The worst that could happen was that they figured out what we did and sent us back to Tote and Carry for the rest of our lives. So I smiled, and Beendohj crossed the conduits, and the door flew shut and sealed us in the room. We pushed and hauled at it for the benefit of Security but after a while, we walked over to where the camera could see us better through the walls and shrugged. The Voice From Everywhere said, "Open the door!"

Beendohj said, "We can't. It's stuck. Get us out of here. And hurry up!"

I knew exactly what he was doing so I said, "Right! And be quick or we'll report you." They were guaranteed to leave us there for hours after that. If they thought we wanted to stay in there, they'd have had a team of Uppers working to free us in two minutes, but since we wanted out and since mere Squats like us were giving them orders, they'd do the opposite. Security was usually Squats too, at least for the violent stuff, but some moved up to Surveillance and they usually forgot where they came from.

Beendohj and I sat down with our backs against the wall and waited. I wasn't Sparkling by a long shot, but I was beginning to

Shine a little and The Ball fascinated me. I sat and looked at it and the longer I looked, the more amazing it seemed. Beendohj looked at it too, but he didn't see it the same way I did. To me it was a marvel, to him it was a mechanism. "That's what keeps us here," he said.

I said, "What? The door?"

He shook his head. "The Ball, idiot. The Ball."

He got up and walked toward it. I got up after him. I wasn't so sure it was a good idea to get so close to it, but the closer I got, the better I felt. By the time we were almost close enough to touch it, I felt like I'd had my head in the Mesh for hours.

"This is what keeps us in our place," Beendohj said again.

He was always on about how Stile City worked and why we were Squats and the Uppers were the Uppers. I guess for somebody as smart as he was, it was a torment to know he'd never rise up the Shaft and get a chance to use it. I knew he was feeling bad about that, and I said what I always say: "It ain't gonna change in our lifetime."

Beendohj looked like he was going to say something, but instead he went over to where Security could see us better. "Get us out of here, you lazy Squats!" he shouted at the camera. "Can you hear me?!" He stepped up and tapped on the glass. "I'm talking to you!"

If they were listening when he started, they certainly weren't listening when he finished. Somewhere a couple Squats were sitting there laughing at his voiceless face. He shouted a couple more times for good measure and came back.

"It could change," he said. "It could all change in a flash. We could turn Stile City upside down."

"Upside down," I said. I knew it meant something to him, but it was gibberish to me.

"In a tall place where the Risers don't work," he said," where's the best place to live?"

That was easy enough. "On the ground floor."

"Right. And what does The Ball do?"

"It keeps the energy in Dynamic Equilibrium."

"And when the energy starts to go up?"

"I don't know," I said. "Uses it up. Runs the Risers up and down faster, cranks the air-conditioning higher, turns things on all over the Peristyle."

"And where does the energy come from?" he said. I could tell he was leading me somewhere, but I couldn't tell where.

"It's just there," I said. "In the System, just like they put it in in the beginning."

I'd seen the holos of how it got started, people in old style clothes checking readouts in a big tube that ran in a circle around Stile City fifty miles across. They spun some little pieces of matter around and around in there and when the pieces got going fast enough, they slammed them together and a flash shot out into the plasma that runs Stile City and lit it up for good.

"The Ball balances the energy in the System," he said. "*In* the System."

"Of course." I had no idea what his point was.

"And if somebody gave The Ball a shove?" he said.

It was a scary thought with him so close to The Ball. If I wasn't Sparkling so much, I'd have started rerouting the door myself.

"Are you crazy?!" I said.

All of a sudden, I could see where he was going with it. There was The Ball, whose little wavers leveraged huge changes all over the System, and all of a sudden its own energy shoots up. Nobody but Beendohj would have thought of adding energy from *outside* the System so they couldn't have a defense against it. "The Ball would think it was the System shooting out of control," I said.

"So what's the only thing The Ball could do?"

"Shut everything down."

It wasn't just some temporary shut down he was talking about. The big tube that put all the energy into the plasma was long gone, disassembled and moved to some other city and probably ten more cities after that. It would take them years to build it all back up again.

"They'll kill us," I said.

"Not us," Beendohj smiled. "Some Upper should have known what would happen if dumb Squats got locked up in this much Sparkle for this long. Besides, Security should've got us out of here quicker."

"Dumb squats do dumb things," I said.

"Especially when they're Sparkling."

I looked at The Ball wobbling and wobbling and wobbling, and I looked at Beendohj. The Ball was everything that kept Stile City running, everything that kept us Squats, and all I had to do to stop it forever was to give it enough momentum to overload the System.

That was what worried me.

"Yeah," I said, "but what if The Ball thinks it's out of control and starts running the energy up instead of down and everything blows up?"

Beendohj laughed like he was glad I was starting to think for myself. "You're only young once," he said. It made me smile.

"Yeah," I said, "and it don't last long."

Then we took a step and kicked Stile City into history.

The Teenage Years of Ed Nimbus
(a moral tale)

Neil Weston

Ed Nimbus had his life
organized early
by medically trained parents threaded through
with fear.

Get him to youth, thrust him to the first colony
Earth creates,
and pray he keeps his head
low.

That was the plan.

The teenage years were going to
be harsh.
No one enjoys those years,
especially Ed Nimbus.

Rebellion, recriminations of
poor parenting
were no different for the
Nimbus family.

THE TEENAGE YEARS OF ED NIMBUS

Ed rarely came home early.
The day he disappeared
was no different, only
he never came home.
The police went searching,
but Ed remained lost
until the podcast streamed through the
Nimbus computer.

Ed Nimbus was taken by the
lurking scientists,
his body of
particular interest.

They were always watching
the Nimbus boy.
No one trusted giving Mr. & Mrs. N.
sentience.

The youth's prosthetic face, limbs,
body (grown from nanotech)
were worth more,
in segments.

As the Gamma Knife did its
dirty work
his parents' screams were heard through
the galaxies.

Ed Nimbus made one final request before fitted as a
head transplant,
"Tell my android parents ... this teenage 'droid is sorry
for arguing."

If there is a moral to this tale—
if you androids build an android boy
don't build him up to be
human.

String Theory

Danika Dinsmore

Alexandra Tate lies in bed testing the ambiance of her room. Posters of bands she has never heard of, like Thunkerpunk and Remode Control, are plastered over every spare inch of wall, making the room dark and cavernous. Piles of clothes take up most of the horizontal space. She reaches up for the metal device strapped to the top of her head. It's still warm. She rips off the white tape that keeps the device's wires stuck to her temples, removes the metal contraption from her head, and sets it on top of some music magazines on the nightstand.

She slips from the bed, fully clothed in ripped black jeans, studded belt, and shredded T, and goes to a mirror on the wall. Hollow eyes look back through a pale face and smeared mascara. Two piercings poke through her left eyebrow, one ring sticks through her bottom lip, five total in her ears, and there's a broken green heart tattoo on her neck below her right ear.

"Oh my God, I'm a goth," she says to her reflection, then sucks in her cheeks dramatically. "Or a vampire."

She pokes around the table for a moist toilette or sponge and knocks over a half-empty beer bottle next to the overflowing makeup kit. A pile of clothes on the floor catches the bottle and the liquid spills out onto a plaid miniskirt. She grunts and dismisses the mess with a wave of her hand, searching the dresser until she finds some tissues.

After she yanks a few from the box, she reaches down to wet them in the spilled beer. She rubs at the old mascara, but it doesn't help much. She finally gives up, runs her fingers through a tangle of blue-black hair and smells her armpits. Body odor and cigarette smoke. Gag. She finds an inoffensive hoodie from a pile of clothes on the bed and exchanges it for her smelly T-shirt.

She grabs a few more tissues and emerges from her room, peering into the hallway. Two closed doors on the left, front door and closet to the right, kitchen straight ahead. Gingerly, she steps into the kitchen and flicks on the light.

To-go containers, bowls caked with dried cereal, empty juice and milk cartons litter the counter. She looks around for a calendar, but the fading yellow walls are bare. The refrigerator boasts a stained poster that claims ICE CREAM IS A FOOD GROUP! below a sundae-shaped food pyramid with a cherry on top.

"Mom?" calls Alexandra as she steps through the kitchen into the dining nook, where a table littered with mail and magazines looks as if it hasn't been eaten at in weeks.

She turns right into the living room. Collapsed in a recliner is her mother, Theresa Tate, looking much older than her forty-two years. Gray hairs stick to her face, which is swollen and puffy from crying.

Alexandra enters the room and kneels down in front of her mom, whom she fears, for a moment, is catatonic.

"Mom?" she waves her hand in front of Theresa's eyes. "Are you all right?"

Theresa moves her gaze to Alexandra's and stares for a few seconds before reaching out and slapping Alexandra across the face. Her daughter falls back and clutches her cheek.

"How dare you!" Theresa hisses and leaps from the chair. "How dare you!" she calls as she crosses the living room into the kitchen. Her heels clip-clop across the linoleum and are muffled by the carpet as she enters the hall.

Alexandra lifts herself to the couch. All righty, then.

A door slams and her mother's clip-clop moves back through the kitchen.

"I'm sorry?" Alexandra offers.

Theresa appears with her purse and keys. "Sorry? That boy may never come out of a coma. Do you understand? I could go to jail for this."

Her mother approaches the couch again and Alexandra cowers.

Instead of slapping her daughter, however, Theresa yanks her coat out from behind her.

"I'm sorry," Alexandra tries again. It's the only thing she can think of saying, and she has found, through trial and error, it's always the best thing to say when she has no idea what the hell is going on.

"For which part? The part where you and your friends decide to throw a party in my lab? The part where you fry your boyfriend's brain? Or the part where my life's work is confiscated by the feds?"

Ah. Things are a little clearer now. Party in lab, accident, friend injured, mom's career demolished. God, what kind of degenerate was she in this timeline? She should just go back to bed. Or maybe raid her room for money and treat herself to a movie. She has yet to visit a timeline without movies.

"What can I do?" she asks instead.

Theresa throws a newspaper at Alexandra's chest and the sections flutter apart around her. "You can look in the classifieds for a job. I doubt I'll be able to support you from prison."

With one final glare, Theresa tears from the room. "Don't talk to any reporters!" she shouts back as she leaves the apartment. "Don't talk to anyone!"

The front door slams.

Alexandra picks up the sections of newspaper and arranges them in order. She has become a fiend for order, for anything she can control. As she flips the front page over, a headline catches her eye: POLICE RAID LAB AFTER LOCAL BOY LEFT IN COMA. Beneath that in smaller type: *Scientist accused of manufacturing mind-altering weapon.*

The date at the top of the page reads Friday, March 3, 2015. With a sigh, she drops the paper back on the couch. She's lost count of how many times she's woken up on Friday, March 3, 2015.

The wrong Friday, March 3, 2015.

Against the wall is a messy roll top desk. She motivates herself enough to get up and go to it, shuffling through the unopened bills, random lists, and strange sketches until she finds a black pen and some sticky notes. She writes GET YOUR SHIT TOGETHER on one of the sticky notes, goes back to "her" room, and smashes it into the mirror.

Don't talk to anyone. Fine. She doesn't feel like going to school anyway, which she rarely does anymore. Too many instances of going to the wrong neighborhood, attending the wrong classes, and, the worst, hanging out with the wrong friends. She now reserves those experiments for days when she's properly desperate and lonely.

She's pretty sure meeting this Alexandra's friends would not cheer her up. There are photographs of them stuck into the mirror frame. Most are of two black-and-metal clad vixens and a dark-skinned boy with a shaved head and round disks in his earlobes. It takes her a while to realize she is one of the vixens in the photographs.

She drops the photos into the garbage, flicks open the dusty window blinds, and starts picking clothes up off the floor. What a mess.

There's no clothes hamper in sight, so she stands in the middle of the room not knowing what to do. Finally, she falls back onto the bed and the clothes slip from her arms. As she stares up at the popcorn ceiling at some kind of brown stain stretching out from the corner, she starts to cry.

It happens. The weight of it gets to her sometimes. The compiled pain and disappointment every version of her has caused in the space-time continuum. Logically, she knows she's not responsible for any of it, only for the crap in her own timeline, which she would happily face.

She rolls onto her stomach and stares into the trash at the boy in the photograph. Even if she manages to find her way back to her own timeline, this boy, in this life, could stay in a coma. This mom, in this life, could spend the rest of her life in prison. How can she forget about them? How are their lives less real?

The light slowly shifts as the sun crosses into afternoon. Eventually, as always, she pulls herself together. She eats a cold piece of pizza and cleans the kitchen. Afterward, she cleans the bathroom. She even mops the floor. She has no idea if anything she does during her one day in any timeline lasts or has an effect on its future. But if in this timeline her mother comes home to a clean house and a semi-rehabilitated daughter, it's the least she can do. She likes to think that in some small way she's managed to make each mother's life easier.

It keeps her sane.

Exhausted from the emotional and physical day, she watches television, eating stale potato chips, until almost midnight. Theresa doesn't come home.

Before bed, even though she's not religious, she says a small prayer that the boy will come out of his coma, her mother will stay out of jail, and Alexandra will straighten up and get a job.

She slips into bed and places the metal device over her head, attaching the white patches to her temples. The sticky note falls from the mirror. She hesitates before getting back up and reattaching it, reinforcing it with black nail polish.

*

Alexandra wakes up and looks around her room. Posters of cheerleaders with life-affirming sayings call from sky-blue walls. Stuffed animals huddle on a white wicker loveseat. The room is large, spotless, and has its own bathroom.

"What new kind of hell is this?"

She leaps out of bed and rushes over the fluffy white carpet to the bathroom. The reflection in her mirror is clean-faced, with shorter highlighted hair and blue baby-doll pajamas. There's also a metal device strapped to her head and four white patches across her face.

"Oops." She pulls the tape off, unstraps the contraption, and places it on the counter.

Back in the bedroom she finds a *Far Side* desk calendar nestled between some schoolbooks and a silver jewelry box.

The current page reads Friday, March 3, 2015 and has a cartoon with two ducks talking. Underneath the date, I LOVE JIMMY – 8 PM is scrawled in red with a little heart dotting the "i" in "Jimmy." She rips off the page.

"So tonight's the night, huh? You little trollop."

She opens the silver jewelry box and examines the collection of gold chains, pendants, and crosses. Inside a little cardboard box, she finds a tiny bag of white powder.

"Tsk, tsk," she clicks her tongue. "Alexandra!"

She takes the little baggie into the bathroom and flushes it down the toilet.

In the kitchen, Theresa, hair pinned up and dressed in a smart gray business suit, drinks coffee as she waits next to a toaster. Alexandra enters with the calendar page in her hand.

Before Alexandra can even test the air with a *good-morning*, Theresa gulps her coffee and cries, "Lexie! You're not even dressed!

You'll be late for school."

The Audubon clock on the sunny kitchen wall reads a house wren past a robin: 7:30.

"What time does it start?" Alexandra wonders if in this timeline she's some dork taking an early "zero" period so she can fit seven classes in per day. That might account for the snorting habit.

She's past judging these things. People are complicated, she's come to realize, and if this Alexandra is a good student, then she doesn't want to mess with her GPA by failing a calculus test.

"Lexie …" The toast pops up and Theresa nabs it, placing it on a plate and going to town with the butter. "You know I can't give you a ride today. You have to take the bus."

"Bus. Right."

"Hello? Earth to Lexie!" Theresa waves the butter knife in front of Alexandra's face. "Remember? I'm flying to the con-ven-tion to accept an award for my in-ven-tion. Hey that rhymes … I should have been a poet rather than a scientist." She laughs at her little joke and throws the knife in the sink.

"The invention was a success?"

"Are you all right?" With a piece of toast in her mouth, Theresa feels Alexandra's forehead. "You don't feel feverish." She glances at the clock and swigs the rest of her coffee to wash the toast down. "Your father's picking you up from school today. In case you forgot that, too."

"My father?" Alexandra's heart starts to pound.

She's had few glimpses of any father in the timelines. When he does make an appearance, it's usually for a few minutes before he rushes off to work and a few minutes after he gets home, before he zones out on TV or hops online in his home office. She's managed a few kisses on her forehead.

Half those times he's been shorthaired and short-tempered, the other half a bit scraggly and preoccupied, but strangely, he's always smelled the same. Like a dad.

"Well, I can't do it. I'll be forty-thousand feet over the ocean by then."

In a daze, Alexandra looks down at the calendar page in her hand. "Mom, who's Jimmy?"

"Is this a philosophical question? Because I don't have time for—"

"I mean why do I love him?"

"How should I know ... because he's captain of the football team?" Theresa rinses out her coffee mug in the sink and places it in the dishwasher.

"You're kidding, right?"

"Are you purposefully trying to make me miss my flight?"

"I think I should just go back to bed."

"Well, then call your father at work, otherwise he'll sit out in front of the school waiting for you."

Waiting for me, Alexandra thinks. I have a father who waits for me.

*

The metal device, an invention of some certified genius at her "real" mother's lab, the mother she's been trying to get back to for hundreds of March 3rds, still sits in the bathroom. She has no idea what it's called or how it works, only that she wishes she'd never placed it on her head in the first place. Never stolen it or taken the dare from her best friend to try it out.

Her best friend. Right. Taylor has yet to even notice her in any alternate timeline in which she's appeared. How odd, right? Shouldn't that say something about soul mates or cosmic connections?

All she knows is that she went to sleep with it on and woke up the same day in a life she didn't recognize. She's been trying to get back ever since.

She grabs the device and goes to her bedroom window, parting the curtains and tapping the metal headgear against the glass. The view is from the second story of a house in an upper-class neighborhood of wide, trim lawns, three car garages and clean streets. It's the nicest neighborhood she's ever transported to, if "transported" is the right word.

It's different every time, but so many things are familiar enough to confuse her. The familiar things always feel out of context, but, really, she's the only thing out of context. The Alexandra of each timeline doesn't think her life is wrong. She might think it sucks, but it's not "wrong." Those Alexandras and Alexas and Lexies and Xans don't know there's any different kind of life they could have, or any different type of person they could be.

But she's seen the best and the worst of her selves. The painful worst of her selves. And she's tired of trying to make up for it all, and she's tired of being alone.

For the first time in all her attempts to get back to her proper place, she is tempted to stay. To give up and just take the best life she can find.

All she has to do, she believes, is go to sleep without the device on. And when she wakes up … the device would be gone, right? At least, in every scenario in her head, that's how it plays out. The invention would disappear and she'd be stuck in that timeline. She'd be stuck, but she would move on. Time would move on.

She looks down at the calendar page, still clutched in her hand.

She could deal with this life, right?

Quit the stupid cheer team, dump the football boyfriend, kick the drug habit, and spend more time with her father. Just having a father would make it all worth it.

Wouldn't it?

Or would she spend the rest of her life missing her "real" mom? Would she always feel like this mom was an imposter?

Would she always feel like *she* was?

Before she can talk herself out of it, she runs to her parents' bathroom and rifles through the medicine cabinet until she finds a box of Dramamine. Not sleeping pills, but she knows they'll make her drowsy, especially if she doubles the dose.

She triples it to make sure.

Then, she goes back to her bedroom, rips the wires out of the device, and throws them across the room. She lies down on the bed, places the metal cap on the nightstand and stares at it, waiting for the medication to kick in.

It will all be over soon. No going back. No staying the same.

"Good-bye, Mom," she whispers to the device as tears stream down her cheeks onto the clean bedsheets. She wonders if some kind of imposter will take her place in her real timeline. Would it be the Princess Lexie version of herself? And if so, would Princess freak and end up in a psych ward?

Or maybe Alexandra will simply blip out of that existence.

She pictures her mother in their apartment, alone and heart-broken, never knowing what happened to her daughter. It pains Alexandra even more than the Princess Lexie psych ward scenario.

"No!" she cries, sitting up. But the medication has kicked in and her head spins.

Getting her bearings, she grabs the metal cap and stands up. Too fast. The room swirls around her and she collapses to the ground. She crawls across the plush carpet, searching for the wires. She finds three of them, but there are four. Two red, two green. It's a white carpet; why can't she find it?

The missing wire is caught in a blanket that has slipped to the floor. She nabs it and leans against the bed, frantically trying to replace the wires.

"I'm coming, mom. I'm coming," she sobs, but she can't figure out how to reattach the wires. Will they work if she twists them together?

Her eyelids are heavy, her brain mush. *I need a soldering iron*, she thinks, and then wonders from what recess of her mind that came. Recess, she thinks. Play. Children. She's an only child. Always an only child. How come none of the versions of her have siblings?

Her head is too heavy; she has to put it down. She drops to the floor and pulls the blanket around her. *I'm an only child*, she thinks. *Only a child.*

*

Alexandra pulls herself awake, disoriented. She slowly gathers herself up from the floor and rests on her bed. She's wearing men's pajama bottoms and a Yosemite T-shirt. She scans the room in a daze. Some textbooks lie on the floor, an overflowing hamper in the corner, a desk with an antique thrift store lamp and a laptop, purple walls, a few Decemberists and Death Cab for Cutie posters.

It's all vaguely familiar. Like a dream.

She crawls across the bed to the window, parts the curtains, and is met with the brick wall of the building next door.

Thoughts come like glue. Why does this seem right and wrong at the same time? She reaches up for the device and it's not there. It takes a few seconds to process this.

She dives to the floor and searches the blankets, remembering I love Jimmy and her father, waiting, and the sickly perfect room and the Dramamine and pulling the wires … it's gone, the device is gone.

Standing up is too hard, so she continues to crawl around the room for clues. A *Far Side* desk calendar has fallen into the wastepaper basket. She pulls it out and stares at the date: Friday, March 3, 2015.

A cartoon of two ducks talking. She drops it back into the trash and manages to stand up. *Don't panic*, she tells herself, and then laughs. She's too disoriented to panic. If there were a fire it would hypnotize her and she'd burn.

She weaves her way down the hallway to the living room.

Her mother, Theresa, is passed out on the couch, a bottle of vodka dangles from her fingers. The early news is muted on TV.

Alexandra sits down on the edge of the couch and brushes the hair from her mother's face. "Mom?"

Theresa stirs. "Alex ..." she murmurs.

"I'm here, Mom," she kisses her mom's forehead. "I'm here."

Theresa pulls herself up a little to make more room for Alexandra. The bottle in her hand takes a moment to register. She attempts to hide it, realizes it's futile, and places it on the table.

"Oh, God, Alex. I'm so sorry."

"It's okay, Mom."

"I'm such a mess."

"No, you're not."

"Yes. Yes, I am."

They both stare at the TV for a moment. It plays a commercial for Dramamine.

"Mom, why aren't you at work?"

"I got fired, sweetie," Theresa runs her hand through Alexandra's hair.

"You got fired?" Alexandra asks, then more tentatively, "From the university?"

"Wouldn't you have fired me? I misplace my keys and Dr. Schefield's prototype disappears? His life's work?"

"Oh, Mom!" Alexandra propels herself into her mother and hugs her ferociously, laughing and crying.

"Aw, honey. I know. I know." Her mother cries, too, "I'm a total screwup and I lost my job and we're broke and ..."

Alexandra pulls back and smiles through her tears. "Mom, it's all right. Everything is going to be all right."

"I hope so," says Theresa, staring at the bottle of vodka.

Wiping her face, Alexandra sighs and laughs. She hugs her mom one more time.

"I think I'll go to school today!"

"You can't, sweetie," Theresa says.

"I can't?" A cold spikes Alexandra's heart. "What do you mean, I can't?"

"It's Saturday."

"Saturday," she murmurs, and then wraps her arms around her mom again and cries and laughs some more. "Oh, Mom! It's Saturday!"

Hollywood Forever

Llinos Cathryn Thomas

I never expected to make it this far. I'm shaking as the doorman scans my palm to read my ID chip. I'm trying not to sweat too much inside my hired red carpet dress. I know it shouldn't matter, but it does. I wish I'd gone for one with a little more material, but covering up doesn't get you noticed here.

Tickets to the Global Movie Awards change hands for thousands of dollars, hundreds of thousands, more. People will pay a lot of money to attend the only official movie awards left on the planet. Since I was a little girl, I was always desperate to go. I knew I'd find a way, someday, and now I have.

I can't remember ever wanting to do anything but act. I remember seeing Amber Westen in *The Unicorn Hunter*, when I was just a little girl, and knowing with utter certainty that was what I wanted for myself.

Amber Westen is probably here tonight. She's up for best actress again. I wonder what I would say to her now, if I saw her.

Maybe I'd tell her about how I just finished high school last year, and I've been trying really hard ever since to make it as an actor. How my dad told me over and over that I didn't have a chance—it's not that he doesn't think I'm talented, he's just pragmatic about how the industry works. I didn't want to believe him. I wanted to think that talent and a bit of luck would set me on my path to Hollywood stardom.

Maybe I'd tell her how that turned out.

The foyer is crowded with people in gorgeous outfits. My dress that seemed dazzling when I tried it on earlier looks childish and old-fashioned now. I was so pleased with how I'd managed to curl my hair, but I can see out of the corners of my eyes that the curls are already dropping out. No personal hairstylist for me. Still, I'm here, and that's what counts. I follow the crowd towards the auditorium, trying to walk like I belong.

I spot Josh Riley, and bite my lip. He's even more handsome in real life. His muscular frame, his gleaming smile, his taut, youthful skin. A year ago I had holo-posters of him in my bedroom. I had the one all the girls had, the one where he leans over and kisses you on the cheek as you come into the room. He always missed my cheek because I'm taller than a lot of girls, but he generally got my shoulder and I'd feel the holo buzz slightly and pretend I was tingling where he'd kissed me.

I got rid of that, after my last audition. I got rid of all my holos and my regular posters. I couldn't look at them any more. I always said I'd do anything to be a star, but that's just what people say. Sometimes when it comes to it, when someone tells you—do this, in this room, right now, with me—you just can't do it.

I was angry with myself afterward for not doing it, but now I'm glad I didn't. I made it to the awards anyway, didn't I? And I'm here for myself, not on some director's arm, acting grateful for his attention.

There's Amber Westen—as I'm moving toward my seat I see her and my heart lurches and for a minute I'm fourteen again and I'm watching every movie she ever made and taking notes and wishing and wishing so hard that I could be like her, because if I could just be like her, I know I could make it in Hollywood and be a big star.

That was three years ago. I know better now. Nobody makes it in Hollywood anymore. And nobody makes it any other way, either. Independent movies were declared illegal before I was born. Nobody makes a movie these days without the official seal of the Global Movie Approval Board.

Not officially, anyway.

I look at Amber Westen again. She was my inspiration, the embodiment of my dream. It's really hard to feel angry with her even though I know I should. I watch her from a distance, the elegance of her movements, the shy smile as she walks past the rows of people who greet her.

I'm not supposed to talk to anybody, in case I tip someone off that I'm not meant to be here. And besides, why would a movie star care about someone like me, someone who couldn't even get a single bit part, even after dozens and dozens of auditions? So I don't know why I do what I do, but when I see her head to the restroom I leave the seat I've barely reached and follow her. I'm not supposed to but it can't hurt, right? Just to get a closer look before ... well, before I do what I'm here to do.

The restrooms are more or less empty when I arrive. There's nobody at the long bank of lit mirrors—probably too busy being photographed outside; it's still kind of early. There's only one stall in use. That must be Amber Westen. I busy myself looking in the mirror, hoping to act vaguely natural when she emerges.

The face I see isn't all that different from hers, really. Large, round eyes, full lips, defined cheekbones. I know I'm pretty, I know I look like a movie star—or at least it wouldn't take much, just a professional to do my hair and makeup—but that isn't enough to make it anymore. Not when someone like Amber Westen—who is already so famous that kids on the other side of the world who don't own a holo or a TV know her name—started with everything I have, plus a guarantee that she'll stay that way.

Over the last year I cried and cried, wishing I'd been born twenty or thirty years earlier. If I had, I might have been starting my career just as the Rejuvelix craze began. It could have been me instead of her. I could be the one with armfuls of awards—she's on her seventh Best Actress Globy now, if she wins tonight—and not looking a day older than when I started.

If I'd had the chances she had, I'd never have got into Indie movies. I can't decide if that's good or bad—I believe in what I'm doing now, and I love my Indie friends, but I can't figure out if I'd have been happier just going along, making it in Hollywood and never having to learn how messed up everything is.

I realize I'm glaring at my reflection. I try to get my face to act normal, and then I hear something.

Someone's crying. But there's nobody in here except me and Amber Westen.

I fight with myself over what to do. David says it's their own fault. He says they deserve what's coming to them. He says anyone who claims to love acting but won't make room for anyone new to get their start doesn't really love anything but themselves. And it's not as though it will matter, when I'm done, whether she was crying or not before it all happened.

David scares me a little.

I'm trying to harden myself like he says we need to, but I hate it when people cry, so I knock on the door and ask if she's okay.

"Yes, thank you, I'm fine," she whispers, but she can hardly get the words out, she's so upset.

"Um … is there anything I can do? Someone I can call for you?" I ask.

"No," she gulps. "Nobody can help me."

Well … damn. This wasn't part of the plan at all but she's *Amber Westen*, and she's crying right there a plywood door away from me, and she sounds really miserable, like it's something awful, not just big night nerves or whatever. And to be honest I'm kind of curious to know what she has to be sad about.

"Hey, come on," I say. "It'll be okay. It can't be that bad, can it?"

I decide to think of it as intelligence gathering. Hopefully David won't have a problem with that.

"It's worse, I promise you," she sniffs.

"Want to talk about it?" I ask.

I'm uneasy about the timing of the mission, suddenly, but if Amber Westen is in here, then I'm probably still good.

After a few moments I hear the bolt slide back and Amber Westen emerges. She even cries like a movie star. Her face just looks porcelain-pink and adorable, with a tiny glistening tear wobbling under each eye. I stare.

"You're really young, aren't you?" she asks. "I mean, you're not Rejuvelixed. You actually are a teenager."

I nod, wondering where she's going with this.

"Don't let them do it to you, kid," she says, sitting up on the long counter and taking the wad of tissue I hand her to delicately dab at her eyes. "Do you know how long I've been a teenager? Twenty-three years. It gets old, excuse the pun."

I'm back to staring.

"Really?" I ask, stupidly.

She nods, takes a deep breath. "Know how many Globies I've won?" she asks.

"Six for Best Actress, three Best Supporting Actress, one for soundtrack," I answer promptly. I must've watched the documentary about her a hundred times.

"Yeah," she agrees. "And every single one was for playing the same character."

I frown at her. "No, it wasn't," I say. "In *The Unicorn Hunter* you played the daughter of a ..."

"I'm talking metaphorically, kid," she says.

It sounds funny when she calls me that—she looks as though we could have graduated high school together.

"What I mean," she continues, "is that I've made a career out of playing the ingenue. I'm sweet. I'm wholesome. I'm sexy in a nonthreatening, accessible way. You know what I wanted to play?"

I shake my head.

"Lady Macbeth," she says. "Or Blanche Dubois, or Ranevskaya. One of those great roles, you know? One of those wonderful, rich roles that one day you dream of getting to. I never meant for all this. I never meant to get stuck playing the same parts over and over."

"So why did you?" I ask. "Why couldn't you just cut down on the Rejuvelix and go for some older roles? People in the industry like you, right?"

"Oh, they like me," she said. "They like me just like this, perky and nineteen." She rolls her eyes at me. "Don't you think I tried? Don't you think I'd have done it, if it were that simple? Of course I would. But I can't. The studio loaned me money to get my first shot of Rejuvelix, but it was okay, because I was making a movie for them, and it was going to make millions. So when they hired me for the next one and it was a condition of my contract that I not age during the filming and promotion, I thought, well, that's okay, I'm in no hurry. Pretty soon I was trapped."

"Trapped?" I ask.

"I got into a situation where I had to Rejuvelix to get the next job, and I had to pay for it with the money I was going to get—and I know you think movie stars get paid a lot but it also costs a lot, a hell of a lot, to keep looking this young. So I'm trapped. Every shot I get means I can earn the money to pay most of it back, but I can't pay for it without the work, and I can't get the work without the Rejuvelix. I'm stuck looking like a teenager forever. There's no other way I know to make money, and I'm so deep in debt most of the time, I'd lose everything if I stopped."

I shake my head. "I had no idea," I say softly.

"That's how they like it," she says, and there's a bitter edge to it that doesn't sound like any teenager I've ever met. "We're most of us trapped—me and Josh Riley and Hunter Murray and all the rest. We know everyone hates us. We even know this whole night is a mockery. But we can't get out."

I stare at her. For a minute I don't know what to think, what to say—I think back to the movies I've seen her in, try to figure out if there was misery behind her eyes, if there was fear.

If there wasn't then, there is now.

"I don't know how I can go through another night like this," she says.

I decide.

"You're not going to," I say. "You're coming with me."

Now it's she who stares, her perfect forehead puckering in confusion.

I was supposed to activate the device at the height of the ceremony, just as they were giving the award for Best Movie. There would have been just about a minute for me to get out safely. And then it was supposed to go off, killing dozens and maiming more.

I can't even remember now why I thought that was a good idea.

I take Amber Westen by the hand and escape by my pre-arranged route. David and the others are waiting in the van.

"What the hell are you doing?" asks David. "We agreed that the …"

He stops midword, his mouth hanging open, as he spots her. When he speaks his voice is a low hiss.

"Traitor," he says to me. "Traitor. How could you?"

"David," I say, "she's all right. She's not one of them anymore. She's with us now."

"Do you realize what they'll do to us if they find her here?" he demands.

"They won't find her," I say. "Not once the Rejuvelix wears off.

They won't recognize her in a million years."

Amber Westen begins to smile as she realizes what's going on.

"You're Indies," she says. "You're making illegal movies—and I can be in them?"

I nod. "You don't have to play by their rules anymore," I tell her. "How does 'starring Amber Westen as Lady Macbeth' sound?"

"It sounds like the role of a lifetime," she says.

Ghost Walkers

Sandi Cayless

The world is old, so old ...
Base metals turned to rust;
The land is barren, cold,
Its people gone to dust ...

A new star lights a dawn
That still in splendor glows
In colors rich and warm,
In shades of dusky rose.
But cold eyes watch the skies
Where fire's the blossom borne;
As scream of retros dies
A ship disturbs the dawn.

They've come again for more—
Rapacious, callous, cold,
With predatory claws
To rake red ash for gold.

They once brought end of time—
Through light and air they came.
Their weapons shook the sun
And left a world aflame.
As firestorm limned the land
And turned the seas to wrack,
They changed rich earth to sand
And fertile green to black.

They've come again for more—
Rapacious, greedy, cold
With predatory claws
And eyes alight for gold.

Boundless ages pass
And yet they haunt the dust;
Still there is spoil to grasp,
And profit for their lust.
But now—a strange unease,
A shiver, born in fright,
As one looks up to see
A shape at edge of sight.

But yet the world is old …
Its metals turned to rust;
The land still barren, cold,
Its people gone to dust …

The darkness, stilled, is dim;
One turns back, unafraid:
The ghost at shadow's rim
Was trick of light or shade.
The world is old, so old …
Base metals naught but rust;
The land is barren, cold,
Its people less than dust.

SANDI CAYLESS

Yet out of loss grew hate:
Ice-crystalled, deathless, bright;
Formless first, to wait
Beyond both air and light.
Shaped of that hatred, we
Who haunt the edge of sight,
We know our time is near …
Our cold eyes wait the night.

Our world is old, so old, so old …
Base metals less than rust;
Our land is barren, barren, cold—
But now we walk the dust …

The Cleansing

Mark Smith-Briggs

Mum cried when they drew Granddad's name. So did my sisters. I didn't. I knew one of us had to stay strong. I just took Granddad's hand and squeezed it a little. He didn't say anything. And he didn't weep like the others. He just stared blankly at the TV while the presenter continued to roll off a long list of names. I guess he was in shock. I figured it was a normal reaction for someone that had just been told they were going to die.

They drew a hundred and fifty thousand names that night from Australia, not to mention the names drawn from all of the other countries; names that rolled across the screen in simple white type like credits to a movie. But these weren't the names of characters from any production. They were husbands and wives, brothers and sisters, parents and grandparents. Real people who in thirty days would die for the good of the nation and the world. They drew out a hundred and fifty thousand names but for the four of us sitting in our living room only one really mattered. Adam Charles Whitaker.

Despite the hot summer rain outside, a chill washed over me.

My mum and sisters crowded around Granddad, hugging him and sobbing onto his chest. He let them hold him, but he didn't hug back. He just watched the screen. Then the phone rang and Mum had to let go of him to answer it. It was her sister. She'd read the name too. That only made Mum cry even more. I told my sisters to go and comfort her. I could have done it myself, but I didn't want to let go of Granddad's hand.

He waited until the last names had scrolled across the screen and then turned off the TV.

"I think I'm going to go to bed," was all he said.

He stood up and left the room. Mum put down the phone.

"Maybe you guys should turn in, too," she said.

The girls wanted to sleep in the same bed. I told them it was okay. I tucked them in and made sure they had their favorite teddy bears.

"It's not fair that Granddad has to die," Tanya, my youngest sister said.

"I know," I told her. It was all I could think to say.

I turned off their light and went up to my room. I brushed my teeth, turned down the bed, changed into my pajamas and punched a hole in the wall.

*

Granddad was the first one up in the morning. I was the second. He put down the paper and offered to make me bacon and eggs when I walked into the kitchen. The paper had a special lift out with all the names that had been on the TV the night before. They were listed under the headline OUR HEROES. I picked it up and searched for his name. It was on the back page.

"They can't do this," I told him.

Granddad cracked an egg on the side of the frying pan and dumped the gooey center onto the pan.

"They have to," he said.

"But what if they're wrong?"

Granddad added a couple of rashes of bacon to the pan.

"You know I've never been called a hero before," he said. "It feels kind of nice."

"You can't be okay about this?" I said.

He shrugged and dumped the eggs and bacon onto a plate. "Here. Get it while it's hot."

Mum didn't come out of her room all day. Not even when the two government officials came to see Granddad. They spoke to him in soft, sympathetic tones. I didn't catch exactly what they said but they used the words "support" and "hero" a lot. When they left they gave him a little pack with pamphlets and phone numbers for special councilor lines and told him to call the numbers anytime. Granddad said he wouldn't need to and gave them back. One of the men left them on the dresser on the way out. They also gave him a gold-colored envelope.

Granddad made me open it in the kitchen. It was an invite to an honorary dinner at a fancy restaurant in the city. The letter said they were holding them across the country for all those chosen in the draw. It said the dinner would be linked via satellite to the others around the world. It said that Granddad should feel proud to serve his country for his fellow man. The envelope contained a gold pin for him to wear on the evening in celebration. It also said the dinner was mandatory.

"They better serve plenty of top-shelf booze," was all Granddad said.

*

The dinner was a huge event, held in a giant ballroom decked out with hundreds of balloons and streamers that dangled above dozens of long, lavish tables. A giant plasma screen filled the far wall, beaming images of the other dinners. If it wasn't for the large banner that read: "To our heroes, your sacrifice will save us all" you could have been forgiven for thinking we were attending some giant birthday celebration.

A pair of smartly dressed waiters smiled as we entered, taking our jackets and escorting us to our seats. Dozens of other families were already seated and spoke among themselves in hushed tones. A quartet belted out an upbeat rendition of a jazz standard in the corner in an attempt to lighten the mood, but from the looks on everyone's faces it wasn't working.

We were served platters of seafood, BBQ and roast, washed down with jugs full of soft drink, juice, and milk. The adults guzzled liters of imported wine, spirits, and foreign beer. It was like nobody had been able to make a decision on what to serve, so they just brought it all out. As everyone ate, the mood lightened and for a while things seemed okay again. We had no idea that it was to be the last meal we'd share as a family.

They broke the news to us in an announcement after dessert. The band cut off midsong and a tall, skinny man with bottle glasses and a blue pinstripe suit took the stage. A nervous silence settled back over the room as we waited to hear what he had to say.

"Ladies and gentlemen," he said. "I want to begin by thanking the organizers for this wonderful banquet to honor our heroes and their families."

The man clapped enthusiastically, urging us to join in. A smattering of half-hearted applause echoed from around the room.

"We bring you together tonight to share news about the New Melbourne Cleansing."

They'd called it the Cleansing because of the purifying effect it was meant to have on the environment, but as many newspaper editorials had pointed out, the name hinted at a darker, more horrible truth. The removal of one third of our elderly population was simply "a slaughter" based on biased data, it argued.

In the Government's defense, it wasn't as if they'd rushed wholeheartedly into the idea. The Cleansing was a last ditch effort.

We'd learned all about it in science class, but it never felt real. They'd identified the problem during the twenty-first century, but even decades of cutting back emissions, switching to cleaner fuel supplies and replanting our rainforests had failed to slow the melting of the polar caps. In the past eighty years, the sea had engulfed five percent of our landmass, driving people inland and placing a greater strain on what natural resources were left. The rising temperature would not be stopped. Medical advancements had seen the average age jump to almost a hundred years. There were more people alive than ever before and the planet was suffocating under humanity's weight.

The proposal to "cull" the human population had first been mooted ten years ago, and shot down amid a public cry of outrage. But as the decade passed, and the ocean levels continued to rise, discussion of the "unthinkable" surfaced again. Then a worldwide summit had been called and the fates of twenty-seven million lives had been set. Tonight we found out when.

"The date for the Cleansing has been pushed forward." The man waited for the news to sink in. The Cleansing had been scheduled for the beginning of August. It was already July.

"Changed? To when?" someone finally called out.

The question was echoed by others in the crowd.

The man behind the podium loosened his tie.

"Sunday," he said.

The room erupted into cries of anger and disbelief. Sunday was only six days away.

"As a result," the man continued, "we believe it is in the best interests of the men and woman chosen to be taken to a secure location where they can be properly counseled for the event."

The hall doors swung open and a brigade of armed soldiers entered the room. They pushed their way toward the tables.

"Now, if I can have all our heroes line up against the far wall, your escort is ready," the man said.

The room broke into movement, but no one headed for the wall. Frantic families clung to their loved ones, pushing their way toward the doors. The soldiers blocked their paths, isolating those with gold pins and rounding them up in the back of the room.

Granddad didn't try to run. He just picked up his scotch and swallowed it in one gulp. I leaned over and hugged him in a fierce embrace.

"I won't let them take you," I said.

Strong hands gripped my shoulders, wrenching me back into my seat.

"Sorry, son," a soldier said.

I struggled to break free, but he was far too strong. Granddad gestured for me to be still.

"It's okay," he said, as a second soldier helped him to his feet. "I'll see you soon. I promise."

I reached for my Granddad's hand.

He took it for a moment, before his fingers slipped from mine and he disappeared into the shuffling crowd.

*

I couldn't sleep that night, nor could my mother. I heard her pacing downstairs, back and forth from the fridge like a starved animal, while I stared blankly at the ceiling and counted blemishes in the paint. It had only been a few hours and already the place seemed so empty without Granddad. I thought of him all holed up somewhere, left with nothing to do but count down the days he had left. I couldn't bear to think that he'd never walk through our front door again, or sit in his favorite chair by the TV. He was still out there somewhere, but to me it felt like he was already gone.

*

Things didn't get any easier during the next two days. We heard nothing from the Government except that "our heroes" had been

191

moved to a secure location within the city. Mum spent most of the time in her bedroom crying, a habit that both my sisters were also developing, or on the couch staring at a blank TV screen. I feared that if we didn't hear something soon, she'd quit functioning completely. Then on Wednesday we got a call.

I was upstairs in the shower when it came. I didn't even know the phone had rung until Tanya banged on the bathroom door.

"There's a man on the phone about Granddad," she yelled from the hall.

"Give it to mum," I called back, my hair lathered with shampoo.

"But he asked for you."

It didn't make sense. I was only a kid. Why did someone want to talk to me about Granddad?

"Okay, okay," I said, shutting off the taps and reaching for a towel.

The phone call was from a Government official telling us that Granddad was being held in a facility on the other side of town. He said that one member of the immediate family could visit him today, and that the rest of us could see him later in the week. He said that Granddad had requested me.

Mum was sleeping, so I caught the train across the city on my own. I'd left my oldest sister Carlie in charge, telling her and Tanya to play inside while I was gone and wake Mum if anything happened. I didn't say where I was going.

*

Granddad was being held in a large complex surrounded by stone walls and razor wire. For our nation's heroes, it looked eerily similar to a prison.

I met him in a small, windowless room with concrete walls and fluorescent lighting. He sat in a plastic chair by a single wooden table. A second chair had been set up on the opposite side of the table. Two armed guards kept watch from the far door.

The artificial lighting made Granddad look pale and miserable, like a sick dog waiting to be put down.

I took Granddad's hand as I sat.

"They're keeping you here?" I managed, stifling back a mixture of anger and disgust. "This place is a prison."

"Was," my Granddad corrected me. "It closed down a few years ago. They say it's the only place big enough to provide for us all."

By "all" he meant everyone selected from Melbourne. Other centers had been set up across the country. I pointed to the guards.

"And them?"

"They're here for our safety. To stop us from trying to do anything stupid like escaping, or killing ourselves."

"Kill yourself? What? Don't want you spoiling their fun?"

Granddad shook his head. "It's not like that."

A tear ran down my cheek. I wiped it away.

"Let's not dwell on what has to be," Granddad said. "But I'm glad you came. There's something I've been meaning to talk to you about."

I fought back a fresh well of tears, trying to put on a brave face. If Granddad could do it, I could at least make an effort.

"When you're father passed away a few years ago I became a kind of father figure for you and your sisters," he began. "I tried to raise you right, as my father had raised me and your dad had started to do. You've developed into a fine young man, but when I'm gone your sisters and mum are going to need someone to continue that role. It's going to be up to you to be that someone."

I tried to say something. But no words would come out.

"I know it's a lot to take on, but you can do it. Here ..."

Granddad reached around his neck and unclipped a silver chain. Dangling on its end was a small, gold-plated compass. Funny, I'd never noticed it before.

"My dad gave this to me on his deathbed," he said. "He was a soldier in the navy. He told me it was time for me to steer the ship. Will you take the wheel and keep the family on course?"

I nodded and slipped the chain around my neck, tucking the compass under my shirt.

Granddad smiled and settled back into his chair. We stayed that way, silent, until the guards told us visiting time was over.

*

They allowed us one more visit with Granddad before the week was out, but I couldn't bring myself to see him. Instead, I waited in the blistering heat outside on a bench in the newly planted rose garden and watched my sisters emerge red-faced and puffy eyed from the building. I told my mum that I couldn't bear to see Granddad in that room again, but the real reason was much more selfish. I was mad that he'd dumped the burden of carrying our family onto my shoulders. It wasn't fair. I was only a fourteen-year-old kid and not ready for that kind of responsibility. I was mad at him for giving up without a fight, even though I knew there was nothing he could do. But mostly, I was mad at myself for being too scared to honor a dying man's wish and become the man he wanted me to be.

*

I sulked in my room that night, away from everyone. I would have stayed that way too if it wasn't for Mum. She got worse after the visit: stayed up late drinking vodka from the bottle and screaming at ghosts who weren't there. I snuck the girls into my room when she began to smash up the kitchen and did my best to keep them calm. I held them both and told them that everything was okay, that the crash of cutlery and string of obscenities were just Mum's way of telling Granddad she cared.

The next morning she didn't even bother getting out of bed. I let the girls sleep in while I crept downstairs and surveyed the damage. Mum had done a real number. The oven door had been torn from its face in the wall, and several holes were punched in the cupboards. The fridge was on its side and gooey liquid oozed into a smelly pool. Shards of broken ceramics and glass littered the floor.

It took me an hour to sweep and mop the mess into two green garbage bags. By that time, Carlie and Tanya had arisen and joined me tentatively at the foot of the stairs.

"Mum's resting," I said, trying my best to hide the two bags of damaged wares and wishing I could hide the oven or the fridge. "Go get dressed for school and I'll fix you something."

I made the girls a simple breakfast of Vegemite and toast, using the few plates that had survived the conflict. They had to be content with washing it down with a few gulps of water from the sink; the cups hadn't been as lucky.

The girls made their bus just as it was about to pull out into the street. I apologized to the driver and saw them off. I thought about catching my own bus, but decided after last night's outburst someone needed to keep an eye on Mum.

That night Carlie, Tanya, and I ate off plastic plates and watched reruns of *The Simpsons* on the nostalgia channel. Later, after I'd tucked them into bed and managed to get Mum to eat something—even if she did it from a cocoon under her doona—I flicked over to the news channel and watched the reports on Sunday's Cleansing.

The station was doing its best to allay the nation's fears. It reported that Granddad and the other men and woman would be euthanized under the most humane conditions using a noninvasive "gassing" technique that would simply put them to sleep, and that their ashes would be spread into a memorial rose garden being prepared to commemorate the brave souls.

Other, less biased sources on a late-night radio show offered a very different take on the process. They argued that the use of hydrogen cyanide was simply a "cost effective" method of killing, and had little to do with patient comfort. They claimed that the gasses were actually quite traumatic for victims, causing them great discomfort before they slipped into unconsciousness. They also highlighted that the mass-grave style incineration and disposal of "our heroes" in a rose garden memorial was an insensitive solution to save space in our already crowded graveyards. Several callers had phoned upset that they would not be able to say farewell to their loved ones with traditional funerals and burials.

The cold-hard truth of what we were about to do was difficult to take, so I shut off the radio. I wanted to believe the fairytales the Government was spinning, but I knew better. We all did.

*

Mum finally emerged from her room the next morning. I found her on the back step, standing in the humid air, sifting through the rubbish shortly after dawn.

"I made a real mess of things, didn't I?" she said, letting the broken crockery fall through her fingers and back into the bag.

"It wasn't that bad," I lied. I guided her hands away from the bin. She had a series of tiny cuts on her palms. It was hard to tell if they were from sifting through the broken plates, or battle scars from the other night. "We hardly even heard you."

"Liar," she sobbed, allowing a small smile to purse her lips for a second. "I went kind of loony."

"Kinda," I said.

We watched in silence as a magpie landed at the foot of the yard and began scratching for scraps by the compost.

"How are the girls?" Mum asked.

"Good. They're sleeping."

"They're taking it okay?"

"I think so."

"And you?"

"I'm okay."

The magpie plucked a worm from the dirt, snapping back its head and letting the writhing creature slide down its throat.

"They say we can visit Granddad beforehand," Mum said.

"I know."

"The man didn't think it was a good idea to take the girls though. Said it could be too traumatic for them."

"Maybe. It should be up to them though."

"Maybe."

Mum picked absently at the cuts on her hands. Some of them looked a little too clean to be made from broken glass.

"Aunt Lyn's not going either. She says it's too hard."

"That's bullshit," I snapped.

"I know."

"You're going though."

"I don't know. Maybe."

"You have to! Think of how Granddad feels."

Down the yard the magpie squawked, apparently sated from its feed. It took off, disappearing over the back fence.

"Will you hold my hand?" Mum asked.

"Every step of the way." I wrapped my fingers around hers; keen to show her the resolve of my promise. She smiled.

"You're father would have been proud of you."

*

Sunday arrived way too fast. Before we knew it Mum and I were driving past the fringes of suburbia and into the mountains to a purpose-built facility where the Victorian leg of the Cleansing would take place. Traffic was heavy, and we arrived shortly after nine to a sea of reporters, protestors, and onlookers. A roughly assembled security line had been created by a score of armed soldiers, and after checking our names from a long, computerized list they waved us through a set of heavily guarded gates.

We drove up a narrow, winding path toward a series of large, white marquees where we were directed into a makeshift parking lot and ushered into one of the tents along with the other gathering families for an information session. The marquee had been decked out like a circus tent with circular, stadium seating and a small floor-stage in the center. When we were seated a pair of men in black suits entered the arena.

"Good morning," one of them said. "My name is Professor John Sawyer and this is my associate, Professor Steve Moore. We are two of the scientists involved with today's Cleansing. We come before you this morning to shed some light on what will be happening today and to make you aware of some rules and regulations in place to ensure the best interests of all involved. Today is a sad day for us all, but we ask that you not forget the greater good for which these brave men and women make their sacrifice."

They went on to tell us about the gassing procedure, likening it to someone going to sleep, as well as the visiting rules for the day. What they didn't tell us until later was that our heroes would be herded into the chambers like animals in groups of two hundred, gassed till dead, and burned in giant furnaces at the back of the property. During question time, when someone quizzed them on the rumors of pain and suffering associated with the gas, the professors quickly assured us that this was not the case. I couldn't help but notice the quick, nervous glances they threw each other and, judging by the ripple of unrest, neither had the crowd.

Following the information session we were ushered into a second larger tent, where armed guards divided us into smaller groups. The smaller groups were then led into quartered off rooms and told to wait. Forty-five minutes later, we got to see Granddad for the last time.

He shuffled into the room with his head bowed, as if he was ashamed for us to see him this way. He was decked out in white cotton pajamas and a pair of slip-on shoes. Both his head and eyebrows had been shaved. The orientation had warned us to expect this. It was designed to cut down on the odor of burning hair during the disposal. When Granddad finally did look up he had tears in his eyes.

"I guess this is finally it, hey?" he sniffed, trying his best to make light of the situation.

The sight of seeing Granddad resigned to death, after he'd put on a brave face for so long nearly tore my heart in two.

Mum and I both lunged at him, cocooning him in a fierce

embrace. Tears streamed down my cheeks for what seemed to be the hundredth time that week.

"I don't want you to die," I wept.

"It wasn't on the top of my 'to do' list today," Granddad replied.

Mum and I laughed, letting him go long enough to sit on one of the plastic chairs they had provided us.

"How long do we have?" Granddad asked.

"Only a few minutes," Mum said.

"Oh," Granddad said.

The three of us sat in silence, unsure of what to do next. People always say the worst thing about death is never getting to say good-bye. Sitting in a room, knowing we were doing it was so much worse.

"How are the girls?" Granddad finally said.

"Okay," Mum and I both answered at the same time.

"They wanted to come, but the Government wouldn't let them," Mum explained.

I knew it was a lie; she'd never given them a choice. But I kept my mouth shut. It wasn't something Granddad needed to hear.

"They said to tell you they love you," I added quickly.

Granddad smiled. "You tell them they'll always be my little angels."

A uniformed soldier knocked on the cubicle wall.

"It's time," he said.

"But he just got here," Mum cried.

"I'm sorry. It's time," the soldier repeated. He took a step into the room.

"Just thirty more seconds," I pleaded. "Please?"

The soldier paused and nodded.

"Thank you," I said.

Mum broke down in tears again, clutching at Granddad with all her might. When she finally let go I stood up and embraced him one last time. I took in all I could about him, from the way he felt in my arms, to the slightly musty smell from the cologne he always used. After today, memories were all I would have and I wanted this one to remain as vivid as I could. Dad had died when I was young and fragmented images were all I had left. I didn't want the same to happen with Granddad.

The guard placed a hand on Granddad's shoulder.

"It's time," he repeated.

Reluctantly, I let him go.

"Remember what I talked to you about," Granddad said. "Keep 'em straight and true."

I clutched at the compass under my shirt.

"I will, captain," I said.

Granddad smiled and gave me a salute.

The soldier led Granddad out of the room and across the tent to a set of large, steel doors. Granddad paused, giving Mum and me one last look before the doors opened and he disappeared out of our lives forever.

*

More than twenty-seven million people perished that month in an organized global operation designed to benefit mankind. Two years later, environmental reports showed a 0.02 percent drop in the spiking global temperatures, and they heralded it a success. That's when talks began about the possibility of an annual Cleansing.

I still think of Granddad every day, even though there isn't much around to remind us of him anymore. Mum said it was too hard hanging onto all his things, like rubbing salt into old wounds. So we turned Granddad's room into a study and took down his old maritime pictures from the hall. I wouldn't let her get rid of his chair though. It remains, empty in front of the TV. I sit in it sometimes late at night, when the rest of the house is sleeping and stare at the compass he gave me. It helps me to keep him close and reminds me of the promise I made. I'm the man of the house now and it's my job to keep us all on course. Granddad entrusted this task to me and it's my burden to bear. I'll never let him down.

Prospect of a World I Dream

Alex Kane

The doorway to the bridge irised open, and I pulled myself inside using the cold handrails on either side of me. In the ice-blue dimness of the spacious room my peers were already present, seated in two semicircular rows around the projection lens. All nineteen of them strapped in, to keep from floating freely in the near-weightlessness of the ship's stationary axis.

Their expressions were grim.

I felt eyes glance my way as I took my place beside the other adolescent girls, fighting to suppress my embarrassment at having arrived last. Again.

Beside me, Jayanti leaned in, her boyish black hair mushrooming outward in the low-g. "Everyone's saying it was a mistake," she whispered. "Sounds pretty bad."

The hushed murmur of conversation died down when ribbons of light blossomed from the pedestal in front of us and coalesced to form a holographic image of the *Canto de Esperanza*—the starship that had brought us here over the span of countless lifetimes while we patiently waited to be born.

Our home.

Silent, unmoving stars shone out in the space beyond the bridge, drenched in the brilliant blue of the projection. I shivered with apprehension, sinking deeper into the beige aerofoam.

A toneless, masculine voice greeted us from several speakers ensconced in the ceiling: "By now you may have heard about our predicament." The voice belonged to Quinn, one of the three overseers who comprised Control. "We will not be colonizing Candidate Number One."

The other overseers, Iris and Komla, said nothing.

I glanced across the room at Ayden, who sat fidgeting with his hands. A sheen of sweat gleamed on his forehead; his spiked brown locks stood in disarray. He made no eye contact, so I turned back toward the projection.

"The nearer we came to our destination," Quinn continued, "the more evidence our telescopic imaging suggested that the system's star had become a red giant sometime in the last several millennia. Inconvenient though it may be, this recent concern has proven correct."

Iris's emulated female voice added, "Consequently, the planet we sought is gone. Consumed by its own dying sun."

The finality of her words chilled me. She'd made it real.

"Even more troubling, there's only one way to make it to the next potential target," explained the third overseer. Komla: the Zen infomorph. Radical posthumanist. "We're running short of reactor mass. A contingency mission, with all-new training, is necessary if we're to have any hope of eventual success."

"Mining," I speculated aloud, barely above a whisper. "You're talking about mining."

"Yes." A long pause, maybe for emphasis. Or was it calculation?

"The nearest asteroid belt," Iris said, "is only a few months' distance at our present vector. It will have large, even *planetoidal* bodies. And if we're lucky, enough palladium crystal to generate the antimatter needed to make up for the time we've lost."

In my peripheral vision, I saw Ayden shaking his head in frustration. "And just how much time *have* we lost?" he demanded.

Iris answered evenly: "Lifetimes."

*

You don't miss what you've never known. The homeworld was just a story we'd all heard a thousand times; a place where our mothers and fathers had died millennia ago. I wasn't going to lose my mind over not getting to settle a planet, mostly because I didn't see it as the tragedy the overseers made it out to be.

I slid the door shut behind me and looked over at Ayden, who just kept staring at the floor with his arms crossed.

"Are you okay?" I asked.

His blue-green eyes glinted with quiet tears in the semidarkness of his quarters. "Oh yeah," he said. "Aside from everything they just laid on us."

"Things will get better. Always do, no matter how messed up everything seems now. And you're strong."

Even if I didn't share his pain, I still understood it. Our whole lives had been spent preparing for colonization: learning to thaw our modest cryostore of old Earth specimens and begin anew.

We'd been raised on the dream of one day making our home on a planet like our parents and our ancestors. Now Control was saying we might never leave the starship. Ayden had every right to be angry.

I wanted to say more, but words seemed inadequate.

Ayden just needed time to heal.

When he finally looked up, he seemed embarrassed. I sat beside him, and he glanced away—toward the shadows in the corner of the room.

"Thanks, Inna." Gently, he placed his hand atop mine.

"For what?"

"Being here. I'm … glad I didn't have to spend the rest of the shift alone."

*

You showed great courage, volunteering for the expedition, Komla subvocalized after the routine call for lights-out. I picked up the tablet from my nightstand and gazed at the illuminated words.

"I don't know," I said into the mic, "it just seemed right. I mean, we owe you, don't we? Without Control, there would be no *Esperanza*, no one to fly it. We've devoted our entire lives to your service, to this voyage, and I see no reason to back down now. Despite whatever setback."

Like I said, he sent. *Courage.*

I shook my head, released a held breath. "Besides, I'll have friends with me. Jayanti, Armando …"

Ayden.

Seeing his name twisted my lips into a smile.

"Yes."

You've always been perceptibly fond of him. For fifteen years I've watched the two of you grow, and you seem utterly enamored with the boy. No doubt he's noticed by now.

"Ayden's a passionate person, but I think girls are the last thing he's concerned with. All he ever talks about is—well, you know. Doesn't matter now."

After a long pause: *He'll liven up a bit, once the shock wears off. Give him time.*

Privately, I hoped Komla was right.

*

Light amplification sensors in my helmet's visor compensated for the dimness as I stepped inside the sterilization chamber and strapped myself into the landing pod. A vaporous mist showered the room, and then a grid of lasers burned away every trace molecule of our vessel's artificial atmosphere.

I turned to face Ayden, felt my breathing grow rapid and panicked.

The hiss of escaping air filled my in-ear speakers before it was replaced by a low, muffled groan like someone screaming underwater.

With a soundless yawn that tugged at my boots, the depressurized bulkhead eased open, revealing a sprawling, cratered mass the size of a small continent.

Ayden's voice broke in on the comm channel: "This is it."

The asteroid filled half the space visible beneath us, its vastness made dizzying by the unending void of glittering black that surrounded it. The massive object spun slowly in the vacuum, drifting away from the ship along its own ancient, chaotic orbit.

"Ready?" asked Zahir, one of three others who had openly volunteered for the mining drop.

Everyone except me nodded.

I took a deep breath and said, "Okay. Punch it."

With a short burst of the landing pod's thrusters, we powered aft toward the fleeing asteroid. I felt suddenly adrift in the cosmos, its full scope revealed all about us like some immeasurable black hand, drawing closed around us as the starship we called home grew distant in our wake.

Zahir's hands were on the controls, but even if I'd taken the yoke I doubted anything could shake the sheer hopelessness that seized me. Our feet hung freely in the vacuum, and the lander lay wide open. No canopy, no solid metal base underfoot; its inflatable impact sphere would decide our fates, once we made contact.

Thoughts of micrometeoroid showers, radiation, and even the possibility of missing our target sprang to mind unbidden. Aboard a spacecraft, these things weren't fatal.

In the meantime, I had only my pressure suit to keep the universe out.

Hundreds of kilometers away, the edge of the asteroid drew up to form a horizon. One more burst of the rockets oriented the lander, and then a knifelike, magnetized stake harpooned out the front and dug deep into the rock.

"Hang on!" I heard Ayden yell across the comm.

Behind her visor, I saw Jayanti screaming.

The impact cushion shot outward around the lander, encasing our bodies as well as the rocket pack in a balloon of smooth nylon nanofiber.

Contrary to our months of training, I tensed as we struck ground, then bounced weightlessly until the magnetism generated by the lander brought us to rest. The force of being tossed about was sickening, and I drew in a series of short breaths to prevent myself from vomiting inside the suit's helmet.

Zahir flicked a switch on the lander's console, and the impact sphere deflated, disappearing into the various compartments that housed its individual slivers.

Landfall. At last.

Not on any place fit for habitation, of course—not without constructing a more permanent, well-shielded installation. But we'd touched down on natural ground; somewhere beyond the hull of a ship.

Beyond the electronic eyes and ears of Control.

With a grunt I unlocked my restraints and crawled gently to a stable place along the surface, where I hammered my own anchor point into the rock. I ran my gloved fingertips along the ground, felt the coarse, porous celestial body stretched out beneath me.

No human being had ever been here before. No one would ever come again. The notion haunted me: the scope of outer space, and the magnificence of all it encompassed …

My helmet's HUD bleeped with all kinds of spectroscopic data, overlaying various preassigned colors upon the visible rock to denote mineral composition in the asteroid's surface: blue for iron; red for magnesium; green for concentrations of rare platinum-group metals, like our precious palladium.

"Damn," Armando said over the comm, "we *made it!*"

Hearing his enthusiasm put a smile on my face, and we all raised our fists toward the stars.

*

Once we were alone and on an isolated comm channel, pulling ourselves into the soft darkness of an unfathomably deep crater, I asked Ayden what made him decide to volunteer for the mission. Why he'd risk his life for a cause he no longer believed in.

"To be honest," he said, "I didn't feel like I had a choice."

The sudden gravity between us was immense. My heart thundered beneath the mining harness and beckoned me to reach out and touch him.

"My hand just went up the second yours did," he said.

I laughed. "Oh, *did* it?"

"This isn't our mission anymore, you know? We're just sort of … along for the ride. Bad luck, if you ask me." He smiled, then got moving again, digging his diamond-bladed climbing axe into the delicate space ahead of him and pulling.

In the low-g, the force of his movement dragged me right along behind him with ease. Viewed through the helmet's light amplification visor, the crystalline latticework of the asteroid's innards gleamed all about us. It jutted from the walls of the crater like so many angry, stony shards of broken glass, and I prayed my spacesuit's armor was as thick as it was heavy.

"Yeah," I agreed. "I guess that's true. But somehow, that makes our role in the overseers' mission all the more vital, doesn't it? I mean, we're their last hope for finding a new world, for realizing their dream of colonizing another planet after *thousands of years.* Everything depends on us." I gestured at the calm blackness all around us. "On this."

Ayden laughed sardonically. "Catching on to that, are you?"

"It's the truth."

"Yeah." Sorrow tinged his voice, now, noticeable even through the comm. He glanced down at me, forced a smile, then got moving again.

Indicators lit up my visor, pointing to a large metal ore deposit just ahead of us. It was tough to make out in the dark, but specks of enhanced light off in the distance suggested a metallic luster.

Ayden sped up before I had a chance to mention it. *He* wasn't wasting any time in this deathtrap, either. Once we reached the prospect, he secured himself along the walls of the tunnel right away by stretching his legs out in front of him and wedging his feet firmly in place.

Like he'd been born for the job.

"Here," he said, and handed me his climbing axe. "Get the bag out and hold it open. We'll get this done in a hurry so we can be waiting at the lander when the others surface. Just to piss them off."

I smiled.

"Plus," he added, "I've got something I want to talk to you about."

*

Ayden shoved his arm down into the bag and tossed a fistful of palladium, most of it small flakes and dust, in with the rest. Now just a single huge chunk, doubtless the crown jewel of the large deposit, remained. He chipped at it carefully, coming at it from a forty-five-degree angle along the point where it met normal rock.

I unsnapped myself from the harness and drifted up alongside him, then used the axe he'd handed me to dig at the opposite side.

He gave me an absent grin, an icy dullness in his eyes, and kept hammering.

Something was on his mind. Something big.

Finally, the last piece of palladium crystal broke off and hovered in the space between us, glittering like a sliver of starlight.

I grabbed it and stowed it away in the bag, then sealed it shut.

"Now," I sighed, and placed a hand on his shoulder, "let's get the hell out of here."

*

There didn't seem to be any more light outside of the crater than in. Looking at all the stars gleaming overhead I couldn't help but wonder just how far away we were from civilization of any kind.

Iris's voice echoed the answer in my mind: *Lifetimes*.

When Ayden emerged behind me, he passed me the bag of precious ore and started toward the lander, walking gingerly over the ragged terrain from his anchor point at the crater's edge.

"Stay here and watch for the others," he said. "Go ahead and keep our signal separate while I activate the beacon."

I nodded, but grew nervous as I watched him go.

What had he wanted to tell me? The secrecy didn't sit well with me. Couldn't it wait until we were safely back on board the ship?

Jayanti and the others were nowhere in sight.

Ignoring his instructions to stay put, I followed Ayden, stopping twenty meters or so from the anchored rocket pack where he was already crouched down, keying in the command sequence programmed to transmit the beacon for extraction.

Suddenly I felt cold, and wanted nothing more than to get back home. And, in the privacy of my quarters, work my way into Ayden's arms.

A kiss, I decided. What I really wanted was a kiss.

The thought lingered as he rose to his feet and approached me.

"Listen," he said, "there's too much to say. Nothing can really articulate what I've been feeling these last few months ... but I want you to know, I couldn't have made it this far without you."

I took a step forward, and traced my fingertips across his face shield. "Is *that* what you wanted to tell me?" I squelched the urge to press myself against him.

"No." He looked at the battered surface of the asteroid underfoot, then pushed something into my hand. "That will tell you everything you need to know. Shatter everything you think you understand about our lives and our purpose." He gestured at the cosmic emptiness that filled the sky.

Black, airless. Passively hostile.

I examined what he'd given me: a data chip. I pressed the tiny button on its side, and an image flowered from the central lens.

A pixelated human face mouthed silent words into the void. Someone's holojournal.

"I found it in one of the empty rooms opposite the main dormitory," Ayden said. "Thick, strange dialect, but the speech patterns and diction are unmistakable. It's Quinn's."

An avatar? My mouth hung open as I searched for the right questions to ask.

I wondered: to us, the overseers had always been faceless; no more than synthetic voices belonging to ancient human consciousnesses stored permanently in the starship's databanks.

"Why have we never seen him like this before?" I asked.

"That thing's from before they left Earth. It's *that old*."

I drew in a deep breath, trying to grasp the enormity of whatever Ayden was trying to tell me.

"The chip explains everything they'd hoped to achieve," he said. "Everything they planned to do in case of failure or unexpected deviation."

"Deviation?"

"Like the one we made to come here. To this damn asteroid." He paused, and heaved a sigh. "They *used us*, Inna. We're just their instruments, their *slaves*."

"What are you talking about?"

"They *knew* that we didn't have a chance of colonizing Candidate Number One. That its sun had gone red giant long before we even came close. They knew *before we were even born*. Inna …" His voice trailed off, and he stumbled backward, putting distance between us. "They birthed us from their store of embryos so we could mine burning mass for propellant. They needed to refuel. *That's it*. It's the only reason we're alive: to land on this damn rock so they can see their own dreams come to fruition."

My mind swam in confusion, chaos. "You're—you're sure? Absolutely sure?"

"Yes, of course! You think I would've shared this if—" He clenched his jaw and curled his hand into a fist. It trembled.

If Control had known well into the outbound journey that it was too late to adjust course without running short of fuel, then what Ayden was telling me was at least conceivable. They would have traveled far enough by then that their only viable option would have been to thaw some of us out to do the work that they, no longer possessing physical bodies of their own, couldn't do.

Their slaves, he'd said.

"No," I whispered, "they wouldn't. Komla would never allow for such, such …"

"I wish you were right. It doesn't make any sense, doesn't accord with his beliefs, his ideals, and yet he let it happen." The triumvirate allowed for a two-vote majority. If Iris and Quinn agreed, then Komla's input didn't matter.

"So, what? You're thinking of telling the others?"

"No." He waved his hand for emphasis. "They can never know. What *I* know—I don't want to burden anyone else with. I had to tell you, though, Inna. I'm sorry. I'd made up my mind to go away, and I just—I needed *someone* else to know *why*. You have to promise me you won't tell anyone about the chip, or what I told you. Promise."

I nodded, unsure of everything. My whole footing on reality had just been shattered. What was I supposed to say?

"I promise."

"Good-bye, Inna," he said, as he unhooked the curved climbing axe from his waist.

"Wait, what do you—"

He plunged the blade deep into the armored chest plate of his pressure suit, puncturing his oxygen canister.

I stretched my hands out to catch him, but he slipped past and dropped to his knees.

His eyes widened as the last of his air supply leaked out into the vacuum in a single violent burst of metal, and he coughed, reaching for something unseen between us as his choked lungs blotted out his life.

For a moment I froze, unbelieving, uncomprehending. Then I stumbled toward the lander and frantically flung open each of its supply compartments, the contents of each spilling into the void: nanofiber patches, emergency maintenance tools, plasma flares ...

And two spare atmosphere tanks.

I seized one and dove for Ayden, scrabbling along the rock on all fours, praying I wasn't too late to stop his final foolish act of defiance.

I fumbled at the release mechanism on his chest until it unlocked, then pried the ruined canister away and tossed it heavenward. I pushed the new one into place from the side of his chest plate, and it slid home with a satisfying crunch.

"Open your *eyes*," I screamed, shaking him. "Open your eyes, Ayden! *Breathe!*"

I cursed; him, the overseers who'd deceived us, the cosmos. I cursed myself for ever befriending him, for ever falling in love with him.

Pounding his armored chest, feeling the sting of sweat on my pores, I wished we'd never spoken to one another. Never tangled eager glances. Never dreamed of one day having children and making a home on a mysterious new world beneath the warmth of some rare star.

And then I wished, as Ayden had, for an end.

For nothingness.

"Breathe," I whispered. "I love you … I love you. Please: I need you to *breathe*."

With gritted teeth and a bass-drum pulse, I didn't notice the tears floating like colorless pearls before my face.

*

I clutched Ayden's clammy hand with both my own, my bottom lip quivering as I choked back the sorrow and confusion that had plagued me since we'd returned to the *Canto de Esperanza*. To the mastership, security, and care of Control.

"Thank you," Ayden said. His voice was a tired rasp.

How many hours had we spent together in tears? He kept trying to explain and I kept telling him to shut up and go back to sleep. Rest. Dream.

"You don't have any reason to thank me," I said. "I'm here, and I'm staying. You're not going to be left alone."

"I have every reason to thank you. I would have died out there, but you didn't let me."

"*Shh*," I said. "Relax. There'll be plenty of time to thank me later." Time to forgive the overseers' deception, to forgive himself, to cultivate our hopes for the future. In my mind I heard Iris's toneless voice:

Lifetimes.

Larvae

Gregory Frost

June 17

The Hawkmoth is very like a hummingbird when it's pollinating
flowers. Its wings beat really really fast, which is not like other moths.
The problem—which is true of a lot of moths—is it's nocturnal, so I
haven't actually *seen* one yet. I intend to stay out here till I do.

Uncle Bart built me this tree house in the big magnolia right at the
edge of The Enclave, where the maintained commonlawn grows into
the wilderness. It's in line behind their house, so he had permission
to do it. Tree houses are usually a boy thing, I know, but Uncle Bart
understood how much I wanted to explore the wilderness and collect
my moths and butterflies. One of the things Mom let me bring with
me was my science fair display from two years ago. I had caught
twenty-three different kinds of butterflies—and that was in the city,
where basically even if there were Hawkmoths, I wouldn't be allowed
out at night to look for them.

I would *so* like to catch a Hawkmoth for my collection, but I don't
know if any have ever even turned up in North America. The way
things are going, I'm almost positive they will, though. Everything is
moving, all over.

Uncle Bart says this all used to be experimental farmland—The
Enclave and the wilderness, too. A company called Messisto owned it

like about a million years ago, but they got into some kind of trouble—with their "geemos", according to Uncle Bart—and the government took the land away from them through eminent domain, which we studied in civics in middle school—how when the climate shifted all over, the government finally had to step in and redistribute land (what they called "holdings") so that people could escape from the flooded cities and the parched towns and not have to live in camps the way they did in California. People and corporations didn't want to give up the land, either, and there were "lots of skirmishes." That's what our teacher, Mr. Anderson, called the Climate and Water Wars, which are still going on in different places every year. In fact, I think one of the reasons Mom wanted me to spend the summer with Uncle Bart and Aunt Julia was that our city is in trouble, too. Aunt Julia said over dinner, "I wish Hermione had come with you." That's Mom. Aunt Julia says my grandparents named her after some character in a book that they read when they were children. Most actual books are gone now because it's too costly on the grid to maintain the buildings to house them—that and, when other fuels dried up, people burned a lot of them for heat in the winter.

In The Enclave, you'd never know deprivations like that had ever happened. It's so quiet and safe out here. Uncle Bart made a lot of money in business, which is how they got invited to live here, which Aunt Julia likes to repeat kind of too often. I guess all the families here must have more money than everybody in the city. Mom said she's allergic to the countryside, but I don't know if she was making a joke or not.

Anyway, they let me sleep in the tree house, provided I pull the ladder up and close the trapdoor so that no one can climb up in the night, although I don't know who they think is going to do that. Jamal maybe. His family sent him out from the city, too. He wasn't in my school, and anyway, I don't think he likes me, because I have a tree house and he doesn't, and his family won't build him one.

Uncle Bart put screens over the windows so I don't have to worry about mosquitoes, which I wouldn't anyhow what with all the stuff Aunt Julia sprays on me before she sends me out for the night. Of course, I don't really go to bed out there. I just pretend to. I think she knows it, but pretends like she doesn't.

I've been climbing down at night with my Maglite and walking all over the wilderness. I'm pretty careful, and I have to be. I've found where there are leftover fences, most of them pretty rusty, which I guess I could get seriously cut on if I wasn't careful. It's impossible to tell now how things were laid out when Messisto owned this land. The fences are buried, completely overgrown.

I *have* caught some new moths: for instance, I have an *Ipimorpha pleonectusa*, which is brownish with spots, and big and pretty common; and a Fern Moth, which is not common—or maybe it is, but because of the way they camouflage and blend in, they look like old dead leaves. Really, that's what got me started on butterflies and moths in eighth grade—how they can make themselves so invisible. You could stare at a Fern Moth in the wilderness for an hour and not realize it if it didn't move.

June 23

Yesterday was a wonderful day. I caught a Brimstone, a *Gonepteryx rhamni*, in the wilderness. I must have been at least a mile from The Enclave, and I nearly missed it. The Brimstone looks exactly like a green leaf. Its wings even have raised veins on them the way leaves do. It's a terribly clever insect to do that. I mean, how does it know what it looks like to the world? I don't even know what *I* look like to the world, and I can see me in mirrors. Uncle Bart looked at it in my killing jar and said, "That's a hell of a thing, Iris."

June 26

Mom called last night to see how I was doing here. I told her all about the Brimstone and what a stroke of luck it was catching it. She said, "It sounds like you're in your element, sweetheart." I could hear that she sounded sad when she said it, as if she understood that her element and mine are always going to be different.

July 1

Last night I hunted again for the Hawkmoth. What I would really like is the one with the Death's Head, the *Acherontia lachesis*.

There was a full moon and the sky was crystal clear. I had my net, and was very mindful of the fences. By now I believe I know where every single wire is. Anyway I still didn't see a Hawkmoth, and finally I went back to the tree house and went to sleep.

I don't know when the storm came. I woke up to a great roaring sound, and I thought that I must have been right under a funnel cloud. It was pitch black, and outside everything seemed to be whirling past. I shone the Maglite through the different screens, but all I could see was how the air was full of tiny bits of things—leaves and twigs and dirt probably. The moon had completely vanished. Stuff kept pinging off the screens. Then I thought I remembered leaving the trapdoor open when I'd come back, but I was wrong. I'd closed it after all, and that was a relief.

I would have run inside, but I was too scared to try to climb down. I don't know why. I suppose I thought I would have been sucked out. But then I realized that for all the whirling, I didn't *feel* any wind at all, and Uncle Bart had made windows on three sides of the tree house, so I would have.

The roar went on for so long that it became kind of soothing. I sat back down. I thought, *Well, if the tornado does touch down here, I guess I'll just fly up into the air and that'll be that.* But it didn't, and finally I fell asleep. I remember that just about the time I did, I thought I heard another noise, like somebody moaning.

This morning when I woke, I looked out the windows. I expected to see something awful, like all the trees pulled up or houses smashed or something, but everything looked fine—so totally normal that I almost convinced myself I had dreamed the storm. "Almost" because a couple dozen small bugs had gotten jammed in the screens during the night. Most of them had burst, too. They had to have been shoved pretty hard for that to happen. I'd never seen any stuck in the screens before. I'd also never observed their specific genus, though I think they might be some kind of tiny Nigetia.

I told Uncle Bart. He seemed sort of distracted. He was looking at the back of his hand, like he had a rash or something, but I couldn't see it. I don't know what he was thinking about. Finally all he said was, "Well, it's just one of life's mysteries, as you are, Iris." Then he smiled and gave me a squeeze on my shoulder.

Aunt Julia slept in half the day. I think she wasn't feeling well and he didn't want to say; but she was up in time for dinner, and seemed okay then. I caught the two of them giving each other looks, which they probably thought I didn't see. I know those looks. Whenever Mom has a new boyfriend and he finally passes all the tests and gets to come for dinner, she's always giving him looks like that. I love my aunt and uncle but I kind of do not want to know about their intimate sex lives—though I suspect it explains where the moaning I heard last night came from.

July 4

I couldn't go out tonight because there was an Enclave celebration, and everyone had to go. They shot off some fireworks, but not many. I remember when I was maybe five, how the city had a big display of them for July Fourth, and Mom and I would go up onto the roof of our building with a lot of the other neighbors and watch them. Now I guess the cities can't afford them. Neither, it seems, can The Enclave. I mean, the children were walking around with some sparklers, but that was it. Even Jamal, though he and I are older than the others. He wanted to know what I do at night in the tree house, but when I told him, he made a face and said, "Why d'you mess with bugs?" I explained that I'm not messing with them, I'm cataloguing them. Like the ones I found in the screens, which I've decided are maybe a new discovery. "I'd like to discover *something*," I said. "Yeah, but why bugs?"

It was clear he would never understand—which is true of most adults, too, even Mom.

*

July 8

Last night I heard the roaring again.

I was in the wilderness with my net, way deep in where it stops being huge weeds and is all trees and brush and high grasses. It was more humid than it's been this week, and the lightning bugs were out all over the place in there. Aunt Julia calls them fairy lights because they don't come into The Enclave, but only flicker around in the taller weeds and grass. If you try to get near them, they move away. She says fairy lights called "will o' the wisps" do that in Ireland. They lure people out into bogs and marshes where they can drown. I asked how the lights could know that's what they were doing, but she didn't have an answer for that.

Anyway, the roaring. There's a thick wooded area to the north where the ground's really uneven, and there's a stream in the middle of it, and the roaring came from the far side of the woods. This time I knew it couldn't be a tornado, because I was staring straight up at the Milky Way, and there were hardly any clouds in the sky. As I listened, the noise rose and fell and rose and fell, and what it reminded me of more than anything was the chirring of insects the way it's described in some of my books. I know there are some, cicadas for instance, that live underground for most of their lives and then emerge in cycles, and they make a noise like that. There are some others—like locusts—that swarm, too. I'm pretty sure the ones in the screens are no kind of locust at all.

I struck out in that direction, but there's a place where the old fencing is really treacherous, even in daylight, and right away I realized I didn't dare try to climb through it at night. I'd have gotten cut bad for sure. Anyway, by the time I neared the fence, the roaring sounded like it had moved to the west, back toward The Enclave. It faded away while I listened to it.

By the time I got back to the tree house, I was soaked from coming back through all of the tall weeds. I *had* caught a Luna Moth, which was pretty cool. The books say they used to be everywhere, but now you don't see them much—at least I haven't.

I wish I could stay here all year round instead of just till the end of July. The wilderness with its riot of wildflowers and weeds seems to attract so many different butterflies and moths and other bugs. I bet if I could stay through the winter, I'd discover *Lepidopterans* that everybody thinks have gone extinct.

July 9

Aunt Julia has finally stopped smearing me in insect repellant. But I'm not noticing any mosquitoes, either. It's like they all left town.

July 10

The humidity got incredibly thick yesterday. You could feel the storm coming. Every breath was like drinking water. So I was surprised that my aunt and uncle didn't turn on the air conditioning. I know The Enclave is designed to have a small environmental footprint and everything, but the houses all have central systems built into them, unlike in the city where everyone has small window units, the kind where you pour water in to get cool. We had three. Jamal told me his family only had one, so when it got really bad in the summer, everybody pretty much lived in that one room. They would sleep on the floor and pretend they were camping out.

It's gotten dark early because the storm's coming now. There's heat lightning spread across the sky behind the wilderness, and thunder way far off. Uncle Bart came out just now and stood under the tree. I heard him call "Iris!" a couple of times, so I opened the trap door. He told me to bring my stuff inside, he didn't want me up in the tree during a bad storm. I've moved back into the house, into the guest room again. The wind's picking up, and a breeze that smells like rain is flowing through the whole house. It's like a river on the air.

July 11

It's after two in the morning. I'm writing this under the covers by Maglite. Something is very strange here.

We all went to bed, I think, before eleven. The storm was still building. I tried to go to sleep but about the time I started to doze off there was a huge explosion of lightning that must have been right next to our house. I jumped up and sneaked to the dining room, where the big glass door is that looks out onto the wilderness. Uncle Bart had pulled the white curtain halfway when we came in. I could see my tree house in the magnolia. The big plasticky leaves were flying all around like giant moths but the tree looked like it wasn't bothered by the wind one bit.

Then there was another really bright flash of lightning. I was standing right next to the curtain, and when the lightning flashed, the curtain shifted. It was so spooky I jumped. That was so weird that I stared right at it. And when the lightning came again, I saw the curtain move again. It was like with the flash its molecules all came apart for a microsecond and reassembled—like the curtain couldn't keep up with the sudden change in light.

I reached out my hand to touch it, and Aunt Julia said, "Iris, what are you doing?" I jumped again. She had come right up behind me and I hadn't heard her.

"God, Aunt Julia!" I was shaking even. I could see that she wasn't really looking at me, though. She was staring out at the storm, too, kind of excited. Then there was another really bright lightning strike behind me. It lit up Aunt Julia, and I'm pretty sure that I gasped. She was just like the curtain—for that one second she looked like a live jigsaw puzzle. Like ten million pieces of her broke up and regathered like a wave that rippled down her body.

Before there was another flash, she reached over and turned on the ceiling lights. "What is it, dear?" she asked. When I didn't say anything, she said, "Oh, it's only a storm and there's nothing to be frightened of, Iris. You should really go back to bed." As if everything was normal.

So here I am. I waited till I heard *her* go back to bed before I started writing this down. I know it sounds really insane. If it had just been the curtain I probably would think it was some kind of optical illusion or something. But I swear my aunt broke apart.

July 12

Insects have known how to disguise themselves for millions of years. I read about one called a *Termitaradus mitnicki* that could sneak into termite towers and live right beside the termites without being detected. It could flatten itself out against the wall and make its body look just like the wall. It even gave off a chemical signature to match the termites.

And there are flies that lay eggs inside honeybees, and when the eggs hatch, the larvae take control of the bees and make them fly at night. Entomologists call them "zombie bees" because they aren't in charge of their own bodies or behavior anymore. I wonder if the bee knows what's happening to it? Does it feel itself disappearing into the flies as they consume it? Is it afraid?

July 15

It's been raining off and on since the storms moved through, so I'm not getting into the wilderness very much, but I am staying up in the tree house. I know Aunt Julia and Uncle Bart can tell that I'm trying to avoid them. When I'm inside, I can't help but watch them really closely. I haven't seen Aunt Julia shift again like that, and I can't tell if Uncle Bart's like her or, if he isn't, whether he's noticed anything. He doesn't seem to have or else I guess he'd be up here with me.

I've invited Jamal up into my tree house about every day now. I like him and everything, and he seems a little more interested in all the butterflies and moths I caught, but really I'm just using him for an excuse to eat dinner up here instead of inside the house. They don't seem to mind it. In fact, Aunt Julia said she was glad I was "socializing." She worried about the way I tend to isolate myself. She'd never said so before. I can't tell if she's worked out what I'm doing or not. Obviously though, I can't stay up here for two whole weeks. And there's another storm coming later, probably tomorrow. I'll have to go inside again, won't I?

July 17

How did I not know?

There was another storm, not as bad as the first one, but I stayed in my room. I wasn't asleep of course. No way did I intend to fall asleep in here. It soon became clear that the storm was just a lot of rain and not lightning, so I decided I could sneak back out into the tree house.

I gathered all my stuff in my backpack and crept out of my room. I'm sure I didn't make any noise louder than the storm, but it's like Aunt Julia had worked out what I was going to do. I circled around the dining table, and all of a sudden the lights came on. Aunt Julia was sitting beside the switch. She didn't look angry or upset, more as if she'd just been waiting for me to come out.

"Iris, dear," she said. "I think we need to talk."

I set down the backpack, then started to back away. I thought maybe I could run out the front door. Only, I heard a sound, and there was Uncle Bart standing in the doorway to the hall. He gave me a smile, but then his gaze moved to Aunt Julia and he said, "She honestly doesn't know."

"That's what *I* thought," she agreed.

"Know what?" I asked.

Aunt Julia pointed at the chair next to her around the dining table. "Sit, honey."

They didn't move, didn't try to make me do anything. They just waited, and I could see there was no other course, so I walked over to the table, pulled out the chair and sat beside her. She looked up and Uncle Bart walked off, back to their bedroom.

"Iris," she said. "Your mother's going to drive here in less than two weeks to take you home. To the city. Now, I want you to think, and tell me how you feel about returning to the city."

This was not the conversation I thought I was going to have—not that I knew what we *were* supposed to talk about. I thought about Mom, about our apartment and all my things there, and I really wanted to fly there right now. But I couldn't hold onto it. I seemed to slide out of the apartment and down to the streets. The concrete and asphalt and the trash. And it made me queasy, like it was all poisonous. I thought of my friends, of school, but the feeling of being sick wouldn't go away.

Aunt Julia must have read all of that in my face. She said, "You don't want to go back, do you?"

I didn't say anything. I still didn't understand.

"Of course, you don't." She leaned toward me. "You belong here now. With us. All of us. And your wilderness." I didn't really notice her hand moving until she had taken hold of mine.

I looked down where she was touching me. She turned my hand over so that hers was underneath. I don't know what she did—I didn't feel the signal. But I watched my own hand break apart and surround hers. Her fingers curled as if cupping my own but they weren't there, and all of me—all of us—was spreading, coming apart. I was still me, though, aware now that when I drew a breath it was as large as the whole of the room, and I—we—were whirling, diving, hovering; and every single bit of me was me, so that I was in a million places all at once.

Aunt Julia stood and opened the glass door, the sound so sharp, like scissor blades. She held back the curtain and I spiraled out and up, and I was the air, the wind, the clouds. My tree house passed below and I dove into the field where I'd walked so many times, threaded the weeds, the flowers, tasted them before flying into the darkness beneath the trees.

Some part of me, a voice I'd never noticed, called and echoed in every one of us, and we spun and spun, and closed and aligned. All of us knew what part we played. Soon there were others with us, in and around us, thrumming. I touched Jamal and so many others who had been in the streets on the Fourth. We heard each other, and blended.

I've had dreams before that I was flying. This was so much better.

*

When I walked back from the wilderness, Aunt Julia and Uncle Bart were there to meet me. They had my clothes, which weren't part of me at all, though I hadn't noticed it. I stared at my hands, my feet, everything that was me, and it was flesh and who I was, and I was legion.

July 18

I threw out the killing jar. It doesn't really bother us, but I don't want to use it anymore.

July 20

Mom called today because she hadn't heard from me. I'd forgotten to call. I said, "Mom, I know how you feel about the countryside, but I really think you should come and stay at least a couple of nights before we go back."

Aunt Julia looked up from where she was reading and smiled at me.

"Seriously, Mom," I said. "It will *so* change you."

The Alien

Cathy Bryant

I came upon her as she quivered,
which is their way of crying,
and I asked what was wrong.
She looked at me, shivered
and told me about it, sighing
in their strange language of song.
She explained in silvery notes
that her fur was far too short,
her foot-scales too small, her throat-noise
inconsistently modulated. Motes
like tears fell from her, and I was caught
by the euphony of her voice,
and the beauty of her physical being;
yet she feared that she would never mate.
Felt ugly, put together badly.
So I realized what I was seeing:
an unhappy teenager, full of self-hate;
some things are universal, sadly.
And I hugged her in silent language
as the stars shone coldly down,
and I wished for more love for them all,
the young ones so messed up, so savage
with themselves, like me, too fat, too brown
or her, feeling adulthood's difficult call.

Over It

Camille Alexa

Lolly was assaulted in cyberspace a couple of weeks ago and she isn't getting over it. That's what her friends are telling her to do: get over it. *Get over it, Loll … it's not like anybody actually touched you or anything.*

She scratches blindly at the cuff of her left senseglove trying to relieve an itch on her arm without removing her goggles and all their attached virt-reality enhancers: they're pressure sealed over her eyes and cheeks and ears and would be a pain to get back on again. She might lose her place in the Scape.

This particular Scape is her current favorite from the countless thousands of free downloads, one buried way at the bottom of the popularity lists where Lolly likes to explore. Its terrain, she knows from sChOOL infoparties, is called a jungle. It's got greenery everywhere, thick, heavy, wet vegetation covered in slimy slug things which are usually pretty small but can grow to the size of your arm. It's got fetid air smelling of rotting wood, and it's hard to walk without slipping and falling on decaying leaves or tripping over exposed roots. There are these huge reptilian birds with feverbright plumage slithering through the upper branches, and sometimes small monkeys screech and throw excrement at you with alarming accuracy, the way non-player characters in other Scapes throw grenades or footballs or axes or frisbees. What's not in this Scape—nowhere Lolly has discovered yet anyway—are *people*.

Maybe people cost more to generate, so they don't want to waste them on free VR sampler apps? But no: there are tons of freebie Scapes with NPC humans. The big corporate developers drop dozens of new downloadable freebies into the net every day, try them out on the general populace, see what goes viral. Enough buzz fluffs up an app's hashtag count and they start charging for it: *First one's free, kiddies! Second one'll cost you.*

Of course most of those freebie Scapes, especially the weirdish ones off the beaten path, aren't worth a second glance and don't last a week; there's some pretty dumb stuff floating around out there.

But sometimes, there's some fun stuff. Or some weird stuff, or boring stuff—*lots* of boring stuff—and when you're like Lolly, skating through a dozen, two dozen, five dozen Scapes a week, logging on every spare hour you can squeeze between sleeping and mealtime interfaces with your fooking parents and the stupid fooking infoparties at your local sChOOL which the law says you've got to attend every day until you're eighteen, well … you also come across some pretty messed-up stuff.

It was in one of these last ones where Lolly got jumped. Carried kicking and flailing into a murky virtual back alley with hardly any decent visual coding but extra sauce on the VR interface olfactories and sensories. She was gagged, held down, beaten, and choked, unable to exit the Scape until the five minutes stipulated by the licensing agreement and user contract had passed and the sonic neural dampeners released the parts of Lolly's brain that let her body move again in real life, let her rip off the goggles and unhitch the sensegloves and gulp air into lungs burning from unspent virtual screams.

Five minutes is standard. Lolly has clicked the *I agree* button on so many freebie Scapes so many times, she never once thought seriously about it. The only reason all those experimental development-phase Scapes are free for download is so the corporations can collect market research: physical reactions and app interface success rates and client return ratios and such. It's unofficially called *guinea-pigging*, after some arcane barbaric research methodology from like a hundred years ago. The worst that usually happens is Lolly has to wander around some flat, colorless, half-sketched reality for five minutes, not enough venture capital investment in the Scape to make her sensegloves work right, no decent sonic neural boosters or anything to give her even so much as a tingle. Five boring minutes of her life she can never get back is all, but nothing, *nothing* like that messed-up snuff Scape she stumbled into. No dry heaves afterward, no uncontrollable shaking, no nightmares from which to wake up struggling for breath.

That's another thing her friends keep saying: *It was only five minutes, Loll. Get over it.*

*

Lolly's mom has always liked retro; today, she's pretending to make breakfast. Lolly knows how people actually used to make breakfast, how they chose eggs from a carton and cracked them into a pan, how they boiled water, how they burned toast in those quaint little shiny machines everyone used to add to their collections of similar items cluttering every surface of their kitchens. Lolly remembers her grandfather making breakfast when she was little, back when she and her mom still visited him at his house by the lake. But Granddad's been in the same bed in the same geriatric VR facility for ten years now, hooked up to nutrient machines, probably golfing every day and drinking virtual martinis and hanging out with friends who died a long time ago. Lolly wonders if he ever makes breakfast in whatever private VR he's been living in this past decade. She wouldn't know; the facility closes its Scapes to visitors so they can keep their clients' Realities intact.

"You don't know how lucky you are to have infoparties every day," Lolly's mother is saying, bending at the waist with a distracted air, mimicking motions of stirring and fluffing as the meal makes itself according to its program. "Before corporate sponsors took over and made everything fun, we had to go to plain old *school*." Lolly's mom makes a face, forgetting for a minute to fake-prepare the food as the program spools on without her.

"Did you have to go every day, even if you didn't feel like it?" Lolly asks.

"Yes."

"Was it usually boring and stupid, and did you usually want to be someplace else?" Lolly watches her mother push a couple buttons on the range to let the appliance plate their meal.

"We thought it was pretty boring, yes."

Lolly shrugs. "Then I don't see how it's any different now."

"Well," Lolly's mom sits down, plunking a plate of perfectly round uniform disks of evenly browned pancakes on the table between their plates of Traditional North American Breakfast #12, "at least you get to see your friends. That was always the best part about school anyway, getting to hang out with friends."

Picking up her fork, Lolly is glad her mother's going through one of her retro-fad phases, accessorizing the kitchen with real metal cutlery with real metal tines and edges and pointy bits instead of modern subsonic cutters and grippers. She stabs the eggshaped foodstuff on her plate, watches the yolkstuff run yellow and viscous into the toaststuff. She can hear her friends already, their boredom with her echoing inside her skull like the punchline for a bad joke: *Get over it, Loll.*

*

Skephanie and Slitch are waiting for Lolly when she steps off her bus. Skephanie's parents are pretty gilded: they buy her as many modification upgrades as she likes, as often as she likes. Today she's got blue skin and her breasts are enormous. Slitch is a pretty low-key guy, rarely goes for faddish lookatme mods. He couldn't wait to get his eight-digits-per upgrade, though, for a total of sixteen toes and sixteen fingers. Says it makes ollies a breeze, and his crazy splayed custom-built shoes have sparked a major trend among the skaters.

When Lolly walks up, Skephanie's expression makes her hunch her head lower on her shoulders. Slitch says that lately it's like Lolly's constantly ducking an invisible punch. She doesn't always notice when she's doing it, but she notices now, and tries to stand straighter.

"Hey, fookers," she says by way of greeting, "what's Scaping?"

"Nada," says Slitch.

But Skephanie frowns. "You de-modded some more, Loll? For real? That's so *un*."

Lolly says, "I didn't need all that hair." Big thick dreads, green and gorgeous. Easy for someone to get a hold of, drag you down to the stinking alley pavement and hold your face to filth.

"Whatever on the hair, Loll." Skephanie lifts a hand to stroke a blond braid, striking against the azure of her single bared shoulder. "It's more the face. You'd finally upgraded to those superluscious lips. And now ... this."

Superluscious lips covered by a huge hand, arm bearing down, crushing, pressing against your windpipe, the interface equipment's sonic neural manipulators making it feel hard to breathe, hard to get air, even though you know inside that you can't die in a VR Scape, can't actually be smothered in real life as some perp grinds his virtual weight on you, bruises you in places you never think of yourself as having with a real body.

Lolly shrugs. "These are the lips I had before upgrades."

"That's what I'm saying," says Skephanie. "You look totally normshy."

Slitch, never still, does a little flip on his board, the deck twirling under his extra digits like a circus baton. "I have tons of friends who stay norm, Skeph."

Skephanie tosses her braid over her other shoulder. "Not on purpose they don't. Only no-gild freaks."

All three turn as music starts pumping from the sChOOL building. It's a retro dance boom, thumping and heavy, loud enough so Lolly can feel the beats pulse deep under her ribcage.

"What's your first party?" she asks Slitch, who's a year younger and still on the sophomore curriculum.

He has to yell to make himself heard over the music, which is escalating to remind everyone the parties are starting and they should all file into the massive building if they don't want to be late. "Requisite Consumerism," he says. "After that it's Remote Sexuality."

By now the music is so loud Lolly practically has to read his lips, but she remembers last year's parties. She nods, returns his little half-salute half-wave as he slaps his board onto concrete and starts rolling toward the multicolored light show flashing above the front doors.

"Don't do anything I wouldn't do!" Skephanie calls after him. It's a joke, though, because practically everyone in the entire sChOOL knows there's nothing Skephanie wouldn't do.

*

The day passes as usual, Skephanie and Lolly wandering from room to room when the music changes at the top of each hour, refilling their drinks from dispensers mounted on the teachers' desks. The teachers themselves smile and nod, watching kids mingle and thumb through corporate-sponsored infoscreens mounted around the room. The sChOOL employees all have middling mods, giving them a bland, attractive, neutered similarity from one to the next, like corporate research indicates teens want their adults. Lolly'd rather have an ugly teacher who stood out, made mistakes, got passionate, ticked students off or behaved with inappropriate crudeness once in a while. She saw a historical movie about a teacher like that once and has never forgotten it.

Ubiquitous shopping kiosks line the halls and stand in the corners of the party rooms. By the third party of the day at least three distinct clique sets have changed their skin tone to a dull orange with light green speckles across their arms and shoulders. After lunch there are lines at all the hallway kiosks as kids with sufficiently gilded parents key in their credit codes and modification requests before thrusting their wrists into hermetubes to get the right nanos shot into their veins. After the last party lets out, even Skephanie is nearly completely russet, though her speckles are more blue than green.

She smooths her braid over her dappled shoulder when Lolly refuses to get the day's fashionable skin mod for the ten millionth time. "Fine," Skephanie says, "but over the last couple weeks you've been getting more fooking boring by the hour. And those tiny weird-modded boobs and fuggy grandpa clothes ..." She jabs a finger toward Lolly's oversized slouchy sweater like a lawyer in a reality courtvid pointing to the witness stand. "It's like you're *trying* to be ugly."

Compared to Skephanie's tight micro cardi and hyper mini, Lolly *is* dressed like a grandpa: *her* grandpa, the way he used to dress back when she was small and he could still cook up thick fluffy pancakes: eggs whipped with flour and vanilla and with genuine milk fats, not even synthetic.

"These are my actual boobs," she mumbles, hunching her head down so her naturally brown hair falls across her eyes.

Skephanie stares at her. "You de-modified your *breasts*?"

No girl in sChOOL has her own chest. Even the androgynes and the transgens modify, not only uberfemmes like Skephanie. That was the first thing Lolly had done when she stopped crying after she got out of that Scape: de-modded her chest. Her cheeks had still been damp when the nanos shot into her wrist with their peppery tingle.

"It's my body, Skeph. I can do whatever I want with it."

But Skephanie's looking at something in the distance, clearly bored by anything close. "Yeah," she says, "I guess you'll have plenty of time to do what you want, because, the normshy way it is now, nobody else is even going to notice."

*

The jungle seems thicker today, the slugs plumper, the vines more ropy and more green. The monkeys haven't shown up, which is fine with Lolly; their preferred pastime is not her favorite element of the Scape.

Insect buzz drones in her ears. Plumed serpent-birds flap-slither from tree to tree, nearly invisible in the leafy canopies, their flashes of bright crimson or brilliant yellow welcome bursts of color against the deep chlorophyll sameness. It's soothing, though; Lolly has to give it that. Soothing and private, and challenging in a physical-exertion sort of way that taxes her muscles rather than her mind. She feels the sonic components of the VR equipment manipulating her neural pathways, knows her muscles are actually getting some measure of workout as tiny electrical pulses travel into the deeper tissue. Her body has almost certainly worked up a sweat in RL. Within the Scape, humidity coats Lolly's lungs from the inside, rolls off her skin in steaming beads of moisture as she hacks her way through the undergrowth with a branch she stripped of its smaller protrusions, slashing a path through dense leaves and low-hanging vines and weirdly tufted ferns.

This time, she gets farther into the jungle than she ever has. Pausing in a small clearing, Scape-Lolly wipes the sweat from her virtual forehead and looks back the way from which she's come. Behind her, a narrow winding path ribbons through the thick vegetation, quickly dimming into the emerald blur of the freebie Scape at the periphery of her vision. Ahead in the small clearing is something Lolly has never seen in all the hours she's spent here: a thing made by human hands.

At least, that's what it looks like. She tries to imagine the agile monkeys with their minuscule, articulated fingers selecting rocks of perfectly uniform size and roundness, digging them out of the root-riddled soil or carrying them from who-knows-where. The shape of the mound looks familiar, and from years of searching for anything interesting in the endless weeks and months of sChOOL, she dredges up a name for the structure from one of her freshman infoparties: *cairn*, like the Vikings sometimes used to bury their dead, or ancient fishermen used to mark safe harbor. The little pyramid of round stones piled almost as high as Lolly is tall is called a cairn.

Unease licks along Lolly's spine. She likes this place, this jungle Scape, because it's *hers*, because she is alone. There's no one to try and convince her to get lookatme mods, no one to tell her how lucky she is to go to sChOOL. No one to grab her from behind, to squeeze her windpipe or press her into the dirt.

Turning in a slow three-sixty, she eyes the lush greenery, looking for signs of another human. But the jungle offers up only its comforting green sameness, and the soothing chirr and hum and rustle which is the ceaseless aural wallpaper of this Scape.

Tension ebbing, she approaches the cairn, finds the small opening at the base. It's built hollow, big enough for Lolly to crawl inside, sit crosslegged, lean her head back against the wall of rounded stones. She breathes deep the cool, oxygen-rich air, and reads the words some freebie-app programmer has inexplicably coded into the calcium softness of the opposite wall: *YOU ARE HERE.*

*

Slitch has pinged Lolly a note: *come 2 the bridge 2day / want u 2 meet somebuddy.*

She hasn't been to the bridge for ages, though she knows the skaters and fixies and other wheelers use the acres of abandoned concrete under the overpass for practice and for hanging out. Thinking about being there gives her a bitter little pang for the summers when she, Slitch, Skeph, and a bunch of other neighborhood kiddies used to lounge around with nothing to do. Back then nobody even talked about mods, except maybe to gross each other out with stories of the stupidity of older brothers and sisters, or fooking embarrassing parents who tried to mod young or get all lookatme. When did that change? It's not like it had felt sudden, but one summer they were all wheeling in the dirt or lounging in the leggy flowering weeds under the overpass, and the next summer they were all hooked up to their VR sets or to lowgrade body mod hermetubes at the mall, since the kiosks in sChOOL before grade nine were pretty fiercely regulated.

The bridge, when she gets there, is exactly how Lolly remembers it. Slitch and a bunch of other skaters are doing aerials off a steep ledge. Even the graffiti looks the same. Overhead is the ceaseless droning rumble and roar of thousands upon thousands of cars rushing thousands of people every minute to thousands of places across the bridge, lifting traffic over residential neighborhoods dating back from the days when old-fashioned freestanding houses were common. When Lolly was young, before she'd met and started hanging out with Slitch and Skephanie, she'd wanted more than anything in the world to live in one of the newer towers along the waterfront. There were bridges there too, of course, though they carried the endless traffic across water, not just over neighborhoods too old to keep up with the city as it quested forever upward like cities do.

Spotting her, Slitch waves, does a last little ollie, and skates over. He has a friend with him: a tall, too-skinny boy with narrow old normshy sneakers like Lolly's. No way would sixteen toes fit under those.

"Loll, meet Hap," says Slitch, clapping his friend on the back. "He's straightedge, like you."

Hap looks sideways at her, like he's too shy to face a girl head-on. His backpack makes him look like a gangly turtle. "Not straightedge," he mumbles. Lolly has to pay attention to understand what he says. "Just not into mods."

Slitch laughs. "VR Scaping doesn't count. There's so many neural sonics in the air, those fooking things would be microwaving your body inside and out every day even if you never *touched* a pair of goggles." Turning to Lolly: "He is kind of an addict, though. Mad hacking skills, too. You should see what he can do with a freebie Scape."

Lolly cranes her neck to look up at the boy, tries to imagine what his entire face looks like from just his profile.

"You're an app-hacker?" she says, not even trying to keep the admiration from her voice. Hacking Scapes is hard; all the major corporations hire fulltime armies of defense coders to prevent that stuff.

Hap turns slightly at the waist, twisting so his top half angles more toward her. His bottom half is still twisted away, his feet splayed goofy-foot, rocking his board gently back and forth as easy as breathing and as unconsciously done.

"I know a few things," he says. Watching his lips move, Lolly can't stop herself from wondering what those things might be.

*

Lolly knows Hap is sitting crosslegged only a few inches away, but with the VR set-up over her face and ears, she can't hear or see a thing. She's drifting in freespace while Hap adjusts the settings on her nanotech, rigging it so they can share her machine though it's designed as a single without multiuser interface capacity.

The immersion process goes way smoother than usual. For the first time in Lolly's experience, there's no user licensing agreement, Hap having hacked past the virtual gatekeeper of whatever Scape he wants to show her, a place he swears is the most peaceful place on Earth. When he'd said that, it made Lolly wonder about the definition of *on Earth*, and whether things and places in RL and in VR counted equally. She'd kept the musings to herself, content to walk slowly back to her house while Hap and Slitch skated lazy circles around her, occasionally taking those little detours skaters can never resist, grinding and sliding along bus-stop benches or steep curbs.

A block before Lolly's street turned off, Slitch had waved good-bye, tucked his board under his arm, and trotted up the row of ragged hydrangeas leading to his dad's house. Without comment, Hap had followed Lolly to her place, eaten the sandwich she'd dialed up for him in the kitchen, and followed her to her room. He'd gone straight to her VR kit and nodded. *It'll do*, he'd said, and pulled an ancient mini, some random cable snakes, and another set of goggles from his backpack.

Familiar greenness surrounds Lolly, falling abruptly from above like a leafy shroud. Greenness and the rustle of countless leaves, the humid scent of undergrowth, and—from someplace far off—the chittering cry of invisible monkeys.

It's way weird to see another human in Lolly's jungle. Is it her imagination, or is Scape-Hap slightly taller than the boy she met at the bridge? He certainly stands straighter. And she hadn't noticed that his eyes are green, like leafy growing things. Like jungle.

"How did you know?" she says. She wants to laugh and be mad at the same time. "This is my favorite freebie Scape. I keep worrying they're going to pull it."

"They won't pull it," he says. "Not this one." His voice seems deeper in VR, richer and more confident. "I built this, only leaving empty licensing stuff to disguise it as legit. But no corpo's watchdogging this place. No money being made, and none lost."

"*You* built this?" She can feel the incredulity in her voice. "But it's so … complex." She looks around, feels the moist air beading on her cheeks, hears the caw of flying-slithering creatures in the upper branches high overhead.

"I scavenged code, hacked a historical wartime shooter, took out all the—"

"Took out all the people."

He smiles. She's glad to see he knows how; she'd been beginning to wonder. "I think of it as taking out all the distractions," he says.

"Distractions from what?"

"The important stuff."

"Like?"

He glances away, putting himself into profile again. "Right now, important stuff like you. *You* are here."

Lolly follows the path of his gaze. Past the splayed fronds of an enormous fountaining fern is the little clearing, the cairn of rocks. She pushes past the fern bigger than a car and walks across the clearing, knowing Hap will follow. Inside the hollow structure the dirt floor is dry and cool. Lolly sits with her back against the round stones, facing the message scratched in the soft surface of the chalky wall, a message no one but this hacker boy in front of her could've—would've—placed there.

The light dims as he blocks the entryway a moment, then he settles crosslegged, facing her. Their knees are almost touching. It hits her: the disorienting realization that this is probably the exact same pose their bodies hold in real life, mimicking VR … or is it the other way around?

It's as peaceful sitting together in the dim cool space as it was sitting there alone. Lolly closes her eyes, listens to the syncopated rhythm of their breathing echo in the small chamber. It's a surprise to hear herself blurt: "Something happened to me a while ago and I don't think I'm getting over it."

A few moments pass in silence and greenness and rock. Then he says, "I see it like this: everything that happens to us gets written into our codes. Maybe we're not *supposed* to get over things; maybe each thing we experience builds us, adds to the stuff that went before. Like bulding a cairn." His hand arcs over his head, following the curve of the fitted stone ceiling. "… Or designing a Scape. All we can do is try to get the balance right, try to keep out as many bugs as we can."

"I wish …" Lolly trails off. His eyes are green even in shadow. His knees are so close, she feels the warmth of their nearness.

"You wish?"

Lolly tries again. "I wish I could be here. I mean really be here."

He points to the stones above his head. Not even looking, he traces the etched words in the rock with one finger. "You *are* here," he says.

"No, I mean …" Lolly leans forward so her knees touch his, and when he leans to meet her, her mouth touches his as well.

Whether five minutes have passed or not is irrelevant, since Lolly now knows this Scape is hacked. In RL, she drags the goggles from her face with fingers made thick by her sensegloves. Hap gets his gloves off first, and helps her with hers, calming her fumbles, taking his time. He studies her face as he unfastens her gloves—hard to imagine he could barely look at her when they first met an hour ago—and when they're off he sets them aside, resettles in front of her, legs crossed, and takes her hands lightly in his. She tries not to picture herself with red lines on her face where her goggles had adhered, with hair sticking up from the earflaps and straps, and with sweat dotting the bridge of her nose.

"I'm sorry something bad happened to you," he says.

There's a faint electricity when her skin brushes close to his. "I think I'm starting to get over it," she says. "Or at least, I'm trying to get the balance right. Trying to iron out the bugs."

She doesn't stop herself from leaning into him for real, and he meets her halfway, presses his mouth to hers. She draws back, and for several beats of her heart gets to watch the way afternoon sun streaming in the window lights up his lashes almost golden. It's kind of like being in the jungle scape, with all the distractions stripped away and only the important details left behind.

"Sometimes," she says, "I just need a reminder of what I'm doing. A reminder of who I am. Of where I am."

His eyes flash green, the green of winged serpents and wide fronds of fern. "You are *here*," he tells her, and Lolly leans into him again, into his solidity and warmth and the electricity of his skin.

The Ghost Hunter

E. Kristin Anderson

More than a hobby, these hallowed darks
    are my calling in a whisper.

    I know you can't hear. My own mother
would have me committed, even having heard so many
muffled voices on these recordings.

I'm here, they say—and they say it so often,
    so well, a shadow in digital,
        somehow lingering.

    And I've felt them, too.
    In hospitals, old hotels.

The fingers of the dead hush and wait and brush
along my shoulders, echo past the dust.

And I say,
    Yes, I feel you,
turn on my microphone.

    Later, on my laptop perhaps I'll see her,
an old woman, a child laughing.

E. KRISTIN ANDERSON

In that second, where her voice cracked
across the planes, the world fell aside.

   And then it is just me, alone,
with all spirits who might breathe the air anyway.

Your Own Way Back

Rich Larson

The mausoleum was all plexiglass and synthetic stone, lit by ghostly blue guide lights in the floor that charted visitors to their particular units. Elliot had free run of the place while his mother and granddad talked. When he was younger he chased the autocleaner, slip-sliding on its slick wet trail until someone glared at him. Now he was twelve and the glossy black floor was only slightly tempting. Instead, he sat outside the booth with his swim bag and eavesdropped.

"You can't afford another year in digital," his mother was saying. "You're shedding memories already. If you stay here any longer, we took out that clone policy for nothing."

"Maybe it's for the best." His granddad's voice was wavery, distorted. Elliot peeked around the corner and saw the projection flickering, face carved in blue hololight. It was blurrier than usual.

"There's the alternative, isn't there?" Elliot's mother said. "What we talked about?"

"Must have shed the memory."

"Don't be like that, Dad. Elliot's fully notched."

That reminded Elliot that he'd loaded a new comic to read. He ran his finger along the inert plastic at the base of his skull, feeling the slot where the new chip was sitting and beneath it the arithmetic he'd loaded from school and neglected to open. Elliot leafed through the pages in his mind's eye but kept listening.

"And he's young enough," his mother said. "He's still got brain plasticity, maybe even for another year."

"Why don't you just ask him?" His granddad's projected face raised both eyebrows. "I expect he's listening in."

Elliot's mother craned around the corner and Elliot rolled his eyes back, pretending to be absorbed in the shifting pictures, but knew he'd been caught out. She smoothed her dark hair and blinked tired eyes. "Elliot, what do you think? Come in here, love."

Elliot stood up and walked into the booth, gangly now that he was finally growing. He waved to his granddad out of habit even though he wouldn't see it. His granddad was a neural web in the dull marble plinth in front of them. The blue ghost was only a projection cobbled from old EyeWitness recordings and follow-cams to give visitors something physical to interact with.

"Elliot, you know what a piggyback is, right?" his granddad asked.

"Yeah. Yes." Elliot felt the nape of his neck again. "My friend Daan's got a tutor AI."

"Your grandfather is not an AI," his mother said sharply.

"He knows that," his granddad said. "What do you say, Elliot? Let the old man bang around your head? It's your choice. Completely your choice."

"Just for the summer," his mother assured, pinching the bridge of her nose. Her nails had chipped. "It would just be for the summer while the clone's growing. It's really much better than keeping him here in the mausoleum."

Elliot thought back to when Daan showed up for class with the shiny AI chip in his notches, how impressed everyone had been. This wasn't the same thing, but it was close. "Okay," Elliot said. "Do you still know how to do algebra?"

His mother's ears went red but his granddad just laughed, a synthesized warble that was almost too loud for the silent mausoleum. Before they left they had him loaded into a bone-white chip, and then that chip was sealed in plastic wrap and dropped into a bag, and Elliot carried it very carefully on the drive home.

*

"It might jolt a bit," the technician said, clipping Elliot's hair away from his notches. Elliot nodded as well as he could with his chin burrowed in a pillow. He was on his stomach on the couch watching rain streak down the wide window. The technician had come over with antiseptic-smelling gloves and a black toolkit because Elliot's granddad was not an AI, and Elliot's mother was not going to take chances with her trembling fingers.

She was washing up, but came into the living room every few minutes, hands red as lobsters and slicked with soap. She had excuses the first few times, but now it was just to bite her lip and stare. She didn't realize Elliot could see her in the window.

"Putting him in, now," the technician said. The chip descended in silvery forceps and Elliot felt something slide and rasp at the base of his skull. It settled with a meaty click. Elliot began to ask if they were done, and then—

Jolt.

His nerves blasted sparks all at once, arched his back like a cat, and split the top of his head with a thermonuclear explosion. His body spasmed. From somewhere far away he heard himself howl. Then his mother was over him, holding him down, swearing a blue streak at the technician.

"It's normal," the man was repeating. "It's normal. He's fine now. Ask him. He's fine. Aren't you, Elliot?" He was folding his gloves, wiping the sweat raised on his forehead.

Something was stirring in the back of Elliot's skull. *Right here, Elliot. Steady now.*

"Are you okay?" his mother demanded. Her nails were digging crescents in his hand. "Just say something, all right?"

"I'm okay," Elliot said. He felt the stir again. "So's granddad. He's okay."

Elliot's mother exhaled but didn't let go of his hand.

*

It wasn't like having a tutor AI. Elliot's granddad didn't switch off or go dormant. He was always there in the back of things, when Elliot woke up in staticky sheets and when he sawed through his mother's half-cooked breakfast sausages and when he walked to the public pool early each morning.

Elliot had scrimped the money for his pass from months of bannering the local chip shop, putting value ads in his slots to widecast on the subway or in the street. He didn't get pocket money anymore, so every time the laser raked his neck and scanned him into the pool he felt a beat of pride.

Elliot liked his swims best in the morning. Only a few others were ever there, usually middle-aged men churning industriously up and down their lanes. The lifeguard bobbed at the side like a plastic jellyfish, monitoring the chlorine level.

His mother had given him a gelatin ("Cover up your blowhole," she'd said, taut smile on her way out the door) and he slathered it over his notches, letting it go dry and shiny before he slipped into the water. The chip tingled in his neck but his granddad remained silent, still curled somewhere in the back of Elliot's head as he swam.

*

At school, his classmates were impressed—for the day. By the end of the week Elliot was starting to hear sniggers and knew something was going to happen come gym or recess.

On Thursday the sky was dark and blustery, and the supervisor watched the footy game from a far distance with her chin tucked into her windbreaker. They were playing with an old Soccket that rattled when kicked and didn't bounce quite right, and that was why Elliot had missed another open shot.

"You're slow, granddad," said Stephen Fletcher, who was small and fierce and had his hair razored around his notches.

"What's that?"

"Your old man chip is turning you slow," Stephen said, grinning like a wolf. "Slooow and stiff."

"Quicker than you," Elliot said, but he knew he wasn't, he was only quick in the water.

"You're too poor to grow a clone for him." Stephen bounced the ball hard against the cement and stuck it on his hip. "That's why you have the chip."

Everyone was watching, now, and the keeper from the opposite end was wandering up from his orange pylons to see what was going on. Elliot looked around, looked at Daan, but Daan was grinning, too.

Steady now, Elliot. It's fine. It's a laugh. Elliot gave a start. His granddad hadn't said a word all week.

"Maybe they can stick him in a baboon," someone suggested. Someone else gave a fair imitation of a monkey screech. Elliot clenched his teeth.

It's fine.

"If your ma's going to make all that clone money, she'll have to work the corner." Stephen pumped his hips. Grinned. "Think?"

The baboon dropped quiet and they all stared. Elliot balled his hands.

Thumb outside your fist, Elliot.

Him and his granddad went in swinging.

*

On the walk home, with the sky still bruising overhead and his face now doing the same, Elliot asked about his grandmother. Rain was speckling the sidewalk and Elliot tipped his head back to wash the scabby blood from under his nose. It was a long time before his granddad answered.

She didn't want storage. Or a new body. She said she'd had her time, and that was that.

"Why'd you stay?" Elliot asked. His granddad didn't answer, and Elliot knew enough to not ask again.

Yellow cabs slid by with rain wriggling down their windshields. Elliot wondered what time his mother would be home.

*

When school finally let out for summer, Elliot could spend all day at the pool. The weather turned sunny and so they turned the smartglass ceiling transparent, drenching the tiles with afternoon sunlight and making the water glisten blues and greens. More people showed up. Some of Elliot's classmates splashed and threw foam balls in the shallow end. Elliot stayed in the lanes. He was working on his breaststroke.

You could hold your glide longer. His granddad said it as Elliot sloshed to the wall in a final burst.

"What?" Elliot panted, hooking his elbows over the pool's edge.

Go again. I'll show you.

Elliot adjusted the pinch of his goggles, inhaled chlorine. There were too many people making waves now and the water was warm as a bathtub. He pulled reluctantly into the lane for a few more lengths. As he did, his muscles seized.

Sorry about that. Here. Relax a bit.

His limbs started moving without him. Elliot leaned into the stroke and felt a hundred small adjustments, how his shoulders sloped and how his hands bit the water. He felt like a fluid. His mouth peeled a foamy grin under the water and suddenly he was smoother than he'd ever been, nothing awkward left in his growing joints, nothing but pure motion.

At the other end, one of the morning men was swilling water in his swim cap. "You're really putting that together," he remarked. "You should trial for the club here, boy."

Elliot nodded and grinned and clambered shaky out of the pool. After that, granddad swam with him and told him stories about how in summer he used to put his clothes in a plastic garbage bag and jump off high rocks into the bay, cupping his balls and holding his nose against the splashdown, and how him and his mates set races from buoy to buoy and bet all their pocket money on them.

*

There was a lot of time for those stories. Elliot generally went home to an empty apartment where he draped himself over the couch and churned through his comics, hair forming a damp patch on the pillow. His granddad didn't like how the comics had all gone back to 2D, but he liked how Elliot could change them as they went along. Sometimes the villain deserved to win, Elliot thought.

When he was hungry he trawled for recipes online and always ended up cooking pasta with mushroom soup from a can. His granddad was no help with that. He did, however, show him how to make coffee. His mother was slightly suspicious of it when she dragged in the door to find a pot gurgling on the counter.

"Tastes good," she admitted, swishing the sample in her mug. "That's it for me, though. Have to sleep. One more way I'm inferior to those damn autocabs, isn't it?" She grimaced and poured her dregs down the stainless steel drain, then disappeared into her bedroom.

She worked more than ever and came home late most nights, complaining about the autocabs taking all the business, even though she had the very newest GPS suctioned inside her windshield. Some nights they played cards, the three of them, with Elliot and his granddad teamed up, but she usually fell asleep halfway through.

*

She works too hard. Doesn't spend time with you. His granddad said it in the night, just as Elliot was drifting off. The constellations on his ceiling were peeling and only glowed when headlights shuttled by outside the window.

While they didn't get physical bills anymore, Elliot could tell when they came in from the tightness in his mother's mouth.

"She has to," he said. "She's saving."

You ever feel tired, Elliot?

"Now, yeah."

Not like this, you don't. Ah. Never mind. Sleep well.

"You too," Elliot mumbled. He stretched his arms and his legs and slept like a starfish, imagining himself afloat in the water.

*

One day Elliot came home from his swim and found the apartment unlocked and smelling like cold lemon. His mother hugged him and asked about his swim times. Maybe he could invite some of his friends to go with him once in a while? For the first time in a long while her nails were painted hard and white.

She picked the small bits of gelatin out of his hair while they ate greasy takeout, and afterward she told him they were going to the FleshFac.

"I thought we were growing a custom," Elliot said, bundling up the paper sheaths. "So it'll look like him."

"Well, it doesn't hurt to see options." His mother smiled hesitantly. "Does it?"

Elliot realized she was asking his granddad, but his granddad didn't answer. He pulled his jacket half on and followed his mother out to the car. When he was younger he'd liked the yellow paint. It looked bad now, too bright and too obvious. He slid into the passenger side and then they drove. The seats smelled like cigarettes.

The FleshFac was on the edge of the city, located near a large warehouse and a hospital. The building was squat and iron gray, like a safe dropped from the sky. The AI greeter at the entrance scanned them in, and directed Elliot and his mother down a peeling green hallway to the clone rooms. Everything smelled like antiseptic.

Clones were lined in scratched plastic shells, shrouded by a poison-yellow vapor. Another family was there for an upload, and while Elliot and his mother watched quietly one of the shells hissed open. Hidden vacuums sucked the fog away. The clone was long-limbed and sharp-shouldered with ghostly white skin that had never seen sun, but after a long silence the little girl said, "Daddy, Daddy, we made your bed for you," and then hugged him. The woman stood there with a collection of red balloons wilting in her hand.

So young. He deserves it.

"You deserve it," Elliot said, forgetting his mother was there with him.

There are so many years in that clone. God. A lot of years.

The family left. The daddy was walking stiffly on new legs and his wife held his hand like it was something foreign, but their daughter skipped ahead happily with the artery-red balloons. Elliot and his mother walked down the row of clones.

They came in two models, basic male and basic female, both with standard musculature and post-racial features. They didn't look anything like his granddad. Elliot could tell that his mother was doing numbers in her head, and with every clone they passed her teeth bit deeper into her lip.

When they got home she locked herself in the bathroom and turned on the fan, but behind the roar he could still hear her crying and crying.

"There's enough," she said, when she came out red-eyed. "There's just enough. We can do it."

Elliot nodded. His granddad said nothing.

*

I stayed because I was scared.

Elliot stood in the locker-room shower with his face up to the nozzle, letting it beat a tattoo against his forehead. "Of being dead?" he asked, swilling water in his mouth.

I suppose. Yes. That. She must think I'm a real coward if she's still up there waiting.

"You must miss her," Elliot said. He dragged his toenail along the crack between two tiles.

Madly. I thought maybe I was staying to help your mother. Since your dad split so early.

"Oh."

But she doesn't need me taking care of her. Not anymore. And she sure as hell can't afford this clone, not even one of those gawky bastards from the factory.

Elliot switched the water off. Drops splashed off his face to his collarbone, trickled from his armpits down his elbows. "What do you mean?"

I'm not going to let her put you two in debt when it's time I moved on. I'm tired, Elliot. I stayed because I was scared, but now I'm tired of being scared. You get me?

Other bodies moved away and Elliot was alone in the changing room, fingers turning blue.

You had a good swim today. What do you say to one more in the morning?

"Here?" Elliot asked faintly.

Not here.

*

In the earliest hours of the morning, when it was still dark outside his window, Elliot found a pen and a pad of paper and closed his eyes. He had never learned to write without a keyboard, but his granddad moved his hand for him in graceful swoops and curls over the page. He filled up four of them and then Elliot shuffled them under his mother's door.

His swim-stuff was wet from the day before but he changed all the same, putting the clammy togs on under his trousers. He let himself out of the apartment and walked down the street with the bag tucked under his arm, past the hazy glow of the streetlamps and a roving autocleaner collecting the trash.

The bay was closed off now, with a wire fence that hadn't existed in his granddad's time, but Elliot had spent enough time clambering after lost footballs to scale it competently, if not quickly. He looked at the murk with trepidation for only a moment, eyeing the bobbing plastic refuse and slippery rocks, then he stripped down and plunged in.

His granddad pulled him off into the bay with smooth strokes, powerful the way Elliot had always thought of seals or sleek dolphins as powerful. They were alone in the water, making the only noises. His hands carved the cold surface and the slapping of his body, the tug of his breath, the water in his ears, all seemed vastly loud in the dark.

When they were finally bobbing far out in the bay, watching the red lights of the skyline, his granddad said it was time.

Expect you can make your own way back.

"Yeah. Yes. I can."

Pull me out, then.

Elliot's cold fingers scrabbled for the gelatin lump at the back of his skull. He pulled it off in clumps, then long strips, then it all came away at once. He winched the notches open and his slippery fingertips found his granddad's chip. He hesitated for a heartbeat, two heartbeats, then yanked it like a tooth and hurled it off into the bay. A spark jumped once. Disappeared.

He swam slowly on the way back, his empty-feeling head held carefully above water. He toweled off and dried the strange tingling hollow at the back of his neck. His eyes stung. Swimming without goggles always turned them pink.

*

Elliot's mother was waiting for him on the curb when he got back home, the pages spread around her bare feet.

"Haven't seen his handwriting in so long," she said, combing a strand of dark hair from her face.

Elliot eased down on the cement curb and his mother wrapped an arm around his shoulders. They sat together watching dawn streak the sky with filaments of red.

Me and My Army of Me

Katrina Nicholson

My lab partner is a douchebag. There. I said it. Mom, I can see you shaking your head and saying: "Miles, that is not the kind of language I raised you to use." But you also raised me to tell the truth, and the truth is that Ralph Mitchell is a massive douchebag. And you can't tell me I'm just being dramatic until you've sat beside the guy for three straight months and put up with him calling you a nerd under his breath while mooching off your answers and "accidentally" spilling volatile chemicals onto your pants hoping to melt them right off your legs (did you ever wonder how my jeans ended up with so many holes in them?) Something had to be done about it, so I did it. Now if you could just bury me under a tombstone shaped like Darth Vader's head, I'd appreciate it.

I suppose I should rewind a little bit and tell you why I feel it necessary to write you an "in case of my death" letter. And *no*, I am *not overreacting, Mom!* I'm dabbling in some serious stuff here, and chances are it's going to blow up in my face. Most of my experiments do, as you well know (sorry again about the chandelier … and the garage door … and the cat). So, I'm just covering all my bases here.

Anyway, it all started last Monday. I was sitting in chemistry class, minding my own business, careful to keep all my limbs and belongings on my side of the invisible line dividing my half of the lab table from Ralph's. Ralph was doing his usual nothing, kicking back with his legs sticking out into the aisle hoping to trip anyone foolish enough to pass within his three-meter zone of destruction. He was tearing the instructions for the day's assignment into little pieces and shooting them through a straw at Sarah Mattingly, who sits in front of us and probably has to vacuum her head every day after school. I was just grateful he was leaving me alone to finish "our" assignment.

Ralph stopped ripping when he got to the materials list at the top of the page, which (unfortunately) contained a warning to be careful with the potassium hydroxide (also known as drain cleaner to you laypersons) we were boiling pennies in for today's experiment. So of course Ralph's elbow "accidentally" slipped and "coincidentally" hit the KOH beaker (picture me using sarcastic air quotes here) which "just happened" to spill right into my book bag, which had been safely tucked under the radiator until a minute ago. It ruined my books, my homework, and worst of all my iPhone, which, I might remind you, is where I keep all my episodes of *Battlestar Galactica*.

I'm usually too smart to call Ralph out on anything he does, but I guess my grief over the loss of Kara Thrace temporarily overrode my self-preservation instinct, because I jumped up off my stool and yelled a whole string of really creative curses at Ralph (which I won't repeat here just in case I do live to see tomorrow only to find out that I'm grounded until my college graduation). And then I told him I was going to kick his ass. The whole room (especially me) was stunned to silence at that one, mostly because I'm the kind of guy who could be confused with wallpaper at first glance and Ralph is a massive bull-necked bruiser who once drove a guy's nose bone into his brain during a hockey game. I might've regained my senses then if Ralph hadn't had the gall to burst out laughing as if that was the funniest thing he'd ever heard (so of course the whole class broke out in sycophantic laughter to avoid future pummelings). When he could breathe enough to speak, he said something to the effect of "you and what army," at which point my inner suicidal maniac responded "me and my army of me," and stomped me off to detention before Ms. Keller could snap out of her trance.

It's not like I haven't been formulating revenge plans for, oh, the entire fifteen years of my life—ever since the day Mrs. Mitchell invited herself over for a play date and little Ralphie booted me out of my own playpen. But unfortunately, most of my plans looked like this:

FIG. 1   PROPOSED BULLYING DETERRENT METHOD #487

In other words: they had no hope of working. But I had to come up with something. I'd called Ralph out in front of the whole class. By the end of the day every kid in Schuster High would know about it. If I didn't make good by Saturday afternoon (the general consensus had scheduled our fight for after the soccer game) everyone would go back to ignoring me like they have for the past ten years and I'd never achieve my dream of being carried through the school on the shoulders of cheerleaders (yes, yes, I know, my plans are much more likely to land me in juvie than anything else, but a guy's gotta have dreams). Oh, and I'd be dead, because Ralph would pound on me until my bones turned into gelatin.

Anyway, the vat of boiling acid thing wasn't doable. We only have about two liters of sulfuric acid in the school at any given time (I know because I checked). Also: my ray gun was a disaster, you removed everything even remotely resembling a weapon from the house after my robot went crazy, and I couldn't think of anything else, so I went back to work on the Discombobulator. I know you said no more playing with black holes. And I know I told you I dismantled it and scattered the parts to the four winds after what happened to the cat, but I sort of lied about that. I actually just took that cage thing that makes the black hole, disguised it as a hockey net, and left it in the driveway (so yes, that thing I told you about trying out for the hockey team was a total lie. Sorry). I dragged it into the basement and locked myself in to work on it every day after school. You'll remember that week, because I took my meals through the cat flap in the basement door and stopped showering.

I finished reassembling the thing on Friday, tweaked it a little to avoid another repeat of the cat incident, and flipped the switch, at which point I blew every fuse in the house. I had to scramble around replacing everything before you got back from your date and I ruined the illusion you like to create that I'm normal and therefore "good stepson material" (don't lie—I heard you telling that guy from the bakery that I was on the lacrosse team). I ran a line directly from the transformer up the street and tried again, and it worked … sort of. You see, the goal of the Discombobulator was to turn things (like Ralph) into other things (like a Cheez Doodle, or maybe a dung beetle).

FIG. 2   DISCOMBOBULATION (THEORETICAL)

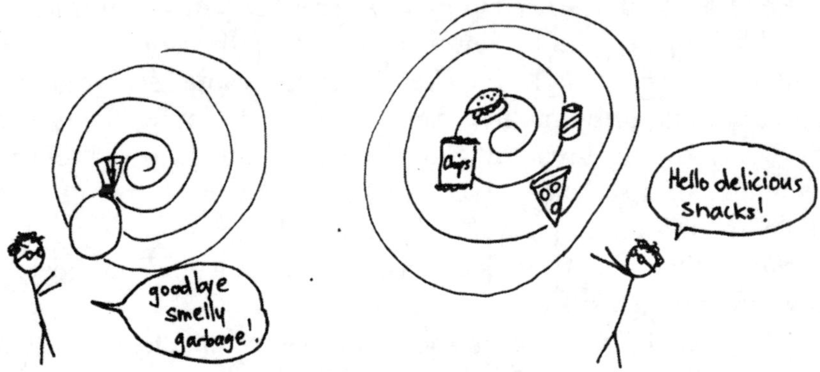

But it's never done that. It's never done anything so far as I can tell, except make a really loud whooshing sound, cause statewide blackouts, and disappear things forever instead of morphing them into snack foods like it's supposed to. But this time something weird happened. When I turned it on, Mr. Fluffles came out. *Yes. Mr. Fluffles.* The cat I accidentally disintegrated in fourth grade had returned from the dead, and I totally peed my pants and jumped on top of a table when I saw him. I've seen way too many zombie movies and I expected him to go for my eye sockets, but what he actually did was sit down and start washing his face like everything was totally normal and he hadn't been missing for five years. And he sort of hadn't, because after I changed my pants I looked him over (very carefully... wearing elbow length welding gloves and a face shield). He was the same as he was when he left. That's when I had the brainwave. What if my Discombobulator was actually a time warp!? So I put Mr. Fluffles in the shed and did some tests (after you read this, you should probably go out there and feed him. He doesn't like brains, just regular kitty food. And tuna.)

After some tweaking and a lot of missing basement junk (sorry about the laundry soap ... and the freezer), I managed to send a pencil, three Hot Pockets, and a mouse three minutes into the future. This was a) totally awesome and b) totally useless, because what were the odds I could get Ralph to come to my basement and walk into a swirly purple vortex that would send him back in time to be mutilated by velociraptors?

FIG. 3   USE OF DINOSAURS AS WEAPONS

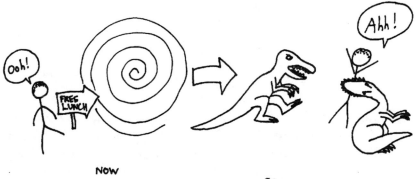

NOW

~ 80 MILLION BCE

I toyed with the idea of disassembling the thing and setting it up in the hockey rink or something, but it would probably cause a panic and/or suck the entire arena back into the Bronze Age. In the end I just went to bed, smelly and unwashed and resigned to the inevitable skull fracture that Ralph was going to give me when I least expected it, if I didn't show up behind the school on Saturday for my obligatory pummeling.

When I woke up Saturday morning I was still smelly and unwashed, but I also had an idea, a *great* idea that had come to me in a dream. Usually my dream ideas turn out to be stupid (cooking popcorn in the tumble dryer, strapping model rocket engines to my bike, etc.), but this one, though still crazy, might actually work: if Ralph couldn't come to the machine, and the machine couldn't be brought to Ralph, maybe I could just use it myself. Specifically, use it so many times with the end destination being the same time that my "army of me" could become a reality!

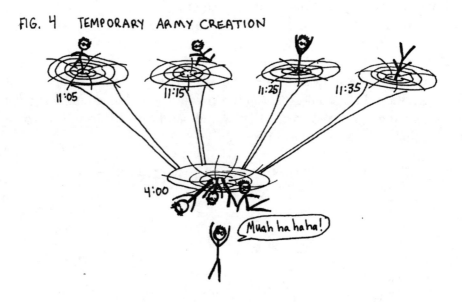

FIG. 4 — TEMPORARY ARMY CREATION

I've got to end this letter now, Mom, because I've got appointments to keep. Lots of them. At 11:05, 11:15, 11:25, 11:35, 11:45, 11:55, 12:05, 12:15 … (you get the idea). I figure twenty or thirty of me will equal about one of Ralph. Wish us luck. And if you could show up at the school soccer field around 4:30 with the van and either a few dozen body bags or a box of Band-Aids (depending on how much faith you have in my [our] abilities) I (we) would be eternally grateful.

— Love Miles(es)

P.S.—Can you set the DVR to tape *Stargate*? You know, just in case I (we) don't die.

Q.S.—Also, we're out of Hot Pockets.

Futuredaze

Author Notes

Over It, USA and Canada

Camille Alexa lives down the street from a volcano in an Edwardian home filled with fossils, shells, branches, and other very pretty dead things. Her stories and poems have been nominated for various awards, and her collection *Push of the Sky* earned a starred review in *Publishers Weekly*. Visit Camille at www.camillealexa.com.

Driven Out, Canada

Steve Alguire is an actor, artist, and first-time publishee. He lives in Toronto with his patient partner Marilyn and two very large cats.

The Ghost Hunter, USA

E. Kristin Anderson is the coeditor of *Dear Teen Me*, an anthology based on the popular website. Her poetry has been published worldwide in many magazines and she is an assistant YA and Children's editor at *Hunger Mountain*. She lives in Austin, TX and blogs at EKristinAnderson.com and www.MetreMaids.com.

Learning How to Be a Cat, Australia

Jenny Blackford's stories have received several Honorable Mentions from Ellen Datlow and Gardner Dozois, and Pamela Sargent described her historical novella *The Priestess and the Slave* as "elegant." Her first poem for decades was the only one included in the *Year's Best Australian Fantasy and Horror 2010*. Visit her at jennyblackford.com.

AUTHOR NOTES

The Alien, England
Cathy Bryant's poems and stories have been published on five continents. She's won many prizes, most recently (2012) the Sampad 'Inspired by Tagore' and Swanezine Poetry Competitions. Cathy coedits the annual *Best of Manchester Poets*, and her collection, *Contains Strong Language and Scenes of a Sexual Nature* was published recently. Visit Cathy at www.cathybryant.co.uk.

Ghost Walkers, Scotland
Sandi Cayless is a research scientist by education and a writer by inclination, science fact and fiction frequently falling from her pen. She holds four degrees, writes astronomy articles, croaks along in a community choir and likes to dig holes in her garden, just in case something interesting turns up. Visit Sandi at www.submartis.com.

Speech Lessons, USA
Alicia Cole, a writer and educator, lives in Lawrenceville, GA, with her husband Roger, their cat Hatshepsut, and two growing schools of fish. An active member of the Science Fiction Poetry Association, her poetry has recently appeared in *Star*Line*, *Goblin Fruit*, *Paper Crow*, *Aoife's Kiss,* and *Through the Gate*. Visit her at http://three-magpies.livejournal.com.

The Stars Beneath Our Feet, USA
Stephen D. Covey (BA, Physics) writes science, science fiction, techno-thrillers, and the futurist (pro-space) blog RamblingsOnTheFutureOfHumanity.com. ROTFOH describes many of his papers and conference presentations on topics from asteroids to space settlements. He is a member of the ITW, NSS, WFS, and AAAS. Visit him at www.StephenDCovey.com.

Market Day, Canada
Anna Della Zazzera spends her free time drawing mermaids and writing about fantastical things. She lives in beautiful British Columbia in an ugly white house with a view of the mountains. Visit her at www.annadz.wordpress.com.

String Theory, Canada
Danika Dinsmore works and plays in speculative fiction with an emphasis on juvenile and young adult literature. She is the author of middle grade fantasy series *Faerie Tales from the White Forest* (Hydra House) and teaches world-building and speculative fiction writing for both children and adults. Visit her at www.danikadinsmore.com.

Larvae, USA
Gregory Frost is a writer of fantasy, supernatural thrillers, and science fiction. He has been a finalist for every major genre award. His latest novel-length work is the YA-crossover duology *Shadowbridge* & *Lord Tophet*, voted one of the best fantasy novels of 2009 by the American Library Association; and also a finalist for the James Tiptree Jr. Award. His previous novel, historical thriller *Fitcher's Brides*, was a Best Novel finalist for both the World Fantasy and International Horror Guild Awards. His novella, "Vulpes," is featured in *V-WARS*, edited by Jonathan Maberry. He is Fiction Workshop Director at Swarthmore College. Visit him at www.gregoryfrost.com.

King and Queen, USA
John Grey is an Australian born poet and US resident since the late seventies. He works as financial systems analyst and has recently published in *Jones Avenue*, *Weber Studies*, and *Big Pulp* with work upcoming in *Poem*, *Pinyon Review*, *Prism International*, and *Evening Street Review*.

Clockwork Airlock, USA
Nancy Holder is a multiple award-winning, *New York Times* bestselling author (the Wicked Series). Her two new young adult dark fantasy series are Crusade and Wolf Springs Chronicles. She has won five Bram Stoker Awards from the Horror Writers Association, as well as a Scribe Award for Best Novel (*Saving Grace: Tough Love*) and a Romantic Times Pioneer Award for her young adult fiction. Nancy has sold over eighty novels one hundred short stories, many of them based on such shows as Highlander, Buffy the Vampire Slayer, Angel, and others. She lives in San Diego with her daughter, Belle, two corgis, and three cats. You can visit Nancy online at @nancyholder via Twitter and at www.nancyholder.com.

AUTHOR NOTES

Pennies and *Things to Consider When Choosing a Name for the Ship You Won in a Poker Game Last Night*, USA

Irving is a full-time web developer and technology researcher and perpetual bad influence on his grandchildren. He lives with his wife near the frozen shores of Lake Ontario and writes science fiction and fantasy poetry in what passes for his spare time, usually late at night when he should be in bed so he'll be awake at that big meeting in the morning. He is an active member of the Science Fiction Poetry Association.

Another Prison, USA

Rahul Kanakia is a science fiction writer who has sold stories to *Clarkesworld, Orson Scott Card's InterGalactic Medicine Show, Daily Science Fiction, Redstone, Nature,* and *Lady Churchill's Rosebud Wristlet.* He currently lives in Baltimore, where he is enrolled in the Master of Fine Arts program in creative writing at Johns Hopkins University. He also serves as a First Reader for *Strange Horizons.* He graduated from Stanford in 2008 with a B.A. in Economics and used to work as an international development consultant. Visit him online at http://www.blotter-paper.com or follow him on Twitter at http://www.twitter.com/rahkan

Prospect of a World I Dream, USA

Alex Kane is a speculative fiction writer and critic whose work has appeared in *Digital Science Fiction* and *Foundation,* among other places. He lives in the small college town of Monmouth, IL, where he recently earned a B.A. in English, and contributes book reviews regularly to Bookgasm. Visit him online at www.alexkanefiction.com

Not With You, But With You, USA

Miri Kim was born in Seoul, South Korea and grew up in Los Angeles. She graduated summa cum laude with a B.A. in psychology, and a minor in screenwriting. Miri enjoys subway rides, cat vocalizations, rooting for the villain, and preparing for the disco zombie apocalypse. Visit her online at mirikim.livejournal.com

Your Own Way Back, Canada

Rich Larson was born in Niger, West Africa, has studied in Rhode

Island, and is now an undergraduate in Edmonton, Alberta. His novel *Devolution* was selected as a finalist for the 2011 Amazon Breakthrough Novel Award. His shorter work has since appeared in *Word Riot*, *YARN*, *Bartleby Snopes*, *AE: The Canadian Science Fiction Review*, *>kill author*, *Monkeybicycle*, *Prick of the Spindle*, *Daily Science Fiction*, and many others. Visit him online at www.amazon.com/author/richlarson

Out of the Silent Sea, USA
Dale Lucas, novelist and screenwriter, is the author of the neo-pulp novel *Doc Voodoo: Aces & Eights* and the e-chapbook story trio *Right Behind You*. His stories have appeared in *Horror Garage* and *Samsara*, his film reviews in the *Orlando Sentinel*. He lives in St. Petersburg, Florida. Visit him at www.authordalelucas.wordpress.com

Why, USA
Evelyn Lumish started writing practically as soon as she could hold a pencil, and she's been writing ever since. "Why" is her first published poem.

Unwritten in Green, England
Alex Dally MacFarlane lives in London, where she is pursuing an MA in Ancient History. When not researching ancient warrior women, she writes stories, found in *Clarkesworld Magazine*, *Strange Horizons*, *Beneath Ceaseless Skies* and *The Mammoth Book of Steampunk*. She is the editor of *Aliens: Recent Encounters* (Prime Books). Visit her online at www.alexdallymacfarlane.com

A Voice in the Night, USA
Jack McDevitt is a Philadelphia native. He has been a naval officer, an English teacher, a customs officer, a taxi driver, and a management trainer for the US Customs Service. Jack's first novel was *The Hercules Text*, one of Terry Carr's celebrated Ace Specials. It won the Philip K. Dick Special Award. McDevitt has produced seventeen additional novels since then, ten of which have qualified for the final Nebula ballot. *Seeker* won in 2007. In 2004, *Omega* received the John W. Campbell Memorial Award for best SF novel. His most recent books are *The Cassandra Project*, *Firebird*, and *Echo*, all from Ace,

and *Going Interstellar*, a Baen anthology on which he served, with NASA manager Les Johnson, as coeditor. *The Cassandra Project*, a collaboration with Mike Resnick, will be out in November 2012. McDevitt claims it will reveal the truth behind the Watergate break-in. Visit him online at www.jackmcdevitt.com

The Stars Beneath Our Feet, USA
Sandra McDonald is a former military officer and recovering Hollywood assistant. She is the author of several books in print and several dozen short stories in magazines and anthologies, including four that have been noted by the James A. Tiptree, Jr. Honor List. She writes for adults and teens, and her collection *Diana Comet and Other Improbable Stories* won the Lambda Literary Award for transgender fiction. Visit her online at www.sandramcdonald.com

The End of Callie V, England
Jennifer Moore lives in Devon, England with her husband and their two children (and six fish). She won the 2009 Commonwealth Short Story Competition and her writing has appeared in publications on both sides of the Atlantic, including *Daily Science Fiction*, *The Guardian*, *Mslexia*, *The First Line* and *Short Fiction*. Visit her online at www.jennifermoore.wordpress.com

Me and My Army of Me, Canada
Katrina Nicholson is a novelist/ screenwriter/ movie reviewer/ freelance writer/ Girl Guide leader/ library clerk, some of which she actually gets paid for. Over the years she has studied engineering, history, screenwriting, Russian, flying, first aid, and cake decorating. She has six published short stories, including one in the young adult themed anthology *Tesseracts Fifteen*. Visit Katrina at www.refrigeratorbox.org

Spirk Station, USA
Chuck Rothman always wanted to be a science fiction writer when he grew up. He has been writing science fiction and fantasy since 1982, with two novels and almost fifty short stories published. He lives in Schenectady with his wife, Susan, and cat, Lightning. Visit him online at www.sff.net/people/rothman

The Cleansing, Australia

Mark Smith-Briggs is a writer from Melbourne, Australia. His work has appeared in more than twenty publications across the US, Canada and Australia. Normally his stories are found lurking in the horror genre, but "The Cleansing" represents his first, and hopefully successful, foray into young adult science fiction. When not writing fiction he can usually be found chained to a desk in the less inventive realm of newspaper journalism. Visit him online at www.freewebs.com/marksmithbriggs

Powerless, Taiwan

Leah Thomas is a recent graduate of Michigan State University. She currently lives and teaches in Taipei, Taiwan. In 2010 she attended the Clarion Writers' Workshop. Her work has since appeared in *Daily Science Fiction* and *Weird Fiction Review*.

Hollywood Forever, England

Llinos Cathryn Thomas grew up in the fairytale land of North Wales and now lives in London with her girlfriend and their family of overflowing bookshelves. She is working on her first novel, a tale of rebellious princesses sticking it to the Man (the Man is dragons). Visit her online at www.llinoscathrynthomas.co.uk

The Myriad Dangers, England

Lavie Tidhar has been nominated for a BSFA, British Fantasy, Campbell, Sidewise, World Fantasy and Sturgeon Awards. He is the author of *Osama*, and of the Bookman Histories trilogy, as well as numerous short stories and several novellas. Visit him online at http://lavietidhar.wordpress.com

The Blue Hour, USA

Brittany Warman is a PhD student in English and Folklore at The Ohio State University, where she concentrates on the intersection between literature and folklore, particularly fairy tale retellings. Her creative work has been published by *Jabberwocky Magazine*, *Cabinet des Fees*, *Mirror Dance*, and others. Visit her online at www.brittanywarman.com

AUTHOR NOTES

The Fall of Stile City, USA

William John Watkins has published over five hundred poems and a hundred stories. His story, "Beggar in the Living Room", was a Nebula Award finalist, and his poem "We Die as Angels and Come Back as Men" won the 2002 Rhysling Award. His hobby is racing motorcycles off road with his son, Chad.

The Teenage Years of Ed Nimbus (a moral tale), England

Neil Weston resides in the U.K. His stories and poems have been published at *Big Pulp*, *Scifaikuest*, *100 Horrors Anthology*, *Space & Time Magazine*, *The Eschatology Journal*, *Grand Science Fiction*, *Fringe Magazine*, among others.

About the Editors

Hannah Strom-Martin's fiction has appeared in *Realms of Fantasy Magazine, OnSpec, Andromeda Spaceways Inflight Magazine,* and the anthology *Amazons: Sexy Tales of Strong Women.* Her non-fiction has appeared in *Strange Horizons Online* and *Fantasy Magazine,* among others. With Erin Underwood she is the co-editor of the *Pop Fic Review.* She currently resides in California.

Erin Underwood's fiction, non-fiction, and interviews have appeared in the *Science Fiction Writers of America Bulletin, Danse Macabre,* and *Bloodstones,* among others. Erin is also the founder and editor of the popular fiction literary blog Underowrds and co-edited the *Pop Fic Review* with Hannah Strom-Martin. She lives in Marblehead, MA with her husband. Visit her online at www.underwordsblog.com.

AUTHOR NOTES

Special Thanks

Erin and Hannah, the editors of *Futuredaze: An Anthology of YA Science Fiction,* offer very special thanks to the amazing people who helped make this book possible by joining our Kickstarter campaign, funding the initial stages of this anthology through their preorders and offering their encouragement. Thank you so much for your kind notes.

We also offer special thanks to our Kickstarter campaign's Supporter and six Sponsors who went the extra mile with their financial support to make this anthology happen.

Futuredaze Supporter
Ed Biggs

Futurdaze Sponsors
Natalie Marie Charlesworth
Alexander Falk
Lucas K. Law
Donovan Pruitt
Philip Reed
Kathleen Retterson

FUTUREDAZE
Spotlights

⋆ july 21 - august 3, 2013 ⋆
wofford college, spartanburg, sc

Shared Worlds is a two-week residential camp for aspiring creative writers where students design fantasy worlds in teams with other young, talented creatives and then write stories set in those worlds!

Students receive feedback from an elite team of visiting writers and faculty. Past writers include Jeff VanderMeer (camp co-director), Jeremy Jones (camp co-director), Ann VanderMeer, Will Hindmarch, Holly Black, Nnedi Okorafor, Tobias Buckell, Karin Lowachee, and Naomi Novik.

Visit our site for more information and to apply!

wofford.edu/sharedworlds

THE FIRST AUTHORIZED,
FULLY ILLUSTRATED RETROSPECTIVE OF

THE VAMPIRE SLAYER TM & © 2012

"This beautiful hardcover book comes in a clamshell slipcase...
It's full of pictures and commentary that give a behind-the-scenes
look at everyone's favorite slayer. You'll learn about the characters
and mythology of the universe...while you drool over the
**120 images of the cast, props,
and show memorabilia.** There's
also a special envelope inside the
slipcase called "Slayer Lore:
Texts and Magicks for the Battle"
with **13 replicas of the ancient
spells and prophecies** that
were used on-screen....
a must-have for Buffy fans."

— *Wired.com's Geekmom*